Shadows:
Book of Aleth
Part One

Michael Duncan

I0629255

Shadows: Book of Aleth Part I

Contact Information: titleadmin@pelicanbookgroup.com

Cover Art by *Pamela DelliColli*

Harbourlight Books
a division of Pelican Ventures, LLC
www.harbourlightbooks.com
PO Box 1738 *Aztec, NM * 87410

Harbourlight Books sail and mast logo is a trademark of Pelican Ventures, LLC

Publishing History
First Harbourlight Edition, 2011
Print Edition ISBN 978-1-61116-120-5
Electronic Edition ISBN 978-1-61116-121-2
Published in the United States of America

Dedication

This book is dedicated to my wife, Patty, to my three children James, Joseph and Joanna, and to all those who have given themselves to a life-long pursuit of the truth.

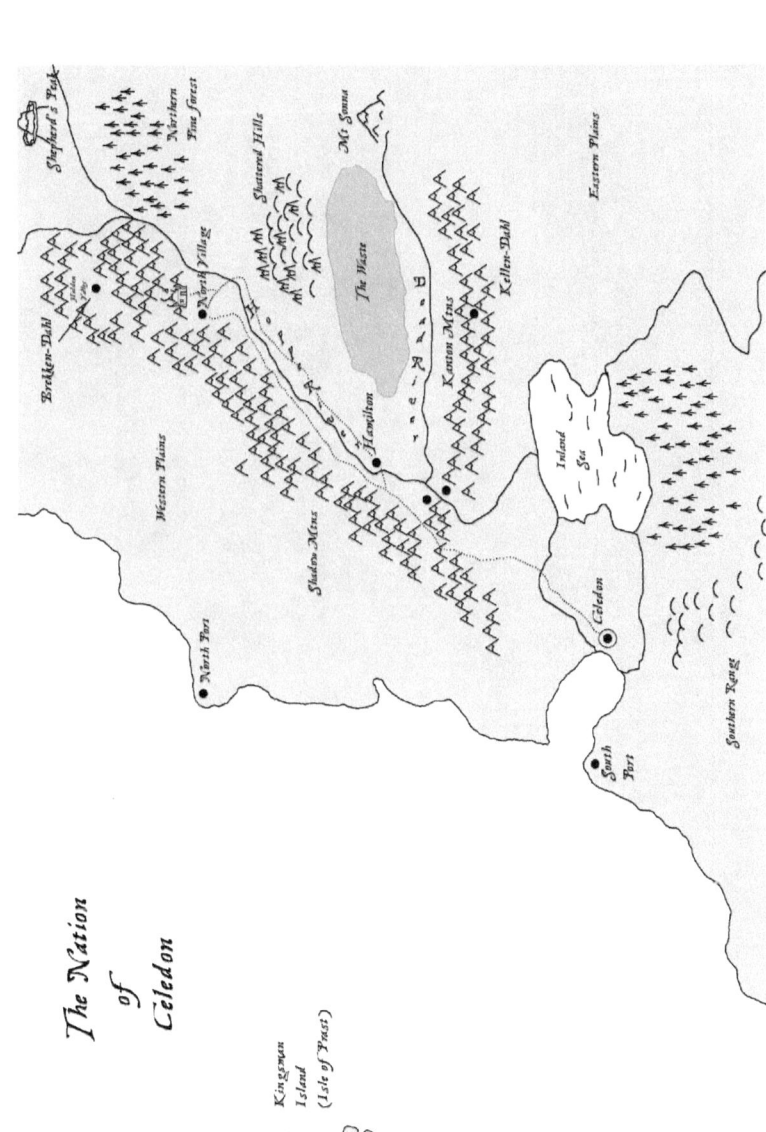

The Nation
of
Celedon

Kingsman
Island
(Isle of Frost)

Shepherd's Peak

Northern
Pine Forest

Broken Dahl

Western Plains

Shadow Mtns

North Port

Shattered Hills

Shepherd Village

Hamilton

The Waste

Mt Somn

Kanton Mtns

Kellen Dahl

Eastern Plains

Inland
Sea

Celedon

Southern Range

South
Port

Prologue

The Coming of Darkness

He stood alone. As the usurper's army approached, the tall, solitary figure kept silent vigil outside the high-walled city of Charis, the last free city of the King. Captain of the royal army, Protector of all Celedon, the lone warrior positioned himself like a bulwark between the unbreached gates and the usurper's evil horde, determined to stop the tide of vile creatures that continued to advance. At his command, those who remained faithful to the King waited within the protective fortress leaving him to face the enemy alone. He gripped his sword. Cold steel flashed with brilliance as the silent warrior waited. A halo of emerald light radiated from a small gem in the hilt and surrounded the protector.

A gentle summer breeze drifted across the vale, but it carried no scent of hope, only the half-dead stench of the usurper's army. Miles beyond the walls, the ancient forest burned unabated and belched thick clouds of smoke high into the air. Acrid smoke darkened the sun and shadowed the world in a ghastly twilight as embers drifted like snow from the sky. Thousands of vile creatures and traitorous men marched against Charis. Their approach echoed like thunder across the valley and shook the ground with every step. Through the haze and smoke, the Protector saw the usurper, mounted on his black steed on a small hill behind his forces.

An explosion of fire shook the ground. The Protector stumbled to his knees and gazed upward at large daemons soaring through an ash-filled sky. The dark, leathery-winged creatures hurled flaming spheres at the lone defender. Each ball of fire burst in a violent detonation that shook the earth, but the sword he held radiated even brighter, its emerald glow thwarting every attack. No magic could penetrate the radiant circle of light. Undaunted, Celedon's captain rose to his feet and held his ground.

The Protector's heart raced with anticipation. In his steeled eyes, a fierce anger burned against the usurper. He knew that his greatest challenge drew near. He suffered no fear, but hungered with the desire to avenge himself upon the hosts of evil. He knew his duty—to protect the King and defend Celedon, and at that duty, he believed he had failed. He thought of his wife and son and all those who remained inside, of those who stood loyal to the King. He gazed back toward the last, great city.

The high, granite walls of Charis guarded the hosts of those loyal to the King. Atop the battlements, the Protector saw archers of the high-born elves, vigilant and ready to defend the city. The tall, oak gates at the center of the city wall remained closed. Along the ramparts, flags displayed the crest of the King of Celedon and fluttered in the breeze. Beyond the massive wall, in the midst of Charis stood the Tower of the Wind, a regal spire of white marbled stone. It shimmered in contrast to the black curtains of smoke. The Protector gazed up to the pinnacle of the tower where he saw a rampart and upon the rampart stood the King.

****

Gazing down, the King of Celedon remained stoic, only the trickle of a tear down his cheek gave testimony to his heart. He surveyed the ravaged land and the burning ancient forest. Then he drew his attention to the mighty host of evil that marched toward Charis. The King looked toward the gates, where the Protector stood encircled by the emerald power of his sword. Foul creatures filled the air, casting their might against the lone warrior but to no avail. Thunderous echoes fractured the silence of the once quaint vale. Soon all would be over.

Ancient yet ageless, the tall King, his black hair blown by the wind, allowed his thoughts to drift in memory. He ruled Celedon without prejudice, dispensing justice and mercy. All seemed in order, and the races had lived together in peace. Then the usurper came to seize the rule of Celedon, to strip the King of his kingdom. This deceiver stirred up dissention between the races and, with his lies, ensnared the hearts of men.

The King's thoughts drifted. He knew the usurper lusted for power. His ancient enemy had long attempted to overcome his rule, but to no avail. Then the usurper turned his evil craft against the race of men. With his lies and powerful delusions, the usurper misled them. He gained followers and through hatred and jealousy turned men against the other races. The usurper then fought against the elves and dwarves. He could not deceive them, so the enemy conjured up vile, monstrous creatures to vanquish the ancient races. Yet, the King alone knew the greater reason for the usurper's arrival and why he permitted such a rebellion in his kingdom. Again the King's gaze drifted across the devastated fields that lay in charred ruins.

Next to the King a stalwart dwarf leaned on the parapet and watched the oncoming horde, his red beard matted and stained with blood from a deep gash across his cheek. "My lord, King!" The dwarf shouted over a loud explosion that burst near the Protector, stirring the ruler of Celedon from his ruminations. The King smiled at his friend, a warrior, dressed for battle with a chainmail shirt and golden helmet, who clutched a double-bladed battle axe.

"Brekken," the King responded thankful to have his faithful friend beside him.

"We must not let this deceiver have his way in our kingdom!" The dwarf lord pleaded. "Call upon your power, and rain fire upon these rebels!"

The King understood Brekken's frustration and anger but would not give himself to hatred. "Shall I destroy the deceived as well as the deceiver? No, my friend, the time has not yet come for such action." The King of Celedon again gazed out upon the hordes marshaled against him. Trolls, daemons, and other evil monstrosities stood together with thousands of men. But he was their King and would not annihilate the people he loved.

"But, my lord," replied Brekken, "We must defend what's left. If the usurper has taken the minds of men, so be it! Dwarves and elves are still loyal to your banner." Brekken paused, thoughtful as he surveyed the fields of Charis. "Where is Mellenden?"

The King continued to stare out at the multitudes

gathered just beyond bowshot. His penetrating gaze, searching, seeking, probing the faces of those who stood beyond the sight of normal men, and fixed upon the one face he sought. High on a hill, at the rear of the advancing force, sat the usurper on his black steed and beside him, astride a pale grey mare sat Mellenden, lord of the High-Born elves. The King knew then Mellenden had betrayed him.

"My lord," asked Brekken, "what is it?"

Sorrow filled the King's eyes. "Mellenden has fallen."

Celedon's ruler watched as the dwarf lord, strong and stout, trembled at the thought.

"Fallen!" Brekken wailed. Anguish overflowed with that single word.

The King of Celedon clasped his friend on the shoulder and resigned himself to what he must do.

"Brekken," said the King, "it's time. I want you to lead the people of Charis into the ancient tunnels beneath the city and escape to the refuge prepared for you. Lead the people to the hidden valley. There you will be safe."

"What? I will never leave your side." The dwarf insisted. "You are my King, and I will stand where you stand and fall where you fall. Do not ask me to do this thing. I will send my sons to lead our people, but don't command me away from your side."

"Lord Brekken," the King said, "you are my friend and have been my companion through many ages, but you must do this. Your sons have another task before them, and it's at hand. You must pass on the wisdom and virtue of our kingdom for the generations to come."

As the two men spoke, the King watched a

commotion at the city gate. Two dwarf warriors hurried out, closing the gate behind them. The King sighed as the two figures moved to stand beside the Protector. Though he could not see their faces, he knew they were Brekken's sons.

"My time has come," the King said. "I must get to the city gate. I will give you time to lead your people out of this place. Soon it will be overrun, and I cannot protect it. Trust me, my friend. In time all things will be restored."

"What do you mean?" Brekken asked.

"A time will come when men will understand the truth, and the kingdom will be restored. Until then, dwarves and elves must remain hidden from the deceptive power of the usurper." The King gazed into the eyes of the dwarf chieftain. "For now you must remain in secret. Take your people and whatever men will go with you and return to your own country. Dwarves must disappear beyond the mountains and elves to the forests."

"But sire," Brekken pleaded, "surely you can return with us? You must survive to return and rule over this land. There is no reason for you to remain if the city falls and we escape! How can I leave knowing you are still here? I owe my very life to you!"

"You must," the King commanded. "In time one will come who can reclaim the rule of Celedon for he will have my spirit within him. This you must believe, for once men stumble onto the truth the time of restoration is at hand. Until then, you must entrust the truth to those who come after you." The King was relieved when Brekken gave up his protests and left to evacuate the people.

The King drew his sword, a magnificent weapon

that shimmered with blue and gold, as if the sun and sky had been forged into its steel. He tucked a small leather tome into his cloak. He turned again to gaze over the field of battle where the Protector waited with two dwarves against an army of thousands.

****

The Protector waited alone until two young dwarf warriors took positions alongside him. Although their crimson beards were not yet long enough to braid, they wielded their battle axes with unmistakable skill. The dwarves rushed into the protective emerald light as two mighty daemons flew overhead. Blasts of fire shook the earth behind them. The three warriors defied the power of the vile creatures, untouched in the emerald circle of the Protector.

Surprised and amused at the two adolescent dwarves, the tall warrior smiled and readied his weapon. Just then the ground trembled. Hordes of foul, loathsome beasts rushed forward in one motion at the three warriors. A cloud of dust and ash kicked up in the wake of the oncoming army. With the first enemy in reach, the Protector filled the air around him with the swiftness of his blade. His sword grew brighter with each new enemy until a shimmering wall of emerald light surrounded him. No enemy that approached could venture into the iridescent halo without being cut down by the might of his weapon.

Overhead, a singing rush of arrows launched from the walls. Daemons plummeted from the sky, pierced like pin cushions. The Protector quickly evaluated the scene. The two dwarves, pressed back to back, fought with courage but lost ground against the overwhelming onslaught of the enemy. The Protector ran his sword through the heart of a troll as the beast raised its knobby club, then rushed to the aid of the dwarves.

He deflected a blow from a massive daemon meant for Brekken's youngest son, spun and cut the legs from under the creature. Then the dwarf raised his axe and struck the beast, splitting its chest. Two more trolls fell as the King's captain fought alongside the young dwarves. Arrows once again flew from the wall as the sons of Brekken and the Protector of Celedon stood their ground. Soon no attacker moved against them, fearing the might of the three warriors.

Beads of sweat trickled down the Protector's face and mingled with his tears. He longed for the days of peace, the days before the usurper came and claimed authority in Celedon. But there they stood: three soldiers against thousands. Though exhausted, the Protector delighted at the fear he saw in the enemy. The usurper's horde remained outside the reach of the Protector.

Then a disturbance attracted the captain's attention, a stirring in the ranks of the enemy. The wall of creatures parted, and the usurper rode to the front line, his black horse pawing at the ground. Pale and gaunt, the usurper looked like a man diseased and possessed. Yet his steel eyes burned with malicious fire. He rode up to the Protector and remained outside the circle of emerald light. His thin smile did not disguise his malevolence, and when he spoke the very air shuddered.

"So," the usurper sneered, "you are the mighty Protector of Celedon." His voice mocked the King's captain. "You protect against what? All of Celedon is with me!" The usurper laughed as he pointed to the hoards of men who stood as his army.

The Protector was not intimidated. "I protect Celedon from evil, and I defend the truth!"

"Indeed," returned the usurper. "I will give you one chance...one choice. Forsake your old allegiance. Turn against your futile King, for he is vanquished. Join with me as others have done, and receive your due reward." The deceiver's words hung in the air like a poisonous vapor.

The Protector sensed the eyes of the two young dwarves set upon him as they waited to hear his response. "To partner with evil one must become evil." Then the Protector gazed upon his adversary. "You may have turned the hearts of others, but mine belongs to the King." The Protector's voice trembled with fury, and he gripped his sword with both hands. The gem in the hilt began to burn with irrepressible light. "Now, deceiver, step down from your mount, and you will learn my answer. I am the Protector of Celedon!"

"Foolish mortal man," mocked the usurper. "Your days of protecting are at an end." The usurper raised his hand. A flash like lightning struck the captain, and he was thrown against the walls of Charis. His sword flew from his hand, and his chest wracked with pain. Gasping for air, the Protector of Celedon clawed towards his fallen weapon as the gates of the city opened. His eyes dimmed; the last he saw was his King step onto the field of battle.

****

The mighty King walked with slow, patient steps toward the usurper as Kellen, the youngest of

Brekken's sons, raced to retrieve the fallen Protector's sword. The dwarf raised the weapon to the echo of wicked laughter from the King's enemy. The green gem faded, its light dimmed, and no halo surrounded the young warrior. Both dwarves raced back inside the wall of the city and disappeared behind the gates.

Reaching the usurper, the King spoke, "Now, Therion, it is time."

"Time indeed! Time for you to realize that I rule Celedon and not you; time for you to die!" Therion laughed at the King. "You think you've come to defeat me, yet you are betrayed by your friends and your captain is vanquished. Celedon is mine!" The air trembled with power at his words. "Now bow your knee to me and surrender!"

"You've cast your web of deceit upon these fair people and have ensnared them. But it won't be long; your lies will be uncovered, and truth will once again reign in Celedon." The King raised his hands toward the heavens and began to speak words of great power in a deafening voice. Reverberations like thunder rolled across the region. The walls of Charis shook. The mighty granite fortress cracked and buckled under the strain of a mighty earthquake. Timbers snapped and buildings toppled. Those outside the city screamed with terror and fled in the chaos. Only the usurper remained unmoved, perched upon his steed in defiance of the King's power.

The King watched as the multitude rushed to escape his unleashed power. Tears filled his eyes and streamed down his face as he held his sword over his head. He spoke again and blue lightning flashed from the blade, then the sword disappeared.

With a great shout, the King lifted his eyes to the

heavens. He raised his hands and the skies filled with lightning that pierced every shadow. Unmoved, he lowered his gaze back to his enemy when the usurper grabbed his spear and hurled the weapon at the King. The cold iron pierced his heart. The King clutched at the wooden shaft that protruded from his chest and collapsed to his knees, blood flowing through his fingers.

Heart failing, life fading, the King expended his final breath to give one last, great shout. Buildings shattered behind him. With a crash that shook the ground, the fractured walls of Charis collapsed, sending dust and debris flying into the air. The earth heaved and groaned under the awesome power the King unleashed. Huge stones broke through the ground, shattering the landscape and sending the remaining army running in fear. The once rolling hills fragmented into shards of massive, jagged rock. Lakes and rivers broke from their banks and rushed like a flood south of the broken city. In a final outburst of energy, the Tower of the Wind exploded in brilliant light and crashed to the valley floor.

The King was gone.

And so passed a thousand years.

1

At the North Village

All was dark...

Overhead, clouds shrouded a waning moon and drifted past the myriad stars that twinkled in the velvet sky, leaving the world in the shadowed blackness of night. The chill of early winter dug to the marrow of the young captain who stood motionless upon the sand. Aaron stared into the blackness beyond his sight and listened as the ocean waves pounded against the shore...and his memories. Like fragments of broken dreams beaten by the sounds of the ocean, Aaron felt a primeval draw to the sea. Shards of dormant thoughts from his long-forgotten childhood stirred in the currents of the ocean and woke to its rhythm.

As he listened, Aaron heard the sound of footsteps shuffle through the tall grass behind him. He turned and watched his longtime friend, Lorik, walk toward him with a torch in his hand that fluttered in the brisk winter breeze. Even at a distance Aaron noticed Lorik's grey hair, blown by the ocean wind. The torchlight danced and flayed and caused shadows to play like children along the sandy path. Aaron took note of the grim expression on his face. He feared Lorik's arrival meant that he, once again, must leave the haven of the ocean.

"What's the word, sergeant?" Aaron asked with dismay.

"Captain," Lorik responded as he continued to approach, "we have received a message from North Village. The thief has been found."

Months had passed since Aaron ordered his entire command to search for the Book of Aleth, stolen from the emperor's royal archives. Scattered across the nation of Celedon, three hundred men, the entire Third Order of the Royal Guard, hunted in vain for the man who stole it. Aaron and his men were commissioned by Emperor Therion himself and ordered to recover the book, but the captain thought the order excessive.

"How many men do we have there?" Aaron loathed the idea of riding over four hundred leagues to hunt down one man.

"We have only one man that far north...a young private named Rayn." Lorik paused. "He sent word by way of the governor of that region. We just received it tonight."

Aaron ran his fingers through his hair as he thought through the situation. "What are our orders then?" he asked with a sigh of frustration.

Lorik pulled a scroll from the folds of his cloak and read:

The Third Order is hereby commanded to proceed to North Village, retrieve the stolen artifact, and destroy the thief by any means necessary.

Lorik glanced up and exhaled a heavy sigh as he handed Aaron the parchment. "Sir, it's signed by Therion himself."

Aaron knew only a handful of men under his command remained in the capital, more than enough to go after one man. "Very well," he continued. "Ready all who are left in the city, and we will gather more as we travel north." He paused as he considered where his men were located. "We can forgo those who are on the northern and southern coast as well as those who are east of the inland sea. We don't need three hundred men to capture one, no matter how dangerous the emperor thinks he is."

"When do you want to be ready, Captain?" Lorik asked.

"We leave at first light," Aaron ordered. "Gather what provisions we'll need and what men you can find. Those who are not ready at daybreak will be left behind."

Lorik saluted and turned to go.

Aaron watched Lorik walk back toward the city, the ruddy glow of the torchlight flickering in the distance. Then it, too, disappeared. Aaron turned back to face the dark, fathomless ocean and listened to the surging waves crash against the breaks. His heart longed for the freedom he felt in the vast expanse before him, and at that moment determined to take an extended leave of absence when the business with the stolen book was over. *Soon*, he thought, *I will be done with this mission*. The captain turned his back on the ocean and walked toward the city, distressed at the thought of a three-week journey north.

****

Hidden in the rugged hills outside the small community of North Village, a quaint cottage sat nestled in the alpine growth. What once was a pleasant, humble home had become a blazing inferno. Trapped inside the structure, an old man, eyes heavy with fatigue, clutched an ancient tome to his chest. Sweat matted his grey hair and dripped like tears from his face. He stood in the center of an open room. The smell of burning timbers filled his nostrils as wisps of smoke danced through the rafters. All hope for escape had vanished.

From within his alpine cottage the man listened to the mocking rants of soldiers who swarmed around his home like a pack of hungry wolves as they laughed at his predicament. For months the wizened man had remained secluded here, certain no one knew his location or what he'd recovered from the archives of the emperor. He was wrong. Despair wrenched his thoughts as tears flooded his eyes.

Clouds of smoke billowed across the vaulted ceiling and fire crackled on the other side of the walls. Under the door, a faint, orange glow heralded the coming flames, growing brighter as the old man watched in horror. The fire would soon engulf the room. He quelled the panic that began to seize him and moved toward a small, raised platform that supported a featureless table and four chairs.

Intense heat dominated the chamber. Two candles that sat unlit upon the table melted, and the old man's wrinkled face reddened as if he lingered too long in the sun. He sat down at the table and waited for his doom that burned just beyond the doorway. He looked at the book in his hands and knew with certainty that the tome was the Book of Aleth. Dunstan had told him what it looked like but now, so close to safety, he faced his own death in the fire set by the emperor's men.

The man held his face in his hands and wept bitter tears. He had come so close only to fail all those who waited for him. So few people remained who believed the ancient truths and now all hope would burn. Smoke filled the room, and the old man coughed and choked with each searing breath. *Soon*, he thought, *my life in this world will be over*.

The flames grew brighter, and the room glowed with the dancing orange light. The air burned his lungs with each forced breath. Rafters smoked and tapestries depicting valiant men from days long ago began to smolder. In a flash, several of the ornamental rugs burst into flame as the inferno burned through the wall. Rafters exploded in fire. The old man looked up in fear as beams which once supported the structure now heralded its final destruction. Flames rushed across the wood as it popped and crackled like kindling.

He had no escape. The fire spread across the roof. Slumped upon the table in final despair, the aged man hugged the book to his chest. With all hope of survival lost, he looked down at the treasure in his hands; its golden emblem reflected the light of the fire that engulfed the room. Tears filled his eyes, and a new resolve burned in his heart to protect the wisdom of the ancient King.

He clutched the tome once again to his chest and dove under the table to escape the ash and debris that fell from the ceiling. Massive timbers fell to the floor. The crash reverberated over the roar of the inferno. A large hole in the roof exposed the room to the open air, and the chamber burst in a massive fireball that shook the foundation of the house.

****

Aaron paced outside the alpine cottage as

darkness fell. A clear, cloudless sky revealed a host of stars that illuminated the velvet blackness of night. The crisp November air clashed with the heat and smoke pouring off the mountain lodge now engulfed in flame. Snow, which once lay like a gentle blanket on the forest floor, melted in the heat and formed rivulets of ash and mud that flowed in random directions away from the house.

As flames consumed the building, his soldiers reveled in the night. Shouts of "We got him!" and "Serves him right!" echoed in a cacophony of other unintelligent expressions. Aaron, however, found no delight in the death of the man within the cottage. *It didn't have to end this way.* Aaron brushed his hair from his eyes, and then rested his hand on the hilt of his sword, as the fire began to die. All that remained was to recover the Book of Aleth from the burned out ruins and return to the capital.

The crisp mountain air brushed against the captain as a slight breeze meandered through the woods, gently whispering in the midst of the pine and fir. The pale light of the full moon illuminated the smoke and haze like ghostly spirits drifting through the trees. Part of the roof caved in, and a massive ball of fire belched from the center of the lodge amid the sounds of crashing timbers. Aaron stepped away from the burning cottage and reviewed the events that ended with such tragedy.

He had arrived in North Village and learned from his private that the old man lodged in the mountains. Aaron pursued him into the hills and trapped him in this cottage. Tired of the chase, Aaron ordered the structure burned with hope that the man would try to escape. He surrounded the structure with his men and gave the order that anyone leaving the building must be captured. Aaron never imagined the man would choose to stay in the house and risk his life for an old book of little value. And Aaron wondered why the man refused to surrender when he knew that the guards were upon him.

"Captain!" Startled from his ruminations, Aaron turned to the voice. A young soldier approached. He was one of the youngest, not more than nineteen years old, a tall, able young man with blond hair and a clean shave. It was Rayn, the private who had found the thief. He was a good soldier, and Aaron appreciated the young private's eagerness to do his captain's will.

"Yes, Private. What is it?" Aaron asked.

"Well, sir, there's not much more to do here. With your permission, some of us have planned a celebration. If you'd allow, we'd like to leave this place and regroup at the local barracks," Rayn said.

The young soldier seemed too eager to celebrate, but that was the way of youth. "That'll be fine. Instruct the men to be ready to return home tomorrow. We've been on this hunt long enough and the task is done. Have Lieutenant Morryn take charge and lead the men back to the barracks at North Village."

"Without you?" questioned the private.

"Yes, Private." Aaron's voice was sharp and huffed with agitation at the young soldier. "I have other tasks to do, and I will be there soon." Aaron just wanted to be done with the entire mess.

But … *why didn't the man give up? Why didn't he just surrender? What caused someone like this man to become such a radical dissident?* Aaron wanted to know, and he hoped to find some clue as to the nature of this man's compulsion. What Aaron didn't want was an eager private snooping around like an annoying puppy and getting under foot. However, the structure was too hot to enter and posed a great risk of structural collapse. He had to wait, but he also wanted to explore the ruined house alone.

In the distance, the captain heard Morryn barking orders as each soldier prepared to return to North Village. The rattle of steel echoed around the ruins as the men mounted their horses and rode off. Aaron alone remained in the glow of the burning building. He thought of the man who lay dead inside. *What was worth dying for?* Aaron shook his head in dismay, returned to his horse, and mounted the patient animal. He hoped in the morning to shed some light on the tragic situation… he doubted he would get much sleep.

The full moon directly overhead illuminated the world in a radiant glow. Aaron enjoyed the crisp, cold night as he followed the rocky mountain path through the snow-covered trees back toward North Village, a refreshing change after breathing dust and ash. He found the trail easy to navigate and the journey gave him time to think.

Shadows played through the trees as the moonlight caressed the branches. The path meandered along the edge of the mountain, silhouetted with many shapes and alive with subtle movements. The path wasn't difficult, but in the darkness and shadows he didn't want his horse to miss a step and suffer injury. A wolf howled in the distance as clouds drifted past the moon.

Aaron stopped on a ledge to look down into the valley. Mist from the river glowed in the moonlight, and the houses and halls of the village radiated the amber light of warm fires and candlelit rooms. On the evening breeze Aaron heard the faint echoes of laughter from his men who rode ahead of him. However, he didn't feel the same joy as his troops. Aaron wrestled with his conscience, pierced in his thoughts about the man who had died. He knew the man was a thief who had stolen from Emperor Therion, but Aaron questioned why the emperor ordered the man's death. He had never before questioned the orders of his superiors, and the sense of uncertainty proved uncomfortable.

"What do you think?" Aaron asked his horse as he gently stroked her neck. The mare gave a quiet whinny and shook her mane, but that was no answer. "Maybe I've become too old and sentimental. I need to put this out of my mind." He gazed down into the valley below. The serene village lay in stark contrast to the chaos of the last few hours. Lights, like fireflies, flickered in the distance. *I will look for answers in the morning,* he thought to himself. Aaron nudged his mare and continued down the mountain path.

The captain approached the main gate of North Village. Its wide, wooden doors were shut to prevent any unauthorized entrance. A solitary soldier kept watch from a rundown shack to Aaron's left. As the captain approached, the guard hurried to open the gate. The tall, wooden door swung outward, and the portly sentry allowed Aaron to pass through without question.

Carts and wagons, pulled by horses and mules, trudged along the snow-covered road, guided by their masters. Children huddled in packs at the edges of houses. Expressive conversations emanated from several doorways and windows as the villagers argued about recent events. Much of what he heard jumbled into a dissonance of innocuous conversations. Then one discussion caught his attention. He stopped his horse and listened as two men bickered upon the front porch of a small tavern.

"Nah… just one man," said the first man. "I heard that they burned the entire place down! Seems a bit much to me."

"Well, now," whispered the other, "I think the emperor has a right to defend his own after all."

"Perhaps," said the first. "But who was this man? Who was he hurting?"

"Watch yourself," whispered the second, his voice resonant with concern. "You might find yourself with these guardsmen at your door next!"

The two men stopped, their words frozen in the air as they noticed Aaron seated on his horse. Both men were old, even ancient in their grey hair and weatherworn countenance. Aaron knew the sight of fear and saw it in their eyes. Silence grew like a wall between the men and Aaron. He nudged his mare and continued, but listened to the faint sounds as the two men continued their conversation.

The fear and mistrust he found in many outside the capital troubled Aaron. He had seen it countless times in villages throughout Celedon, but until now, he'd dismissed it. That last conversation, however, echoed in his mind. He struggled with the same thoughts and questioned the need for such force. With resignation, Aaron continued up the road toward the barracks.

As he passed, people disappeared into homes or businesses with looks of fear upon their faces. One mother grabbed her young son and rushed him through an open door then slammed it behind them.

Aaron heard the lock snap as they barred their home.

He approached the end of the lane and noticed the governor's house at the top of a high hill, overlooking the town. An elegant home for such a village, and from every window a warm, amber light glowed. Aaron's duty required he report to the governor, but he found that most politicians were overfed, under-disciplined men more concerned with their own table than with the people they ruled. Though he loathed the responsibility, Aaron knew he must present himself, and he would do it. First, however, he wanted to see his men.

At the base of the governor's hill resided a long wooden building. Its peak showed the evidence of winter's arrival as snow covered the roof like a blanket. Smoke rose from three brick chimneys that reached up from the rooftop. A chorus of voices echoed from within the hall as shadows passed by the many curtained windows. This was the barracks of the local guard. Two men maintained a sentry post on either side of the single door at the end of the longhouse. Aaron noticed both were low-ranking recruits, perhaps new to the regiment and called to stand watch—a rather monotonous duty reserved for the young and inexperienced. They came to attention when Aaron rode up to the barracks. He dismounted, haggard and weary.

Aaron approached the nearest soldier. "Private?"

"Yes, sir!" A rugged youth with broad shoulders trembled as he responded.

"At ease." Aaron didn't have the time or inclination to stand on formality. "Take my horse to the stable and see that she's tended. I'll be inside with the men. I expect they've been well cared for."

"Oh, yes sir!" The private took the reins of the black mare. "We'll take good care of ya," the recruit spoke to the animal as he patted the mare on the neck. "You're the captain's horse, and we've got a right special place for you!" The young man led her around the back of the barracks.

Aaron stepped through the door and entered into a smoke-filled hall. Pillars stood in single file down the center of the large room. In the middle, a large fire pit crackled and popped, while embers twirled through the air and up the conical flue. At the end of the room, a door opened into a torch-lit corridor. Scattered throughout the room men from the local and Royal Guard sat around assorted tables, enjoying their favored drinks and hearty conversations. Through the haze, the captain recognized the faces of his own men.

At a round table on his left Rayn and two sergeants of the local guard enjoyed a spirited banter. On his right, Lieutenant Morryn sat and sulked into a pint of ale. Two others were at his table, men Aaron did not recognize, and carried their conversation in low tones. They wore heavy, hooded cloaks and kept their cowls low upon their brows so their faces were concealed. They spoke in careful, hushed voices, sharing words and gestures with Morryn.

"Lieutenant!" Aaron spoke over the clamorous noise in the room.

Morryn glanced back, eyes widened at the sight of Aaron. He jumped to his feet and barked a command to the entire room: "Attention!" In unison the men in the room stood on their feet. Even in the casual atmosphere of the barracks' common room, these were disciplined soldiers. Aaron appreciated that.

The room fell silent as the soldiers waited to hear

from the captain. "I just wanted to congratulate you, men, on a task well done." Aaron tried to sound encouraging, but his words came from a heart plagued with questions and doubts. For his men, though, the captain conveyed nothing but confidence. "Be at ease, men. Enjoy the night, and for those who are in my detail, be ready to leave two hours after daybreak." The men shouted a cheer and lifted their drinks to offer a toast to the captain; then turned their attentions back to their own tables.

Aaron took a seat next to Morryn, and the two men left the table without a word. He looked at Morryn and wondered if his lieutenant had the ability to command the men. The lieutenant presented a formidable figure: tall, a full three inches taller than himself, with broad shoulders and muscular arms. Even seated, the strong, stern man held an aura of intimidation. Morryn's face displayed the scars of combat. He bore a scowl, and no smile ever cracked his chiseled features. His short brown hair stood like bristles on his head and the gaze from his steel blue eyes plunged like daggers into those unfortunate enough to catch his attention. Even Aaron, for all his experience, had never encountered such a soldier.

"Lieutenant," Aaron began, "I want you to take command of the men. In the morning you will lead them back to the capital. We've spent enough time away from home. You can ride to the city of Hamilton and…"

"With all due respect, Captain," Morryn interrupted, his baritone voice echoed around the room. "I know the way home. Won't you be returning with us?"

"I have business here, so you must lead the men. I

will also have a message for you to give to the emperor," Aaron said.

"What is so important that you must stay behind?"

"That, Lieutenant, is not your concern. I'll see you and the men off after breakfast. Don't look so concerned, I'll be back in the capital before you even miss me." The levity didn't seem to affect the lieutenant one bit; Morryn's scowl never wavered. Aaron remained convinced that Morryn was the most emotionless man he had ever met.

"If those are your orders, sir, I will follow them."

The captain stood to leave, and Morryn stood as well. "Enjoy a good night's rest, Lieutenant. I'll see you in the morning." Aaron wondered if Morryn enjoyed anything—even rest. He left the table while the crowd of men continued with their conversations, intermittent laughter erupting from various tables. Aaron turned his attention to the governor. He doubted the meeting would go as well.

Aaron stepped from the barracks into the chill night air. The Shadow Mountains towered in the distance; their heavy snows glistened in the rich moonlight but only served to remind him of the night's activity. The same two young men guarded the door and snapped to attention when they recognized him. Aaron stopped on the steps of the longhouse and gazed out over the quaint alpine community.

North Village lay quiet and most of the lights in the windows no longer flickered in the dark, cold night. The streets became the haunt of the local guard. A three-man patrol, dressed in brown, plain uniforms, walked along the main street, casually watching for any sign of trouble. Aaron fixed his gaze up the hill toward the governor's house. Still loath that he must report to some self-indulgent politician.

The lights of the governor's house burned bright and smoke issued from the chimney. It appeared warm and inviting, but Aaron always approached politicians with caution. The majority of local magistrates he had encountered claimed some sort of distant relationship with the emperor. Aaron found them just too eager for recognition. He breathed deep and bolstered himself to do his duty—no matter how distasteful.

"Goodnight, sir," said the guard.

Aaron startled and remembered that the two soldiers stood next to him. "Oh, yes, goodnight men." Aaron said then stepped out of the doorway.

Just beyond the barracks, a long, steep walk led to the governor's home. Aaron hoisted his cloak upon his shoulders, checked his appearance, and then began the long climb up the hill. Halfway up, a high stone wall encircled the hill like a crown. Aaron's path took him to a narrow break in the wall that permitted access to the governor's mansion. To the right of the break stood a small, round guard tower from which voices echoed through the chill air. Through a window, Aaron noticed the figures of two men inside, unmoved at his approach.

"Maybe I'll just sneak past," Aaron muttered, frustrated by the inept soldiers. He just wanted to meet with the governor and finally be done with his day. To announce his arrival he kicked some rocks and made enough noise for the soldiers to hear him. He chuckled when he heard the clatter of gear and sound of anxious voices from the small tower.

The two soldiers exited their shelter, torches in hand, and stumbled through the snow before they took vigil in the middle of the path.

"Halt! Who goes there?" The guard on the left, a stalwart man, shorter than Aaron but with a broad chest and a thick, muscular build, spoke with authority and brandished his flat-bladed spear that glinted in the moonlight as the guard trembled in the cold.

"I am Aaron, captain of the Royal Guard! Let me pass, I have business with your governor. Stand aside!" Aaron, who also shivered beneath his cloak, had no patience for this show of bravado after such incompetence. While the man on the right jumped at Aaron's words, ready to let him pass, the man on the left stood his ground, his spear leveled at Aaron's chest.

"We'll see," said the soldier. "His lordship will first know of your arrival. Come forward and step into the light!" The burly guard leaned over and whispered to his companion then motioned toward the house. The second man ran up the hill and disappeared into the darkness as Aaron stepped into the light of the torch.

"As you can see," he said, pointing to the gold emblem of the Royal Guard emblazoned upon his cloak, "I am who I claim to be. My attire is that of a soldier of the Royal Guard and my insignia proclaims my rank. Or do you doubt your eyes?"

"A beggar may stand and proclaim himself a king—and have fixed himself with fancier clothes than you. You may be who you claim, and if you are then you'll understand me—but if you're not..." He let his words trail off, but the message was clear as he brandished his spear.

"I get the point," Aaron said. "Can we at least wait in the tower? This night will not get any warmer."

"After you." The guard motioned for Aaron to proceed then followed close behind as they entered into the tower.

The scent of boiled beef permeated the air. A fire crackled and radiated its pleasant warmth from a hearth just left of the tower's entrance. Over the fire, precariously perched on a small tripod, an iron pot hissed. Though cramped, the small tower provided adequate shelter from the frigid winter that lingered beyond the stone walls. A small table with two chairs placed beside the window provided a perfect view of the entire hillside. However, a small handful of dice, two cups, and a decanter decorated the table.

Aaron stood near the door and waited as the small torch danced with the motion of the skinny guard. *I hope this doesn't take too long.* The torchlight stilled, then, moments later, it was on the move again. The guard, a dark spot against the white snow, slipped and stumbled his way down the hill.

The thin sentry rushed into the small tower. Despite the cold, bitter air, beads of sweat glistened on his forehead and steam rose from his cloak. The guard panted as he spoke, "Captain, the governor has verified your claim."

"Ah… so I am who I claim to be. That's good to know," Aaron said.

"You are commanded to come with me and report to the governor."

"Yes, let's go up this hill and meet with your governor." Aaron rolled his eyes as they exited the guard tower.

The thin man held up the torch as he and Aaron began the cold climb up the hill, leaving the stouter guardsman to stand watch. The way proved steep, steeper than Aaron first believed. He sensed the weight of the day's events as he willed his exhausted legs to continue up the path while all around him, eerie shadows played in the darkness. Aaron thought he saw movement from the corner of his eye and turned to look—nothing, just more shadows cast by the torchlight.

The hair on the back of his neck bristled as he listened for any activity in the brush just beyond the reach of the light. The sense of being watched unnerved him, and he tried to dismiss the idea as simple exhaustion. He glanced toward the shadows again and hoped to see some animal, nothing. *You've had a busy day and exhaustion's got the best of you.* Nonetheless, he straightened his cloak and rested his hand on the hilt of his sword.

The governor's mansion boasted an elegance Aaron didn't expect. Four white pillars supported a second story balcony and large bay windows shone with the amber glow of oil lamps. At the entrance, on either side of the door, two great statues stood in silent vigil. One looked to be a lion, with powerful jaws and emerald eyes and the other a creature unlike any living thing Aaron had ever seen. It appeared to be a mythical gargoyle, with long talons on its hands and horns protruding from its forehead and a snarl on its face. Two torches, mounted in gold sconces, illuminated the doorway but did nothing to alleviate the uneasiness Aaron felt. At the main entrance of the house were two large mahogany doors with brass rings clutched in the jaw of a lion's head. Both lions also cast ominous gazes at the captain, as if their jeweled, orange eyes scrutinized him to the soul. The carved relief of violent battles, etched upon the massive doors, only added to Aaron's apprehension.

The captain reached for the brass ring and struck it

against the door. A hollow echo resounded within the house. Moments later a servant opened the door. "Ah, you must be the captain from the Royal Guard," he said in a low, graveled voice.

"Yes, I must be." Aaron said with dispassion.

The servant, a short, older man with the shape of a wine cask, possessed a firm countenance. His face was etched with the lines of past troubles. Old scars and a perpetual scowl gave him a churlish, fatigued appearance. A bushy moustache covered his upper lip and thin strands of grey hair circled his balding head.

"Come in, sir, and enjoy the hospitality of our fine governor." The servant motioned for Aaron to follow.

The captain turned to dismiss the guard and found his escort had already started back down the hill. As Aaron entered the mansion, he again thought he saw a shadow pass, this time overhead. He dismissed the sight as a trick of the moonlight but his wariness remained.

The mansion was grand to the point of extravagance. To Aaron's left, a spiral staircase wound its way up to the second floor. All around him candelabras, gold and ornate, provided ample illumination for the house. A door to his right stood open and revealed a library with shelves of books lining the walls. And directly in the center of the room, suspended from the ceiling upon a thick gold chain, hung a crystal chandelier. A large, round table with several chairs rested underneath. A balcony looked down upon the foyer, and upon which stood a man—tall with a pale complexion, short dark hair and long, bony fingers.

"I am the governor of this region," he said, brimming with self-importance, "and you must be the captain of the Royal Guard. Take a seat at the table and we will talk." His authoritative tone punctuated every word.

"Thank you, sir. I appreciate your hospitality at this late hour. I apologize for the delay." Aaron's perfunctory and disciplined manner gave no hint to his apathy. He took a seat at the table.

"Captain," said the governor as he descended the stairs, "I have much to tell you, and I expect you to heed my instructions. As governor, I have authority to retain you for a mission of utmost importance." He sat at the head of the table and continued. "There is reason to believe that a small group of disloyal rebels exist beyond the borders of Celedon. It is suspected that this man whom you destroyed wanted to make his way back to these rebels and deliver the book he stole. First, you will find the book and bring it to me."

"But that man was destroyed and whatever he carried must have been burned up in the fire. There's no way that the book survived."

"There can be no speculation!" the governor shouted. With a deep breath, he regained his composure. "Bring me the book." The governor's face took on a cruel expression as he gave Aaron his orders. "I am aware that you plan to take some time away from your duties. That is most inadvisable. Your oath and your obligation to Celedon are far greater than personal needs." The governor pierced Aaron with his gaze. "However," he continued, "I can see that your long journey and experience on the mountain have left you weary. Be here tomorrow at dawn for further instructions. You can select one other to accompany you, but plan on secrecy."

The governor paused. He cocked his head as if he

heard some distant noise then returned his attention to Aaron. "Now, captain, you are dismissed." With that, the governor stood and left the table. He ascended the stairs and disappeared into the shadows of the hall above.

The portly servant returned to his side. "It's time to go, captain," he said as he motioned toward the exit. Aaron followed him across the room to the large, ornate doors. Without even an obligatory farewell, Aaron left the mansion.

At the foot of the stairs the same young guard waited for him. With torch in hand, he motioned for Aaron to follow him. "Well, sir," said the guard, "quite a man, our governor."

"Yes, quite a man," Aaron echoed. He followed the guard to the barracks, found his room and fell into bed, exhausted.

2

A Thief in the Night

In a snow-covered glade, a monstrous creature stood
over the fractured body of a man. The beast stood almost ten
feet tall, skin the color of charcoal and leathery wings folded
upon its back. Through the protective cover of the forest
undergrowth Aaron watched in horror—helpless, and he
shivered more from panic than from crawling upon the
frozen ground. The monster drew to its full height and
roared in triumph over the fallen man, malice burned in its
grizzly face.

The creature gripped the limp body with its massive
claws. Blood flowed from the dead man and pooled in the
snow beneath him. Fearful of even the slightest crackle from
a winter leaf, Aaron moved a small branch to gain a better
view and continue to watch. Struck with horror, he noticed
the gold insignia on the dead man's cloak—a soldier of the
Royal Guard. Slaughtered by a beast escaped from a
nightmare. He never imagined a creature so malevolent, so
evil.

Aaron lay motionless on the frozen ground and watched
the daemon. The creature's eyes sat under heavy, dark brows
and blazed with red fire, as if a furnace burned inside the
hideous beast. The creature turned and fixed its eyes where
he hid. The forest undergrowth provided no protection
against the monster's gaze. Aaron feared that it felt his

presence!

It moved toward Aaron with slow, deliberate steps. A low guttural growl rumbled from its throat. He had to decide—fight or flee, but he knew he had no chance to outrun such a monstrous creature. With iron determination, the captain gripped the leather-wrapped hilt of his sword. Slowly and quietly, he unsheathed the cold steel blade. Strike first, he thought, and strike hard.

The daemon drew nearer and steam rose from its footprints, as if a hot iron pressed the snow. Whether from the cold or some smoldering fire inside the beast, its breath billowed with heat. The creature neared Aaron's position. He rejected the cold chill of fear that tried to steal his courage. He must strike first and catch the monster off guard. Sword in hand, he…

…woke, trembling and drenched with sweat. His dark, cold room only heightened the anxiety of his dreadful nightmare, even as he pulled the wool blanket tighter around his neck. A faint glow radiated from under the door and cast a pale light upon the wooden floor when a shadow crossed the light. His dream still fresh in his mind, Aaron almost jumped out of bed when someone pounded on the door.

"Captain!" a voice called from the corridor. Aaron calmed his nerves and rubbed the sleep from his eyes.

Again someone knocked. "Captain! Captain, are you awake?" The unfamiliar voiced called into the room.

"Yes, yes, just a moment," Aaron replied. *What a dream.* He remembered the terrible images that had plagued his sleep. A cold sweat hung upon his skin like a mantle and intensified the frigid atmosphere of the room. Aaron just wanted to huddle deeper under the blankets.

Reluctant, he stood upon the cold wood floor and shuffled to the door. He glanced back at the frosted window—the world remained shrouded in darkness. Aaron hoped the person at the door was prepared for a tirade. With the blanket wrapped around him, he unbolted and opened the door. Light from the hall burst into his room like a flood, and Aaron shielded his eyes from the intense brightness. He squinted in a vain effort to relieve his vision and looked at the young soldier who had disturbed his sleep.

"Yes," he said through a prodigious yawn. "What is it?"

The young soldier at the door wore the simple brown uniform of the local guard. A light dusting of snow covered the young guard's hair and cloak. "Sir," said the man, "I am sorry, but it is near daybreak, and I had orders to wake you."

"Yes, soldier, I understand." The tone of Aaron's voice amplified his displeasure. "I'll be along in a moment."

"Y-yes sir." The man stammered. "I hope you don't mind, but I have set orders for your breakfast. It waits for you in the common room. Also, I was told to wake another of your guardsman. Who do you want me to get, sir?"

The captain hadn't thought about it since the previous night. His mind raced through the soldiers under his command. It was too early, and his thoughts staggered in drowsy confusion. He mentioned the only name that came to mind, "Rayn... go get the private, and tell him to report to the common room as soon as he is ready. Also," ordered the captain, "have a breakfast delivered for him—we both will make an early start."

"Yes sir!" The soldier saluted and sprinted away.

Aaron shook his head, turned back into his room, and let his own door close behind him. The darkness engulfed him. He stumbled back to his bed and cracked his knee against the desk that sat beside it, a sturdy, wooden nightstand with a small drawer in the front. Aaron fumbled around the drawer's contents, a collection of cast-off writing quills, parchment, and assorted other items, until his hand rested upon a box that contained several wooden matches. He retrieved one and struck it against the edge of the desk. It ignited in a shower of spark and flame, and he lit the diminutive tallow candle that stood on the desk. Aaron dressed quickly then hurried out the door.

The hallway glowed in the smoky light of several torches that hung upon the wall. Aaron turned to the right and passed through a single door at the end of the passage and entered the common room. A fire roared in the center pit as smoke rose through a cone-shaped flue that reached through the ceiling. He noticed a table set with two decanters and other utensils, as well as a large covered tray. No sooner did he sit down than a man rushed through the main door of the hall. Steam wafted off the newcomer's back, and he breathed heavily with exertion, groaning under the weight of a large metal tray.

The newcomer hurried to Aaron's side. "My... apologies... sir." The man panted as he tried to catch his breath. Dressed in simple leather clothes with a tan apron around his waist, the servant took a deep breath and spoke again. "I didn't mean to interrupt your meal, sir, but I had orders to bring another breakfast to the common room. I'll just set it here and leave you alone to enjoy your morning." Without another word, the servant set the tray down and departed the way he came.

When the servant left another person entered, a soldier. Tall and ruddy, with a boyish appearance, quick eyes, and a mischievous smile, Rayn strolled through the dormitory door and across the room to the table. Young and eager, he paid no attention to his commander and began to explore the contents of his breakfast. Rayn uncovered his tray to reveal generous portions of scrambled eggs, bacon, strips of boiled beef and fried potato wedges. In a large container in the center of the table stood a decanter of water and, next to it, a piping hot jug of coffee. He poured the coffee into a ceramic cup and began to devour the meal.

"Good morning, Private," Aaron said, chuckling at the display of such a voracious appetite. Rayn looked up and, for the first time, noticed who it was that shared the table with him.

"Oh, Captain," came his quick response. Any infraction of etiquette often brought dire punishment. "I am sorry for my behavior...I didn't know that you were you...well, that you were who you are...I mean that you..." His sentence trailed away.

"I can see that you were more troubled with appetite than manners. Carry on soldier, and we will enjoy a silent breakfast together. We have much to do and must be on our way soon. We might need an extra packhorse, though, if this is the way you eat!" Aaron smiled at the private and lifted the cover from his plate to examine his own breakfast. His heavy-laden tray contained the same substantial meal as the private's and together they ate in the silent solitude of the empty hall.

Aaron listened to voices echo through the

barracks. Soldiers woke with a myriad of inseparable noises as doors slammed and booted feet stomped in the hallway leading to the common room. Several servants entered and set tables in preparation for the rush of hungry soldiers. The room soon became a hub of activity as Aaron and Rayn continued to eat. One servant, a young boy no more than twelve, came in with a heavy metal poker to stir the fire in the central fireplace which sent up a shower of glowing embers with the smoke.

Aaron glanced up as Lieutenant Morryn entered. The tall lieutenant dwarfed everyone in the room and commanded attention as he moved through the crowd. Men, both soldiers and servants, gave Morryn a wide berth as he strode toward the captain's table. His hard eyes examined everything in the gathered throng of soldiers. The lieutenant's gaze fell upon Aaron, and a puzzled look crossed Morryn's chiseled face as he made his way through the sea of tables. He stood at the table's edge, his jaw firm and stance erect.

"Please, sit down Lieutenant," Aaron said. "There is no need to stand on ceremony at breakfast."

The lieutenant took a seat but nervously continued to look around the room. "Sir," Morryn said, "I am eager to get the men ready and be on our way. I don't trust this place."

"This is out of character for you, Morryn," Aaron said as he set his breakfast aside. "What don't you trust?"

Morryn's uneasiness resonated in his voice. "I don't know, sir," he said. "I just know that the farther away from the capital, the more uneasy I feel."

"Oh, a homebody, eh?" Rayn quipped through a mouthful of food. Then the private stopped chewing, and his eyes widened.

"Private… your opinion was not asked for!" The lieutenant glared at the young man. "It may be that you'll need some remedial discipline before we make it home!"

"My apologies, sir, I… I didn't think before I spoke!" Rayn's voice trembled as his eyes darted to the captain then back to Morryn.

"At ease men," Aaron interrupted. "Your discipline will have to wait, Rayn, since you're still coming with me. Lieutenant, what is it that you sense? Tell me."

"Sir, I just don't know. I am not one given to fear or imagination, but these northern reaches harbor strange creatures, and these villages are more prone to their own rule than that of the emperor." Morryn paused as if he tried to gather his thoughts. "Sir, last night when the men were in their rooms, I thought I saw a…well…a creature. I was up late and walked the streets of this village when the snow began to fall. I went to the main gate and found it locked so I started back. When I turned, something flew over the roof of the barracks. I didn't see it clearly through the snowfall, but it appeared rather large, in shape like a man but with massive wings. I questioned the guards when I returned, but these local guards are as useless as blunt swords." The lieutenant took a deep breath. "I'll be glad to find my feet upon the streets of Celedon once again."

Aaron's mind raced back to the nightmare that had plagued his sleep. He shuddered at the prospect that the malevolent beast which ravaged his dreams now lurked in the shadows of reality.

"Sir, what is it?" Rayn asked.

"Nothing... it's just that I had a dream last night, and in it I saw a creature similar to what Morryn just described."

Dread filled Morryn's eyes. "Sir, with your permission, I will assemble the men, and we'll leave at once."

Aaron wasn't sure what to make of the lieutenant's expression and dismissed it. "Yes, by all means, the men are under your command, and you are free to depart at your convenience. The private and I have other duties that require us to remain behind."

"Thank you, sir." Morryn stood and saluted. He turned to leave but stopped and faced Aaron again. "Sir," he said, "you mentioned a message I was to take back to Emperor Therion?"

Aaron nodded. "It's nothing. Just tell the emperor that Rayn and I have remained behind to continue the task."

Morryn gave a questioning glance, nodded, and then left the common room back to the dormitory.

After Morryn departed, men from both the local and Royal Guard gathered at the assorted tables and tore into their breakfasts like pack wolves at a kill. Servants, men and women, entered with full trays and departed with empty ones. Several times the young boy came to tend the central fire, to bring wood or stir the coals.

"Rayn, we need to go." Aaron stood and finished the last dregs of his coffee.

"Sir," said Rayn, as he stood, "I don't mind telling you that I'm a bit worried. If we encounter a creature like the one the lieutenant described, the two of us might not be enough to handle it." The private's carefree attitude was replaced by a look of serious concern.

"Rayn, don't get caught up with dreams and shadows in the night." He tried to sound confident, to reassure his young companion, but inwardly Aaron felt a growing apprehension. "We need to see the governor and receive more instructions. He has retained us for a task he thinks is most important. Get your cloak; it's snowing." Both men wrapped their cloaks around their shoulders and meandered through the crowded room to the exit door.

Outside they were greeted by a morning of heavy grey clouds and an onslaught of snow. A sparkling blanket of white covered the world as servants and merchants bustled to and fro. Their footprints filled with fresh snowflakes even as they passed. Large evergreen trees, with branches like massive arms, drooped under the heavy weight. A hazy, pale glow on the eastern horizon signaled the arrival of morning.

On every street people bustled about. Servants, laden with trays of steaming food, whisked their way past the two soldiers and entered the barracks. Merchants pushed carts stockpiled high with products along the main thoroughfare as shopkeepers opened doors and shoveled snow from the front of their establishments. Aaron hoisted his cloak a little higher on his shoulders and, with Rayn at his side, stepped down from the barracks and turned toward the governor's manor.

At the gate two guards kept vigil in the tower. *Certainly*, Aaron thought, *these two guards will be more capable than guards on duty last night.* The two on duty proved more alert than their evening counterparts and came out to stop Aaron and Rayn. They both wielded long spears with flat-bladed, metal tips, polished to a mirror-like sheen. Their brown cloaks wafted in the cold breeze as snow began to light upon their heads, yet they held their posture with discipline.

"Halt!" Spoke the guard on the left with a deep, resonant voice. "Identify yourself and your companion!"

"I am Aaron, captain of the Royal Guard and this is Rayn, a soldier under my command. We have business with your governor this morning." Aaron hoped the two men were informed to the business of the day. He didn't want to revisit the situation of the previous night.

"Yes, sir," the first man said. "We have been told of your appointment and are ordered to escort you to the governor. Please follow me."

Thank goodness! Aaron thought. He pulled his cloak tighter to ward off the cold morning air and defend himself from the continual swirl of snow. Aaron looked up at the snow-covered hill, untouched by any footprint. The soft, white blanket had hidden his tracks from the night before and gave the hillside a look of unspoiled beauty. But for the reasons they were there, he might have enjoyed the serene quality of the early morning snowfall. Aaron saw lights glowing through the frosted windows of the governor's home, and a hint of smoke drifted from the chimney.

Snow crunched under their boots as they walked through the gate and toward the house. Hiking through knee-deep drifts, they pressed on. At the mansion, Aaron appreciated the shelter of the balcony overhead which shielded them from the relentless attack of winter. All three men stomped their fur-lined boots to beat off the caked-on snow. The escort reached up and pounded the gold knocker against the heavy mahogany door. The door swung open at once, and the same cantankerous servant from the previous night stood before them.

"Ah, Captain! It is good to see you again on this fine morning!" The man seemed in high spirits, far better than he had exhibited the previous night as he welcomed them into the home with enthusiasm.

"Is the governor ready to meet with us?" Aaron asked.

"In a moment, sir. But please come and enjoy a warm cup of coffee." His graveled voice contrasted with his pleasant disposition.

The escort spoke to Aaron, "Captain, by your leave, I will return to the guard tower."

"Oh, yes, of course," Aaron replied. "There will be no need for any further help, the private and I will make our own way down." The guard raised his hand in salute and departed without another word. The door closed with a dull thud and left the cold morning air outside. Aaron and Rayn took seats at the large central table where three cups and a large decanter of coffee awaited them. Rayn filled two cups as they waited in silence for the governor.

From upstairs, the resonant sound of booted feet moved toward the staircase. Heavy footfalls echoed through the quiet hall, growing louder until they reached the stairs. A tall figure stood at the top of the staircase and spoke with a deep voice, clear and direct. "Gentleman, I am glad you have come."

Aaron and Rayn stood as the tall, thin man, dressed all in black, descended the stairs and approached the table. The newcomer carried himself with an air of dignity and importance. His angular nose and jaw accentuated his narrow face, and bushy eyebrows grew over eyes as hard and dark as obsidian. Long, black hair cascaded from his head and rested on his shoulders.

Surprised by this unknown figure, a sense of caution welled up inside of Aaron. "Where's the governor?"

"Don't worry, young captain. The governor is detained with…ah…other business, and I have come to speak on behalf of the emperor himself," the stranger said.

"Oh," Rayn interjected, "and just who are you?"

Aaron exhaled in frustration. "Private, don't forget yourself," he snapped.

"It is no matter." The stranger raised his hand to calm Aaron's agitation. Then he turned to Rayn. "Young man," he said with calm, stern authority, "I am as you, a servant of the emperor. I am his emissary and have come to deliver his commands to your captain. You will do well to listen and let your superiors discuss matters unsuited for you." The emissary took a seat across from Aaron.

Rayn squared his shoulders and drew his breath to respond but Aaron interrupted, "I think that once we hear what you have to say both of us will know the course of action that we must take."

"Indeed, you are right Captain. You will understand the bidding of your emperor." A hint of malicious delight resounded in the dark stranger's voice. "The emperor knows that this traitor intended to take his stolen prize beyond the borders of Celedon. There are rumors an ancient enemy of the empire still thrives just beyond our borders and looks to overthrow the emperor and plunge our country into war. You must uncover this enemy and ascertain how they plan to invade before they strengthen their position against the empire. It is understood the man you tracked here belonged to this group. The book he stole is quite valuable, so it is of great importance to the emperor that you recover it."

"As I explained to the governor," Aaron said, "the man in question was burned in a fire and everything he possessed, including that book, must have been destroyed as well."

The stranger pondered the statement. Then he leaned close to Aaron and whispered, "Don't be so foolish, Captain. This book is protected by great magic. It cannot be harmed, even if dragon's fire is used to burn it. No, it is not destroyed, and it must be kept out of the hands of those who want to use it against the empire."

Aaron heaved a heavy sigh, frustrated he was ever picked for such an assignment. "Sir," he said, "if this book is so highly valued, why send me and my private to try and retrieve it? Send an entire division of troops from the local guard to bring this thing back."

The stranger replied, "Lord Therion cannot trust the men of this region. Many have been corrupted by the power of this book, and the emperor will allow only those he can trust to lay hold of it. No, Captain, he will trust only someone of Celedon, a member of the Royal Guard with such a duty. The task falls to you, Captain—you and your private."

Aaron continued. "How far am I to search for these others?"

"Your orders are to recover the book and find the conspirators. How long it takes you and how far you go will depend on the circumstances of your mission. When you've finished you will report to the emperor directly. Speak to no one concerning your task." The stranger stood.

"If that is all, then," Aaron said, startled at the abrupt end to their conversation, "we will ready ourselves and begin."

"Very well," the emissary said, turning his back on Aaron as he left the table. He stopped at the foot of the stairs and looked back, his eyes hard and cold, "When I return to the capital, I will inform the emperor you have begun. Remember the urgency of this undertaking. Let no other activity distract you from your purpose." He turned, walked up the stairs, and vanished in the darkness.

Aaron sat in stunned silence as the fire cracked and popped.

"Captain," Rayn said, "if you're ready, let's get out of here."

"Absolutely," Aaron said.

They rose from the table and immediately the portly butler was at the door. "Captain," he whispered, his raspy voice barely discernable, "don't assume that everything is as it seems." The butler glanced up to the top of the stairs as his hand trembled on the door-latch. The aged servant opened the door and a rush of cold air blasted the men. With a quick farewell, the old man ushered them out the door and closed it behind them.

Aaron and Rayn stepped off the porch into a carpet of new snow and sank to the top of their boots in the white powder. The clouds had thinned and only a powdery mist wafted through the morning air. Like spears from heaven, shafts of golden light pierced the drifting clouds and fell upon the earth to illuminate the world with scintillating brilliance. Trees glistened with wintry reflections as if thousands of crystals hung on the limbs and branches of every tree in North Village, creating a scene of mystical enchantment. Rooftop chimneys puffed out billows of grey smoke that drifted in lazy procession over the cottages and hovels.

Down toward the barracks, Morryn moved through the ranks of the guard assembled in the square. The lieutenant checked and rechecked the men under his command, barking orders in the cold morning air. Within minutes the men of the Royal Guard were mounted and in formation, ready to depart. Morryn waved his hand in the air and Aaron heard the lieutenant shout, "Move out!"

In silent consternation, Aaron watched his men depart.

"Captain?" Rayn interrupted Aaron's troubled thoughts. "Shouldn't we be going?"

Aaron sighed. "Yes indeed. Let's get our gear and return to the ruined cottage. Perhaps there is some burnt remnant of that book. I don't know how much of what we heard is just ancient myth, but we need to start somewhere and that's the best place." The captain hoisted his cloak around his shoulders and trudged down the hill, followed by his companion.

As they plowed through the snow, Aaron tried to walk in his previous footprints, but no amount of effort made the journey back to the barracks any easier. When they approached the guard tower, Aaron gave no thought to the two guards and pressed through the gate, unhindered. Back at the barracks door, Aaron instructed the guard to have their mounts prepared to depart.

"Sir, will you return today?" the guard asked.

"No, we'll need supplies for at least a week," Aaron replied. The guard saluted then ran off while

Aaron and Rayn entered the common room to wait.

Both men sat down at a table nearest the central fire to warm themselves when a young woman entered with a decanter of warm ale and two mugs. Aaron offered his thanks to the girl and poured himself and Rayn a generous helping of the drink.

Rayn spoke first, "Sir, what of the information that we were told? There's something unsettling about this entire mission."

"Well," Aaron said, "I am not sure. I have heard stories about people who live beyond the borders of Celedon. I have never seen them or dealt with them. I don't even know if I believe they exist, but we will find out. One thing is certain; anyone who has opposed the emperor in the past has suffered greatly. So, if there are rebels living outside our borders, the emperor will deal with them. In fact, if you remember your history lessons, the reason the Royal Guard came into existence was to protect the empire. Our mission is no different. What this book is all about or why the emperor wants it, I'm not sure. I am sure of this, however, you and I will find out."

"That's what I'm afraid of." Rayn said with dismay. "What of the dream you had and the creature the lieutenant saw? Do we just dismiss them?"

"No, we don't dismiss them, but don't be taken to fear by them either." Aaron tried to sound dispassionate. "What we'll do is take the next step in the course that is before us. We don't have enough information to do much more than that." Just then, a messenger entered the common room.

"Captain," a young boy interrupted. "Captain" — he panted from his haste—"your horses and provisions are ready."

"Let's go," Aaron said.

Aaron stepped outside to find the world bathed in light as clouds parted, and the brilliant sun burned over the eastern horizon. A hazy layer of mist drifted just above the snow as the sun's warmth permeated the region. Aaron shielded his eyes against the glare and took the reins of his horse.

As they rode through the center of the village to the main gate, Aaron contemplated the conversation he'd overheard the night before as he passed the two old men. He barely noticed the people of North Village as they bustled throughout the hamlet. Silent, Aaron rummaged through his own nagging thoughts. They exited the gate, ignored by two young boys who persisted in a valiant snowball fight, and started on the trail to the cottage.

The track twisted through the trees. Both horses climbed the rugged terrain with ease, unhindered by drifts of snow that collected along the path. The evidence of their previous night's trip still lingered on the trail despite the early morning snowfall as evergreen trees formed a canopy of reaching branches and protected the path from most of the winter weather. Around them, the crash of small avalanches echoed through the woods as snow cascaded from over-laden tree limbs.

Occasionally, the path opened to look down upon the valley sprawled below them. Clear skies, deep and rich in stages of blue, hosted a scattering of gentle clouds, while the valley floor glowed in brilliant white, covered in a blanket of snow. Aaron stopped his horse long enough to drink in the sights, awed at the majestic scene on display. Several hundred feet below, and slightly south, Aaron looked upon North Village. Thin wisps of smoke hovered over houses crowned in white. Far in the distance, to the edge of the horizon, the eastern plains spread out like a painter's canvas, white and barren.

Aaron gazed over the vista desperate for the tranquility he observed. "Peace..." he said, thinking aloud as he stared toward the horizon.

"What?" Rayn asked.

"Oh, nothing," he replied with a sigh. "Just that I've longed for peace, for an end to constant conflict, and I look out over the horizon and from here it all seems peaceful." Aaron shook his head and turned his horse back to the path. "But peace is just a dream." He rode up the trail in silence.

They continued into the forest, again sheltered by trees that kept it passable, though both mounts took measured steps in the increasing drifts. Slow and careful, they rode up the mountain until they came within sight of the burned remnants of the old cottage.

A bleak reminder of the activities of the previous night, snow that surrounded the cottage had become grey with ash. Tall pines, lush and green, bore the scars of the inferno with needles charred brown and branches scorched. The simple, elegant architecture reduced now to little more than charred ruins. Astride his mount, Aaron looked at the scene with dismay and wondered if any room had escaped the fury of the fire. Even as he watched, thin wisps of smoke drifted up from timbers that continued to smolder.

Both men dismounted and tied their horses to nearby tree limbs. Aaron walked toward the burned-out house and hoped there was nothing left but the charcoal remains of an ancient book. "Private, I want you to look in the back, see what you can find. I'll enter through the front and together we can investigate the entire building in a short amount of time."

"Captain, what am I looking for?" Rayn asked.

"Maps, documents, books, anything that might give us a clue to this man's associations." Aaron gripped the pommel of his sword and approached the ruins as Rayn walked around to the back.

The captain approached the front door with caution, concerned that the blackened shell of the cottage might collapse and fall in on the both of them. He walked up the stone stairs to the double doors and tested them to see if they would open and felt the radiant warmth of the charred timbers. Both doors collapsed inward when he touched them, their hinges were burned through and the frame scorched. Aaron did a double-take when he noticed two rhododendron bushes on either side of the entryway undamaged by the fire, just a few scorched leaves on the outer branches.

Aaron passed through the main door into an entryway, smoke-stained and burned. To his left he noticed a small room with its door burned beyond recognition. Inside the room, two chairs still smoldered. On his right stood a small closet with empty hangers that dangled on a round beam. Garments, burned and frayed, lay sprawled on the floor. In front of him another set of doors, broken and scarred, had fallen to the floor and exposed a large central chamber.

Aaron stepped with caution through the fractured entryway as the heat of the inferno still lingered in the air. The hall glowed in the sunlight as a massive hole in the ceiling exposed the room to the sky. Light filtered in like streams of ribbon that reached from heaven. The room was larger than Aaron expected and boasted several benches and tables with a raised platform on the opposite wall from where he entered.

On the dais, a scorched and overturned table caught his eye. Snow had settled in the room and swirled in the air, mingled with dust and ash. Aaron approached the platform, and the acrid stench of charred wood filled his nostrils. Through a closed door on the right side of the dais, he heard a crash and presumed Rayn knocked over some furniture in an antechamber.

As Aaron approached the overturned table, a sense of dread fell upon him. His eyes narrowed. He drew his sword, and it rang with metallic vibrations as it cleared its sheath. The hair on his neck bristled as he drew nearer to the platform, not sure what to expect. Then he saw it. Crouched and slumped over behind the table sat the figure of a man. The man's arms were folded in front of his chest and he sat with his knees pressed up against them. His head bowed so that it almost pressed between his knees and no signs of breath or life issued from the figure. Aaron let out a sigh as his tension dissipated. He examined the old man, bewildered when he saw no trace of fire or smoke upon the body.

The man's hands were positioned so that he gripped an item to his chest. He used the tip of his sword to jostle the man's arms free and discovered— two empty hands. Though the man's hands were clutched as if he gripped an object, he held nothing. Aaron looked around but found only ash and dust. Then he saw the faint imprint of large booted feet next to the body.

Aaron followed the prints and discovered some

intruder had come through a breech in the east wall. The footprints entered and departed through a hole made by the fire and collapsed timbers. Aaron paced back and forth across the dais. As to the identity of the perpetrator, he didn't have the first clue. *One thing is certain*, Aaron thought, *the book has been stolen again.*

Aaron listened to the clattering of Rayn as he worked in some back room.

"Captain! I think I've found something!" Rayn called out.

To the right of the platform a small, narrow door exited the hall. Aaron ventured through it and found Rayn busy searching through the contents of a small desk in the center of the room. Shelves of books lined the walls. Some burned beyond recognition; others lay scattered on the floor. Rayn shuffled through a pile of papers on the desk. It was to the pile that Rayn directed Aaron's attention.

"What is it Private? What have you found?"

"Well, sir," Rayn said, "it seems our thief was well acquainted with a group of people who live in some region known as Hidden Valley. I found what might be a personal letter to the man who died."

He handed the letter to Aaron.

Derrick,

It is with a heavy heart that I hear of your trouble. I want you to know that you are not alone; there are many here who have not given up hope for the Restoration. Bring the book! We are anxious to have you and it safe with us. We need you. Come to Hidden Valley. Make your way through the mountains and you will be safe. We eagerly wait for your arrival.

Dunstan

"Well, now," the captain said, "it seems that we

have a clue after all. Good work Private—"

A loud crash from the central hall shook the building. Both men drew their swords. Without a word, they rushed toward the sound. In the center of the chamber stood a large, winged creature. Its leathery skin was the color of dark ash with its wings folded against its ridged back. Powerful claws gripped a long, black sword and heavy brows loomed over eyes that glowered with red flame. The creature of his nightmare stood before him. Aaron's courage melted like wax in the presence of the hideous beast.

"Old man, where is the book?" The monster's voice rolled like thunder from its throat as it stepped toward the place where the fallen man lay. It tossed aside tables and chairs like toys. Each step brought it closer to the dais. Steam, or perhaps smoke, issued from its mouth with each breath, and its footprints seared the wooden floor as with a branding iron.

The beast reached the table that concealed the fallen man then it tilted its head as if it listened to some call. Aaron heard no sound but the creature stretched its massive wings and took flight through the hole in the ceiling. Rayn, eyes wide with fear, looked at his captain speechless.

"I think," Aaron said, "our mission has just become complicated."

3

Road to Revelation

While Aaron shuffled about the room, Rayn sat on the platform in stunned silence. His sword lay forgotten on the floor at his feet. Aaron, white knuckled, gripped his sword as if the creature might return at any time, though he took no stock in his ability to defeat such a monstrous beast. Leaving Rayn to his thoughts, he stepped around the overturned furniture and burned artifacts to examine the decimated room. He stooped down to inspect the burnt imprint left by the creature, tracing his fingers along the ridges of the mark upon the floor. The smoky scent of charred wood still lingered, and the print felt warm. Aaron's brows furrowed and eyes narrowed as he wrestled through fragments of old memories, desperate to recall some long-forgotten knowledge.

"Captain," Rayn broke the constricted silence, "what are you looking for?"

"I'm not sure," Aaron replied. "I wish I could remember."

"Tell me Captain, was that the monster in your dream?" Rayn's voice trembled.

"I don't know," Aaron said. "I've never met such a creature, but it resembled the beast from my dream. But that's not what I'm struggling to recall...if only I could remember."

Rayn sat, his fists clenched and sweat beads glistened upon his forehead. "Well, I don't know anything about it, and I hope I never will! I'll tell you, if that is what we have to face, I'm rather concerned."

Aaron was gripped by the same apprehension. "That monster had the power to shred us to pieces and, if I am not mistaken, we're still here." He tried to reassure his young private, "Let's look around some more because the book is gone, and it appears that more than just the emperor wants it."

"But what was that creature?" Rayn asked. "Do you think the thief was in league with such a monster?"

"I don't know," Aaron said. "I've read legends that spoke of such creatures." Then he smiled with delight, as if he stumbled upon a lost treasure. "That's it!"

"What's it?" Rayn asked.

"I just remembered where I've heard of that creature," Aaron said. "Years ago, when I studied at university, I remember reading some of the ancient myths of the Elder Days. One such legend spoke of great winged creatures, dark and powerful. As I recall, they were said to have fought during a great cataclysmic war." Aaron paused as he thought. "In fact," he continued, "the story said that a king ruled Celedon and creatures like that were in league with his enemy. And—"

"Sir," Rayn interrupted, "I think we have just encountered a creature from that tale. What you've studied as a myth, the both of us can describe as firsthand knowledge!"

"Perhaps," Aaron said. "All myth has some basis

of fact, and that creature might fit the description. However, I don't hold any stock in the ancient legends, and you shouldn't either. We've met a hideous beast, but let's not start believing fairytales." Aaron's words, however, felt empty in his own heart as he silently wondered if an ancient legend had come to life.

"What do we do, then?" Rayn asked.

"We follow our orders. We have a mystery in front of us and very few clues in hand. Our task is to find this book." Aaron sensed he was in a race against time to regain the stolen book. "Our duty is clear so let's get to it."

Rayn began to relax. "One question, sir, do you think that this book might be an artifact from those days? Isn't it said that relics from those days possessed great power? Could that be the reason why it was stolen in the first place?"

"*One* question," Aaron quipped. "That sounded more like three." He continued. "It's possible, there is no way to know," Aaron replied. "All we know is that we have too few clues and too many questions, and less time to conduct our search. Standing around here doesn't get us anywhere. So on your feet private, let's see if we can discover a better clue than 'a hidden valley' in some mountains."

Rayn stood, and retrieved his sword. He wiped the soot and dust off the blade and returned it to its leather sheath. The chill morning settled into the room and penetrated to Aaron's bones. He rubbed and patted his arms to keep warm as a gentle snow began to fall.

Rayn took the captain's order to heart and returned to the small antechamber to investigate the undamaged documents while Aaron continued to examine the body of the fallen man. Aaron knelt down beside the remains and rummaged through the man's pockets with the hope of finding some clue. He found nothing.

"Captain, I found another note." Rayn shouted and waved a document in his hand as if it were a treasure map. "I think that this also might be of interest." He handed the parchment to Aaron.

Derrick,

We are eager to see you. We know that your time is spent in desperate circumstances, and you have been in constant peril, but we need your wisdom and skill. We have taken our clan and are hiding in the Heart of the Mountain. We believe that we are safe here; no one else knows the location, save you. Come quickly if you're able; we will stand together with you. We know that once the Book of Aleth is recovered the time of Restoration is at hand, and the world will forever change. Send word.

Farik

Aaron looked over several other documents, but to his dismay, none of the correspondences contained any information about the location of the people mentioned.

"This *is* of interest," he said, "but I have never heard of such a place. We now have references to an unknown mountain location and to a hidden valley," Aaron's frustration mounted. "What we need is someone who can lead us to these locations or someone who knows where they are!"

"Yes, sir." Rayn sighed. "Any ideas as to where we can find such a person?"

Aaron paced around the small room with the letter in his hand and kicked at burned and broken debris. He ran his fingers through his hair in frustration and tried to think through the circumstances that surrounded his mission. Rayn watched and waited for Aaron's decision.

Silence filled the chamber except for the gentle whisper of a late-morning breeze. Aaron chased through his mind for some understanding, but for all his effort, he had no idea where to find either location. Aaron knew that his only choice was to return empty handed. "Private," Aaron said, "we must return to the capital. There is nothing more to find here. We need more information, and Celedon has the best historical archives in the empire."

"Yes sir!" Rayn smiled. "It will be good to be back in a warmer climate! One thing, sir, will we be going through Hamilton?" Eagerness filled the young man's voice. "You see, I grew up in Hamilton and would like a chance to visit on our way through." The delight in his eyes betrayed his youthfulness.

"Yes, we must take the road through Hamilton. It is a week's ride there, and we will have to re-supply before we go on. Let's make a start of it."

The men left the burned out shell of the cottage and found their horses still tied to the tree branch. The sun was high in the sky, and its warm light reflected off the snow with the sparkle of thousands of tiny diamonds.

"Before we go, sir" Rayn interjected, "may I ask you a question?"

"Certainly, Private. What is it?"

Rayn hesitated. "Sir, do you think we might encounter that same creature again?" His voice trembled.

"I wish I knew." Aaron took a deep breath, desperate to keep his own nerves in check. "All I know is that I hope to never see one again. It ignored us the first time, so perhaps we are of no concern to such creatures." Aaron tried to convince himself, but his own fears were not so easily dismissed. "Perhaps when we leave this area, we will leave all these concerns behind."

"No offense, sir, but I don't think you believe that."

"Well, whether I believe it or not, what I do know is that we need to move out. We've lingered here too long." Both men left the grim scene behind and rode their horses back down the mountain path.

****

Aaron and Rayn traveled past North Village and began their long journey southward. The road kept close to the swift Hoppe River on their right as the majestic Shadow Mountains guarded the western horizon. The mountains, heavy with snow, hid their peaks behind a wall of grey clouds. The Hoppe River rumbled like the continual roll of thunder and exhaled a steady mist that covered the bank and trees in white frost. Massive cedars hung heavy with large icicles that dangled like spears from their thick branches. Aaron listened to the sounds of the forest around him and heard the occasional swoosh of snow as it fell from the tops of the trees.

The road they traveled was broad, a main thoroughfare used as a highway between the city of Hamilton and the northern regions of Celedon. Trees stood silent as their branches formed an archway over the road. Since the arrival of winter, few travelers ventured to the northern reaches. Aaron and Rayn journeyed in isolation, though on occasion, Aaron noticed the imprint of a deer or elk that had crossed the road to get to the river. The uneventful ride continued for miles with an occasional scent of smoke wafting through the air from some unseen house in the woods.

As the sun fell behind the Shadow Mountains, an eerie gloom descended on Aaron's thoughts, and he looked toward the sky. High above, in the red and gold of sunset, he watched clouds pour over the mountain peaks. The chill winter air turned biting cold. The mist from the river grew thick and hung heavy on the trees. Small flakes of snow drifted from the clouds like advanced scouts, the foreshadowing of a storm.

"Captain," Rayn asked, "where is this snow coming from? There was no sign we were going to face bad weather."

"I don't know, but we need to decide quickly what we're going to do. I had hoped to reach the hostel by nightfall, but if this storm finds its strength we'll be in for it." Aaron knew of no lodging or shelter, so he and Rayn pressed on against the ever-increasing wind. High clouds looked like dark shadows in the dim twilight. The large, snow-laden messengers of a storm drifted from the north as if they pursued the two companions.

Like the rush of an angry army, large flakes fell upon the two travelers. Aaron wondered if the heavens themselves had set its strength against them. With a desperate need to retreat, Aaron looked to the woods to find some protection from the storm. The snow fell so thick he could not see beyond the edge of the road. It piled higher and higher until their mounts struggled to take another step in the deep drifts. Aaron was anxious, and Rayn began to panic as the storm continued.

"Captain, we must find shelter!" Rayn's voice faded as the storm howled through the forest.

Aaron nodded his agreement, and the two departed the road and entered into the woods. Even in the protection of the trees, they were beset with difficulty as the winter storm dispensed its flurries of snow and ice. In the darkness, they heard the churning waters of the Hoppe River. Overhead, the clouds continued to empty their payload upon the earth with no end in sight.

Cold and weary, Aaron and Rayn pressed through the woods along what seemed to be an overgrown trail that meandered through the dense forest. Under the branches they were less exposed to the elements and pushed on with a renewed hope of finding some cave or large tree to camp under for the night. The trail led on, and without any other direction to follow, the two soldiers continued through the undergrowth.

"Captain," Rayn now had to shout to be heard over the wind. "Captain, look there!" The private pointed ahead through the dense trees. Through the heavy snow, in the midst of the woods, stood a solitary house. Smoke rose from a central chimney, and every window glowed with warmth.

They rode up to the structure, dismounted, and tied their horses to a wooden post in front of the house. Engulfed in the near blizzard and the darkness of night, Aaron sighed with reserved gratitude. Chilled to the bone, the thought of a warm fire and a hot meal buoyed his spirits.

Unsure of what to expect, Aaron approached with caution. He kept his hand on the hilt of his sword, but hoped that the occupants who enjoyed a warm fire might be equally warm towards him and Rayn.

Aaron walked onto the covered porch, and the wood planks creaked beneath his weight. He reached up to rap on the door, but at that moment, the door swung open and Aaron found himself looking down at an old man, bent and grey.

"Ah, young master," the old man said, "have you come to stay the night?" The man's voice cracked as he spoke, but there was an air of delight in his expression.

"Indeed we have," Aaron said as his teeth chattered with the cold. "Are you the keeper of this house?"

"I am. My name is Kaylan, and I have kept this house for many years—long before you were born I suspect!" The old man chuckled and welcomed the two men into the home. "Now, the both of you come in out of the cold and warm yourselves by the fire. I'll see that your horses are stabled and will be back in half-a-moment." With that, Kaylan disappeared out the front door while Rayn and Aaron took the old man's advice.

The house was simple, quaint, and designed to keep travelers. To the right, built into the wall, a stone fireplace crackled with a welcome fire that illuminated and heated a large common room. A round table placed in the center of the room had seven chairs around it. On the wall near the fire were several wooden pegs and upon these Aaron and Rayn hung their cloaks. To the left of the entrance door, a narrow stair led up to a landing with several doors that Aaron assumed were various sleeping chambers.

Under the stairwell, a hallway led to rooms unknown, and across from the main entrance stood a closed door. Aaron grabbed a chair from the table and sat near the fire, eager to enjoy the warmth and stave off the chill that had set in. Rayn followed suit. A cast iron cooking pot hung on metal brackets over the fire and bubbled in the heat. Steam escaped the lid and carried the pungent scent of a boiled roast.

Kaylan entered, stomped his feet, and beat the caked-on snow from his shoes. "Fortunate for you that you arrived when you did. A winter storm has settled in, and the snow is falling hard outside."

"Yes, indeed," Aaron said. "If it wasn't for your generous hospitality and the fortunate location of your home, my companion and I might not have made it this night."

Kaylan waved his hand, as if to say *think nothing of it*. Then he disappeared through the hall under the stairs and returned with three large bowls, a two-pronged serving fork and three smaller forks. "Come, sit at the table and let me get you some dinner." He took the bowls, plunged the large fork into the pot and pulled out three large portions of meat. "Not much," he said, "just some boiled beef. But it's hot and there's plenty to spare." He served the men and sat down to eat.

It was just as he said, hot and plentiful. Aaron enjoyed the dinner immensely. His heart lightened from the day's events, and he felt warmth return to his limbs. He looked at Rayn and noticed a smile on the young private's face.

Kaylan rose and grabbed some wood stacked next to the hearth. He cast the fuel onto the fire to a small eruption of embers. "When you've finished dinner, join me by the fire and we'll talk." Kaylan walked from the room and vanished through the door under the stairs.

****

The night passed as Aaron and Rayn listened to Kaylan tell of his many experiences. "In years long ago," he chuckled, "I used to wander the countryside in search of adventures. Oh, I've been to the tops of mountains and across the Great Plains. I've stood on top of the world and found myself in its depths, but you know what I found?" Aaron shook his head. "I've found that after wandering the entire world, I seem to always come back home." He laughed at that. Then he stood, collected the dinner dishes, and took them down the hall. Aaron and Rayn listened to their host as he laughed and talked with himself over the clink of rattling dishes.

"Sir, this man seems to have been around. Perhaps he knows what we need. He must have heard about or seen the places we're trying to find."

"Perhaps," Aaron said, reluctant to trust their cheerful host.

Kaylan returned with a jug of ale and three cups. The brew was warm, and its heady aroma filled the room. Each man took a cup and poured a generous amount of the draught. "Now, young masters," said Kaylan, "what is your story? Two soldiers don't wander around the country in the dead of winter without a purpose." The old man hoisted his cup to his lips and took a large gulp of the warm drink, leaned back in his chair and settled in for a lengthy tale.

"Well," Aaron began, "there's not much to tell." He didn't want to explain the events of the past few days. "We were on a mission to stop a thief and recover what he had stolen; ultimately it led to our arrival at the village a day's ride north of here. He fled, and we cornered him in an old cottage and, unfortunately, he was destroyed. When we looked, we didn't find the artifact and are now on our way home." Aaron hoped the brief, general account of the events satisfied the curiosity of the old man.

Kaylan shook his head in mock disappointment. "I can see you need to learn how to tell a story. How about you, young man?" Kaylan directed his attention to Rayn. "Do you think that you might tell it better than that?"

"Sir," Rayn replied, "my captain gave you an accurate account of the circumstances. I don't think that any information I might add would impress you."

"Good!" Kaylan exclaimed. "You do your captain credit. He doesn't want to share any more than he did, and you keep his secrets well. You must be commended. But, to tell you my little secret, I may know more about your story than you suppose."

"And what is it you know? There is not much more than what I have already told you." Aaron tried to sound nonchalant but he was troubled.

"Oh, don't worry Captain. I won't share your secrets with anyone else. Perhaps, though, I can be a help to you on your journey. What I will tell you is this; I know about your quest to recover the Book of Aleth, stolen from the royal archives." Kaylan paused and Aaron's eyes grew wide with apprehension. "You see, Captain, I know more than you about this and might be able to help."

"Who else..." Aaron stuttered. "Who else knows about this?"

"All of Celedon—that is to say, a Celedon you've never known—is aware of the fact that the Book of Aleth is missing. Whoever possesses that book will be hunted by more than just the emperor," Kaylan said.

"What do you mean, *a Celedon I've never known*? I've been in every province, in every major city and most of the minor ones, in hamlets and villages from the coast to the eastern border." Aaron grew perplexed and frustrated by his wizened host.

Kaylan stood and stretched his arms. "Wait here and I will return with something that might interest you." Kaylan entered the door to his private chambers. Aaron listened to the clanking of unseen objects as Kaylan voiced a stream of comments about the untidy nature of his room. A few minutes later he emerged with a large leather satchel over his shoulder.

"Come, sit closer to the fire," Kaylan directed.

Aaron hesitated. "It's late; can this wait until morning?"

"No Captain, I think you will want to see this."

Aaron's curiosity overcame his exhaustion, and they sat with Kaylan by the hearth. The old man opened the brown leather bag, weather-worn with a strip of rope for a shoulder strap. From the bag, he pulled out a wooden box, old and frail. The box boasted no great marks or designs, and the hinged top creaked when he opened it. Inside was a smooth, clear glass orb. It fit in the palm of his hand and when held up to the light of the fire, it began to flicker as if a small flame burned within.

"What is that?" Rayn asked.

"This is a… a tool," Kaylan said. "It is called a fire orb, and it possesses qualities that permit some who gaze into it to see events that…well…that are of great importance to the one who looks. I can help you, if you wish." He turned toward Rayn. "Young man, reach into the bag and retrieve the stand." Rayn pulled out a three-legged, round metal stand, its silver surface reflected the light of the fire. The top was fashioned to allow the orb to sit in its center without falling through. "Put that in the fire...Yes, just like that, so that the top is over the flames." Then, with great care, Kaylan placed the orb on the stand. It began to glow with the light of the fire.

"Well now, Captain," Kaylan asked, "do you want to gaze into the orb?"

"What will I see?" Aaron was reluctant; the day had already seen its share of strange sights.

"You will see only those things that are important to you." Kaylan spoke no more, but seemed to take on a new, serious expression with a wisdom reflected in his penetrating gaze.

The orb sat on the metal stand and began to glow. The flame within, like an all-consuming fire, intensified until it burned bright and hot. Aaron felt the warmth as if it radiated to engulf his entire being. The fire of the hearth dimmed in the sheer brilliance of the orb's influence as red flames danced inside the sphere. Aaron was amazed the crystal did not shatter. He took the center seat and stared into the red flames that seemed to swirl like liquid fire. He locked his gaze on the flames within. The brilliance of the sphere intensified until the only light in the room emanated from the small object. All others dimmed as if they cowered in the strength of the fire orb. A sudden flash like red lightning burst from the center of the orb, and Aaron was engulfed by the light.

Aaron found himself transported, whether in a vision or in reality he didn't know, to a ledge. High on a mountain cliff, Aaron looked down upon a dark crevasse. The wind howled and whipped against his face, and snow swirled around him to bite into his skin like tiny needles. In every direction stood high mountain peaks that reached their stony fingers into the grey blanket of clouds.

Along the high cliff, a narrow path followed the contours of the mountainside like a precipitous walkway across the dangerous range. Several yards ahead of him a young girl crouched on her hands and knees as her dark hair whipped across her face in the strong wind. Aaron knew the young woman was in distress. He watched as she shouted into the dark chasm. Her voice trailed off, useless in the howling wind. Aaron wanted to move closer, to help her, but the narrow ledge offered a perilous place to stand, and he feared any movement meant a rapid descent into the darkness below.

With a flash of red light, Aaron found himself looking again at the fire. The vision had passed, and the orb sat perched on its stand. The fire radiated bright and warm, as if nothing had happened. Aaron reeled from the event, and tried to catch his breath. He had never experienced such awareness—like being a phantom on a stage, able to watch the drama unfold all around him and experience every sensation without the power to participate in the experience. Flushed with exhaustion, Aaron fixed his gaze on Kaylan. The old man sat motionless, his brown eyes stared straight ahead under his grey, bushy eyebrows, as if he were in a trance.

On his right, Rayn simply stared at him with furrowed brows. "Sir, are... are you all right?" Aaron heard the desperate concern in Rayn's trembling voice.

"Yes, Private...I am OK. But it was more than I expected," Aaron said.

Just then, Kaylan blinked as if he woke from a

spell that held him. He took a deep breath. His voice cracked in a whisper as he spoke to Aaron. "I've helped many to bring forth a vision from the fire orb; but you... yours was the most powerful I've encountered since..." His voice trailed off as he stopped himself in mid-thought. "What you have experienced is a vision—a prophecy if you will—that concerns a decision which awaits you in the future. I've not used the stone for quite some time, and you seem to have an immense draw on its power. My strength is laid waste. I am spent and must rest."

Aaron tried to interrupt with questions.

"No, young sir, I am spent and will discuss nothing more." With that, he slowly stood and stretched.

"One thing," Aaron interrupted, "who are you?"

"I am... well let's just say that I am someone that can help you discover the path you are meant to travel. I am a friend, though I can see by your expression that you've not had a friend like me." Kaylan waved his hand and stopped Aaron before he asked another question. "Keep your thoughts and save your questions for tomorrow. Speak with your own heart and seek understanding there. Goodnight."

Kaylan made his way to his chamber, stooped over with exhaustion. He closed the door behind him and it locked with a snap—his final word for the night.

Rayn looked to Aaron. "Sir, I'm not sure that I understand what just happened. Can you tell me what is going on?"

"No, I don't think I can." Aaron paused, thoughtful. He had no answer for himself, let alone for Rayn. He lifted his head. "What I know is that we have a job to do, and we will investigate and employ all available resources to that end. Our task, no matter what else surrounds it, is to find the book. I am just as puzzled by these other encounters as you are…but I had hoped that this experience might somehow help lead us to the book."

"For now," Rayn quipped, "I guess that the most we can do is to decide which room to take for the night. You look like you can use the rest. I know I can."

"I couldn't sleep now even if I wanted to. My mind is a flurry of thoughts, and I need to think through these recent experiences. You go and get some sleep."

****

Rayn disappeared into one of the upper rooms while Aaron sat near the fire. He stared at the diminished flames in silence as his mind wandered to the image of the woman on the ledge…*who was she…what does she have to do with me…what part does she play…does she have a part in my search for the book*? Questions wove in his mind as he thought through the circumstances that possessed him. He felt like, somehow, he had tumbled into the floodwaters of a turbulent river and was unable to overcome the current.

Events swirled around him like a torrent—the dream, what Morryn saw, the strange emissary in the mayor's mansion, the visitation of the beast at the mountain cottage, and now this strange old man who had shown him a vision of someone he'd never met. All were incomprehensible, and yet they were his experiences of the last two days. "Let it rest," he told himself. "If I get too caught up in trying to think this through, I'll just paralyze myself."

All was quiet—so quiet in fact, that Aaron heard the gentle whisper of Rayn as he slept. The fire had died down in the common room; small flames and the glow of embers were all that remained. Aaron felt as if time stood still, and he found himself daydreaming of his many adventures in the service of the emperor. At thirty years of age he had become the youngest man to achieve the rank of captain, and he was given command of the Third Order of the Royal Guard. It was a high honor, bound with many responsibilities as well as a multitude of privileges. He enjoyed his position, and for the last three years performed his duties with excellence.

Now, however, Aaron felt frustrated in his position. He didn't know why, but his heart longed for more than service as a soldier in the guard—even if he was in command. Old snatches of childhood memories crept into his dreams and mingled with his unsettled restlessness. He wanted— needed—a chance to explore the hunger in his heart, but the oath he swore bound him to his service and could not be broken.

He stared into the fire and noticed the orb was still perched on its stand. A slow, red glow swirled within the sphere as it captured the diminished light of the embers. Aaron was mesmerized by the light as it moved like liquid flame within the orb. He wanted to know more... he wanted to see the woman again and to help her in her distress. He stared at the orb. The lights within moved faster and held his gaze. Then the same flash of red light burst upon his eyes, and Aaron stood in a large hall.

He looked around and guessed that the hall was the chamber of someone important. Large tapestries with images of mighty battles and grand heroes decorated the stone walls. Twelve massive stone columns lined both sides of a marble walkway which ended at a platform. Upon it sat a magnificent marble throne inlaid with gold. Statues of mighty warriors, each wielding a large iron axe, kept silent vigil at the base of each pillar. Atop the throne sat a rugged, bearded man—but shorter and broader than any man Aaron had ever seen. In each corner of the room oil-filled braziers burned with intense fires and black smoke wafted up to a small hole cut in the center of the roof. The lights of the braziers made shadows flicker along the walls.

Aaron, slow and cautious, walked up to the dais, unsure if he was noticed by the one who sat enthroned. He observed the man wore a slender circlet of gold around his head, adorned with diamonds and a single, brilliant emerald at the brow. *Obviously a man of rank.* The bearded man's eyes were fixed upon a scroll in his hands.

The man tore the scroll and shouted, "Get my attendant!" His cavernous voice echoed in the stone hall.

The sound of a latch snapped and another man entered from behind the throne. In appearance, the second man was much like the first, bearded and short, with a broad chest. The man rushed in and knelt before the first. "My lord," he said with respect.

"How long?" He threw the torn scraps of parchment at his attendant. "When did you receive this notice?"

"Sir, I just received this today...this very moment in fact...from the messenger. I was told he received the news just two days ago." The attendant's voice trembled.

"So the book is lost! How could this have happened?" The man stood and began to pace across the platform.

"My lord, it is thought the book was taken by the men of Celedon, those of the Royal Guard. It could very well be on its way back to their emperor as we speak."

The attendant's words sent his lord into a rage. "Send for the seer! I need to know what has happened. I need to know if the book is lost to us! This can't have happened; the world hangs in the balance, and the key to victory makes its way to our enemy. Quick man, get up and go get the seer!" The second man rose and ran behind the throne to disappear with only the sound of a door latch to signal his departure.

Aaron watched the tirade, bewildered at what he saw. It was apparent to him the players in the drama that unfolded before his eyes were unaware of his presence. He didn't know these people but they must be the ones in league with the thief. Aaron took great interest in the fact the Royal Guard was mentioned by name, and that they mistakenly thought he possessed the Book of Aleth. *If only that were true*, thought Aaron. *I could go back to Celedon and be done with this.* He continued to watch the bearded lord pace back and forth on the platform.

In a flurry of activity, the attendant returned. Close on his heels followed another of the short, but unusually stout, men. Bearded like the rest, he wore a hooded robe and carried a large leather satchel over his shoulder. The hood was loosely draped behind his back, and the newcomer quickly assembled a tripod stand with a small fire pot underneath. Then, much like Kaylan, he took an orb from within the satchel and placed it on the stand. The robed newcomer set fire to the fuel in the small pot and it began to burn with great intensity. The orb swirled with a fire within, growing in brilliance until it outshone every other light. The hooded man's attention disappeared into the currents of light within the small crystal. After a brief time he looked up, his eyes fixed with fear. "My lord," he said with a shudder. "I have seen the man who has the book!"

"Who?" Demanded the other and pounded his fist on the throne. "Tell me now; we must make plans to retrieve it!"

The hooded stranger knelt, appearing more exhausted than reverent, and spoke with labored breath. "My lord, it is with a man dressed in a soldier's uniform, a uniform that bears the insignia of the empire and with the mark of the Royal Guard. And, sir, he leads a company of men—soldiers all. He was a tall man, even for his kind, stern and fierce in his appearance. He was on no road that I could see, and led his men southeast."

"Morryn!" Aaron exclaimed.

With a flash of red light, Aaron found he looked upon the dim fire in the hearth and the small orb perched upon its tripod. He turned to see Rayn behind him, a worried, puzzled look on the private's face. Kaylan stood next to Rayn. The wizened man stared at Aaron with strong disapproval. Aaron was out of breath, exhausted from his experience with the orb. He looked at Rayn with a sunken weariness. "We need to turn east," he panted. "Morryn has taken the book." Then Aaron collapsed, unconscious.

4

A Bitter Betrayal

Lieutenant Morryn sat tall upon his steed, a sly smile on his face. He was glad to see the miles between him and his captain continue to grow. He reached down and touched the leather saddle bag at his side and checked that the book was secure. It was. Behind him twenty mounted men rode in silent procession, careful to follow their new commander and more careful to keep a safe distance from his hot-tempered reach. Morryn sat amazed at how simple it was to acquire the treasured Book of Aleth. He just slipped out in the evening while the men in the barracks slept, made his way to the burned out building and walked away with the prize.

However, he didn't foresee his captain giving over command of the squad. Morryn intended to slip away in the still quiet of the winter night, but after being ordered to take command, his disappearance would have been suspicious. He looked back at the score of soldiers who rode in silence. He needed to be rid of them soon.

Ahead, spanning the massive Hoppe River, a single bridge reached to the eastern bank. A heavy mist shimmered in the cold morning air, churned up by the torrent. Morryn led his men across and then turned southeast toward the Shattered Hills. Whispers of discontent and concern about the change in direction swirled within the company, but Morryn knew that they feared to question him directly. He liked it that way.

They rode at a steady pace through drifts of new fallen snow as the sun started its ascent into the pale blue sky. The chill November air penetrated to the bone as a light breeze whipped up an army of snowflakes that clung to both man and horse. They passed through a sparse, wooded glen, illuminated with sunlight that filtered through the trees. Skulking shadows writhed in silence as the trees swayed in the wind.

They continued for several miles when one of the men spurred his horse to catch up with Morryn. It was the sergeant, Lorik, older than the rest, a seasoned veteran of countless years of service in the Royal Guard. A keen awareness flashed in the sergeant's eyes—the awareness of experience. "Lieutenant," he said as he approached, "the men need a rest. I know this area, and there is a clearing about two miles east. We can break formation there and allow the men and horses to recover a bit from this ride."

"Very well, sergeant," Morryn said, frustrated by the delay. "Make sure that you tell the men that this will be just a brief rest. We must arrive at the edge of the Shattered Hills before nightfall tomorrow. Now if you know the way, take us there." Lorik saluted and turned back toward the men behind them. Morryn had to keep up appearances, to feign command until he reached his destination.

He listened as Lorik spoke loud enough to be heard by everyone "Men, we have just a couple more miles to go, and we will take a rest." A collective sigh of relief went up from the men. They rode on with renewed vigor. Lorik returned to Morryn's side and took the lead through the forest. Branches, burdened with snow, sent showers of winter upon the small contingent as they ducked beneath them. Groans reverberated from the men as they cursed the snow and winter.

An hour passed and they came to the edge of the clearing. It was a gentle vale, a quaint, snow-covered meadow nestled in the pine forest. The thin trees provided some protection from the swirling wind. High now, the sun sent down a remembrance of warmth, but was unable to stave off the encroaching cold. The men dismounted and tied their horses to the trees at the edge of the glade and began to scavenge for various branches and sticks, enough to have fuel for a campfire. Lorik helped three other men dig a pit in the snow for the fire.

Soon a large, warm blaze cracked and popped with all the men gathered around. The entire band stood near and stretched their hands out to capture its heat. Lorik retrieved a saddlebag from his horse and passed it to the men who had circled the campfire. Inside the bag was a treasure of dried beef and assorted dried fruit, as well as hard cheese and bread wafers. There was plenty to go around and each man took his share.

"Sergeant," a young, rugged soldier asked, "what are we doin' out here? I mean, I thought we were headin' home?"

Lorik saw a reflection of his own apprehension in the young man's eyes.

"Soldier," Lorik replied, "the captain gave the

lieutenant command of this squad and that is enough for you and me." Lorik looked over to where Morryn warmed his hands by the fire. "Don't be troubled over a detour. If the lieutenant says there's a good reason to be out here then there's a good reason." Lorik spoke more to convince himself. He glanced at Morryn again. *Where is the lieutenant taking us?* He determined to keep a wary eye on his temporary commander.

****

"Soldiers!" An hour had passed when Morryn barked out his command. "Mount up and move out. We must be through these woods before nightfall, and we only have four more hours of daylight. There's a chill wind from the north, so we can expect snow tonight. I plan to have tents pitched before then. Sergeant, get these men moving!"

Morryn mounted his horse and checked his saddlebag to ensure the book was still secure and unnoticed. Several men grumbled about the necessity to ride out on what was sure to be a bone-chilling exercise, but they mounted their horses as ordered and formed two columns. The men rode through the trees in as good a formation as the forest allowed.

"Sergeant," the voice of one soldier rang out from behind Morryn and he eavesdropped on the conversation. "Are we really heading to the Shattered Hills?"

"Yes," Lorik replied.

"But sir...the Shattered Hills!" The young soldier's voice broke with disbelief. "I've heard horror stories of the creatures that live there. Trolls and worse...that's all we will encounter!"

"It's good you're with us then!" Lorik sounded impatient. Morryn listened as the sergeant continued. "Keep your courage; we won't encounter anything that we can't handle."

Morryn smiled a deceptive smile. Lorik's duty was to ensure the men obeyed all his orders and maintain discipline. He glanced back at Lorik. The sergeant's duty would be put to the test.

The rest of the day passed without incident or conversation as each man kept his thoughts to himself. Morryn's forecasted weather, in the form of heavy grey clouds, rolled in from the north, drifting over the Shadow Mountains with long sheets of snow painted in streaks upon the horizon. Clouds shrouded the sun and cast the world in twilight. The pale light projected ghostly images and engendered the forest with eerie shadows that moved like specters. Trees stood around them as frozen sentinels, grasping at the soldiers with gnarled branches. Morryn watched the ominous approach of the winter storm. He knew they had less than an hour.

The regiment arrived at the edge of the forest with both man and beast tired and cold. Many men groaned with fatigue, relieved that they were at day's end. As they passed beyond the eastern edge of the woods the wind, which blew from the north, bit into them with renewed ferocity. Frigid air mingled with swirling snow and caused even the hardiest soldier to shiver in the bitter flurry. Just beyond the tree line, Lorik located a patch of level ground to set their camp and barked out orders in the blustery wind.

"Men, get these tents assembled quickly and prepare a bonfire to ward off the cold." He pointed to the men who stood to his left. "You gather wood and other fuel and build a fire; and you"—he pointed to the rest—"set up the tents. Make sure that they're arranged with the flaps inward, toward the fire. Now gird yourselves up, men, and we'll have ourselves encamped before the sun sets."

Despite the bitter cold and blowing snow, the men responded with the discipline of trained soldiers. Each man took to his responsibility; half gathered loose wood and other debris and piled it in the center of the campsite. The rest of the men moved in almost synchronous motion and prepared twelve tents in a circle around the pile just as the sergeant ordered. When they had gathered enough fuel, several men from the fire detail retrieved their flint and tinder boxes and sparked a massive, crackling blaze.

All the men huddled near the fire, the only relief from the bitter cold. Several bags were passed around containing more dried meats, fruits, and hard-cheese. As they ate their cold meal, the sun gave up its last rays of light with shafts of orange and purple that streaked across the sky. Then it left the world to the cold shadow of night.

Most of the men sat in stillness, occupied with their own thoughts. Lorik heard some of the men quietly talking with each other. "What are we doin' out here? We ought to be on the road home."

Another whisper was heard in reply. "Just shut up, will ya? It doesn't help to think of what we don't have!"

By the light of the campfire, Lorik walked among the troops. Occasionally, he would stop and speak a word of encouragement to a sullen soldier, pat another on the shoulder and keep him focused on his duty. The darkness outside the circle of the campfire deepened, and Lorik wanted to get the men set for the night. He gathered them around him.

"All right, men," he said. "We've had a long march, and it's cold. Get some rest and be fresh for tomorrow. Each tent will be responsible for a one hour guard duty. The lieutenant and I will take the first watch and will wake the next tent in sequence. Get some sleep; you have a long, hard march to the Shattered Hills tomorrow."

The men paired up and entered into their various tents. Most left their tent flap open to try and capture as much of the heat from the fire as possible. Even with the fire, the tents were uncomfortable and chilled.

With the men in their shelters, Lorik ventured over to find Morryn who sat motionless and alone. "Sir, if you like, you get some rest. I can handle the first watch—it's still early and there's no need for the both of us to be out in the cold."

Morryn looked up at the sergeant, as if he were surprised at Lorik's presence. "Are you going to check and secure the animals?" His question carried a tone of frustration at the prospect.

"Yes, sir," Lorik said. "It is standard procedure to secure our mounts and check all gear."

"Don't bother," Morryn said. "I'll do it—you tend to the fire."

"As you wish, sir," Lorik said. He looked at Morryn with a puzzled expression, not sure what to make of the officer's demeanor. Lorik saluted and returned to the fire, *a warmer companion than Morryn*, Lorik thought. He tossed two more branches onto the blaze and sat down on a nearby rock. *Something's wrong*, he mused. *I can't place my finger on it, but something's wrong*. He stared back toward Morryn, the lieutenant's tall frame illuminated in the glow of the firelight. Morryn sat unmoved and looked like a weathered statue. For the first time in his military service, Lorik sensed a strong, unsettled apprehension about the man who commanded them.

The first hour passed in cold, uneventful duty. The snow that fell at first like gentle feathers now came down with renewed vigor. Large, cold flakes of the winter's blast dominated the atmosphere and weighed down the tents. The fire voiced its strong disapproval of the snowfall and hissed with every flake, but Lorik's diligence kept the fire alive and warm for the troops who slept.

The air was thick, alive with swirling white reflections and reduced visibility so that Lorik had to squint to see the far side of the campsite. Yet, across the small compound, he spied the shadowed form of Lieutenant Morryn, motionless near his tent. If Lorik hadn't known who sat there, he might have assumed that it was the projection of a fallen tree or the trick of shadows. However, worry as he did, it was time for him to rouse the next shift and take to the comfort of his tent.

Lorik approached the tent pitched to the right of his own. Snow had accumulated all around the entrance and drifts had built up along the edges. He opened the flap to see two soldiers. They were awake and talked with each other in whispered tones. "Not sleepy?" Lorik questioned. "Well, it's time for the both of you to get your gear and take the watch. Snowfall is heavy tonight so bundle up."

The two men nodded in acknowledgement and the younger of the two spoke up, "Sergeant?"

"Yes, what is it?" Lorik asked.

The young man continued, "Well, I am... I mean, we were wondering, how long do you think that we'll be here? I don't want to complain, sir, but we've been gone from home a long time."

"I don't know what the lieutenant's purpose is or how long he plans to remain in this place, but the captain left him in command," Lorik said.

"But, Sergeant, what are we doin' here? The captain always told us where we were goin' and why. What does the lieutenant want out here?"

Lorik felt the same frustration but needed to maintain discipline. "Soldier, that's not your concern. You don't have any other purpose than to obey the commands of your superior, and right now, that is Lieutenant Morryn. Until that duty is done you will follow his orders." Lorik tried to sound steeled in his resolve, but his own thoughts waivered with anxious doubts.

"But Sergeant," the other soldier chimed in, "this doesn't make any sense." He stood and paced back and forth within the cramped space of his tent. "With the captain, we knew what his orders were—and why. It seems all we know is that we are camped on the edge of perhaps one of the most hostile regions in all of Celedon. Now, don't get me wrong, sir, it doesn't scare me to be here, but to be here for no reason...well...that concerns me."

"That'll be enough from the both of you. We are here, and we will do what duty demands. The time has come for the both of you to take watch. Keep an eye on the horses, and watch the perimeter. Keep fuel on the fire, and wake the next tent in an hour. We'll have no more discussion about why we're here." Lorik crossed his arms and waited as the two men strapped on their swords.

They exited the tent, and the sergeant noticed that Lieutenant Morryn no longer brooded in solitude. In fact, Morryn was nowhere to be seen. Lorik dismissed this and hoped the lieutenant had retired to bed. He reiterated his orders to the two soldiers and made his way through the onslaught of snow to his own tent. The wind whipped the canvas in rhythmic motion, sometimes in gusts, other times like a gentle whisper.

Lorik unrolled his sleeping mat and unpacked two heavy wool blankets. He tied the entrance flap down to prevent the chill breeze from blowing in and propped his sword against the center pole. With a sigh of exhaustion, he flopped onto the mat and rolled himself up in his heavy blankets. *Ah, sleep*, he thought to himself.

****

Morryn watched as Lorik vanished into one of the tents and, with no other guards on duty, he snuck back to the horses and retrieved his pack. At the rear of the encampment, the horses huddled close to one another in an attempt to share warmth and protection from the cold. Inside his saddlebag, the leather-bound tome waited. Its parchment pages crackled as he removed it. He feared someone might discover his prize and didn't want to risk the possibility the book would be brought back to Celedon and the emperor. *He had other plans*.

Morryn covered the book with his cloak and took it back to his tent without any notice. He paused for a moment and listened to the muffled voice of the sergeant in a nearby tent, and then Morryn dashed back to his own quarters. To hide the book, he wrapped it in a cloth, and placed it within the folds of his blanket roll. He was sure no one suspected, and he believed that his plan would deliver to him what his heart craved—power.

The snow fell unabated and started to fill the gaps between the tents. Morryn listened as the guards fought against the winter blast, desperate to keep the bonfire ablaze. He knew the men suffered discouragement, that their hearts longed to return south, but he needed to make his rendezvous. The winter storm, however, did not bode well for his plans. *Patience*, he thought, *that's what it will take*. He had already put the pieces together, now he just needed to wait and let the picture unfold.

The night passed without incident and, despite the snow, the soldiers proved their worth and kept the fire ablaze. Lorik emerged from his tent just as the dawn opened up, grey and dismal, to shed its ruddy, pale light upon the world. The last two guards on duty cast more wood upon the fire which sent a shower of embers into the air. The snowstorm ended as it came, with soft snowflakes that drifted with sporadic laziness from the sky. Then the clouds separated to unveil a crisp, blue sky—a welcome sight to the shivering soldiers. The two guards on watch began to wake the rest of the men, moving from tent to tent until the entire squad had roused from their slumber.

Against the pristine beauty of the new fallen snow, the Shattered Hills lay in dark contrast, a shadowed remnant of an ancient nightmare. Broken crags, large spires, fractured rock, and sharp pinnacles, mysterious and bleak loomed in defiance over the men. To Lorik it appeared as if some great giant had smashed the earth with a cudgel and left destruction as far as the eye could see. A hot breakfast worked well to warm body and spirit and many of the men began to laugh and joke about their destination.

"Bring on the trolls!" One soldier shouted to the hills. "I'll take 'em down myself!"

"Yea, with your breath!" joked another soldier nearby who then elbowed his companion in the ribs.

Each soldier jumped into the conversation to deliver their verbal jabs as they sparred with each other. Lorik was glad to hear the camaraderie among the soldiers and hoped their morale was strong enough to withstand the Shattered Hills. He looked around for Morryn but didn't see the tall lieutenant anywhere among the men. He dipped out a bowl of the hot broth and took it to Morryn's tent. "Lieutenant," Lorik announced his presence. "Sir, with your permission, may I enter?"

"Yes, get in here," the lieutenant's voice sounded harsh and disturbed.

Lorik entered and saw Morryn erect, with his sword strapped to his belt. "Sir, I brought you some breakfast. It's not much, but it's hot."

"Thank you, Sergeant," Morryn said as he retrieved the bowl of warm liquid. "Tell me, how are the men after the night that we had?"

"Their spirits are up, and they are ready to ride out at your signal. Will we break down the tents or leave a contingent here?" Lorik tried to hide the sense of mistrust that he felt toward the lieutenant.

Morryn paused, as if he tried to gather his thoughts before answering. "We will need a small band to venture into the hills. Select eight men and we will leave the rest here." Lorik saluted his commander and left the tent.

"Fall in!" Lorik barked the command. "Lieutenant Morryn has ordered that eight of you will join us for an expedition into the Shattered Hills. Get your gear and be prepared to leave within the hour."

****

Morryn knew it was risky to take anyone with him, but concern for the creatures in the Shattered Hills overrode his fear of discovery. He also knew who waited for him and he didn't trust them. Wizards were, after all, rather unpredictable. But the guild's promise to give him power—power enough to overthrow the emperor—prompted his decision to deliver up the book to them.

Morryn left his tent and looked over the men assembled around the fire. The laughter continued as they joked and talked among themselves. One young soldier who stood in close proximity to Morryn's tent noticed their commander and called the men to attention.

"At ease," Morryn said. "Who are the men that will accompany me into the Shattered Hills?"

"Sir," the sergeant replied as he approached Morryn, "These eight men have volunteered to accompany us," he said as he pointed to eight soldiers gathered behind him. "We will be ready to ride out with you within the hour."

"Very good," Morryn replied. "Make sure you ready my horse and prepare for a two-day expedition. Come and get me when you're ready, I'll be in my tent." He turned and ducked back through the canvas flap and disappeared.

Excitement filled the camp as the eight men

readied their packs and gear for the journey. Morryn could hear their voices, some muffled, others whooping in anticipation.

Time moved slowly as Morryn waited. He opened his pack and took the treasured book from its hiding place. With care, he traced his fingers along the gold emblem on the worn, leather cover. The book felt ancient, with its crisp pages and strange markings. A malicious grin crossed his face.

"Sir," Lorik said, "we are mounted and ready!"

Startled, Morryn quickly hid the book in his pack and strode from his tent. He hiked his cloak high on his shoulders to ward off the chill. He mounted his stallion, its rich black coat and solid build made it a perfect companion. Morryn held up his hand, "Move out!" he shouted and signaled for the men to follow. They left behind the sparse forest and the rest of the men.

Lorik followed Morryn with the eight others in close formation as they rode east into the broken, harsh terrain. Despite their earlier bravado, each step closer to the Shattered Hills brought a deeper level of anxiety among the men as they murmured their concerns to each other.

It wasn't long before the base camp disappeared in the distance behind them. Ahead of them loomed the Shattered Hills. The rock formations possessed no gentle slope or tender rise. Each elevation of shear, sharp rock jutted out of the ground like mammoth shards of broken glass. A pass meandered through the fractured terrain, little more than a narrow corridor that weaved throughout the entire menagerie of outcroppings. The air was cold, as if icy fingers grasped through the skin to freeze the very marrow. In the dismal reaches of the hills, even the sun had no power to warm the earth and the blue sky only intensified the sense of chill.

The men rode single file through the gap as they quietly progressed along the rough terrain. Hours passed in silence, not even the sound of a bird's cry, just the rap of shod hooves on the frozen rock.

"Do you think that trolls actually live here?" whispered one stout soldier. His voice echoed in the unnatural stillness.

"I don't know," another soldier answered. "I've not been in a place like this ever before." He glanced around as if he half expected to see some hideous form leap out of the shadows.

"Quiet!" Lorik whispered as loud as he dared. "We ride in silence." With that, the men before him refrained from any further conversation. Even the horses seemed to know better and kept their opinionated whinnies to themselves. Only the rhythmic stroke of hoof against stone gave voice to their journey.

The sun had reached its zenith when Morryn raised his hand to signal a halt. The men seemed as hungry, cold, and saddle-sore as he was. Quite a few moaned in grateful acceptance for the opportunity to dismount and walk off the stiffness in their legs. Soon after, several sacks of rations circulated through the ranks. The men expressed their misery to one another in whispered discontent, but no one dared to voice displeasure to Morryn.

One soldier started to light a bit of twigs and a small pile of dried grass.

"Soldier," Morryn barked under his breath, "no fire!"

Shortly they were back on their mounts, riding into the depths of the Shattered Hills. They reached a broad area, a cul-de-sac, with enough room for all the horses and men to stand abreast. Massive rock spires rose up around them like fingers desperate to grasp the sky—and they stood in the palm. In front of them, on the eastern wall, a small cave disappeared into indefinite darkness. From the mouth of the cave, rough hewn steps descended into the depths of the earth.

Morryn dismounted and approached Lorik. "We will remain here tonight, have the men arrange themselves and post a watch twenty paces down the path."

"No disrespect, sir, but what are we doing here?" Lorik voiced the question that rested in the heart of all his men.

"We are waiting; that is all you need to know. Prepare camp for the night and post the guard."

Morryn returned to his mount, checked his saddlebag and unpacked his gear. He listened as the sergeant gave the orders and arranged the schedule for the watch. *Just a little while longer,* thought Morryn. The men assembled camp on the north side of the ring of spires. They made a campfire with wood they brought. Everyone stood close to the heat and tried to keep warm.

Morryn paced around the camp. His eyes continued to drift toward the small cave on the eastern wall. He heaved a sigh, anxious and unsettled.

The hours passed with slow monotony. A hint of new snow appeared as light flakes drifted in a casual pageant through the air. The men huddled near the fire and arranged their beds and gear to capture as much of the heat from the conflagration as possible. Lorik and another, younger soldier stood near the fire as they stirred a small cook pot filled with another mixture of beef and water. With the men preoccupied around the fire, Morryn slipped unnoticed into the eastern cave and disappeared down the steep stairs.

The cavern was dim. Filtered light from the entrance trickled in and illuminated the ancient stairwell. As night closed in upon the world outside it left the catacomb in repressive darkness. Morryn took a small, luminescent stone from a leather pouch. It radiated a pale blue light, not much brighter than a candle, but in the darkness of the tunnel it was enough for him to navigate the narrow staircase. The ancient tunnel descended into the depths of the earth. His height forced him to take care as the passage was little more than five feet high. The walls were cold and damp, and the stairs slick with moisture.

He continued, plunging deeper into the musty darkness. The echo of the cavern forced him to ignore the sound of extra footfalls. On one occasion he stopped to listen, cautious that he wasn't followed, and concerned that some unseen intruder tried to match his steps. If Morryn had been given to fear, the dark cavern would have paralyzed him.

Time seemed to stand still in the depths of the earth. Morryn had lost track of how long he had navigated the passage when he found himself at the bottom of the rough stone stairs. He stepped out of the stairwell and felt the enormity of a cavernous, dark hall. His faint light failed to illuminate more than just the few paces before him, but the sense of a vast room was undeniable. To his left two faint red lights bobbed like will-o'-the-wisps. He knew these were the two men who arranged the clandestine meeting. Morryn navigated through broken and fallen rocks, around fractured pillars and several ancient statues to reach the two lights that waited in the distance.

"Seems you were delayed," said one raspy voiced man. "We waited far longer than agreed." His speech triggered an immediate distrust in Morryn, but he needed what these men offered, a weapon of great power.

"I apologize for my delay, gentleman." Morryn voice dripped with sarcasm. "It was unavoidable. I couldn't just sneak off in the night; my duties would not permit such a disappearance. But I am here, and am ready to finish this business." His patience was thin, and his desire to be back above ground grew with each breath. Morryn disliked the cold, damp claustrophobic feel of the ancient hall and distrusted the two men who stood before him. His skin crawled with the sense malicious eyes watched his every move, eyes that stayed just beyond the limited reach of his light.

"Yes, of course," the first man said. Morryn equated the man's voice to that of a serpent. He was aged, almost ancient, and seemed to fit the dark environment. A hooded cloak covered his face so just his thin pale lips were seen. The wizard reached into his cloak and uncovered a box, jeweled and ornate with gold characters inlaid upon the lid that glimmered in the dim light of the stones. It was small, just big enough to hold a small talisman or jewel.

"Is that it?" Morryn demanded. He expected to receive a great weapon, not a small, jeweled case.

"Fool," the old wizard hissed. "This box contains an object more powerful than your limited wit might imagine. It holds the key to power, enough power to displace the emperor himself." He held the small case in his hand and displayed its ornate markings to the lieutenant. "You know," the wizard continued, "the emperor has lost his mind in his desperation to recapture the Book of Aleth...the book you now have. He is obsessed with it, and will destroy his own empire to retrieve it. You came to us to deliver the empire into your hands and we will do it—just give us the book!" The wizard's words were harsh and firm, and carried a sense of undeniable power. Even the air seemed to shudder at his voice.

Morryn felt a strong compulsion to hand over the tome. "I have it here," he said as he reached into the folds of his cloak. He pulled out the book and held it in view of the two men. Morryn looked at the small box, eager to gain its hidden power.

Morryn clutched the Book of Aleth, and the power of the wizard's voice vanished. A moment of clarity rushed through his mind as he stared through narrowed eyes at the wizards. His heart raced, and he knew the two men were about to betray him. "Leave the box on the ground, and I will leave the book. We'll trade places and have what we've come for." Morryn, with his eyes fixed upon the wizards, placed the book on the floor at his feet. The two hooded figures did the same with the box, and the three men began to move toward each other and their desired artifacts.

Hidden by his cloak, his hand gripped cold steel. As Morryn walked past the wizards, he drew his sword and struck. In fluid motion, he decapitated the first man, pivoted, and ran the second man through the heart. The wizard looked down, eyes wide with horror at the sword that protruded from his chest. He clutched at the weapon and then collapsed to the ground, dead.

Morryn chuckled and retrieved the book from the floor then gathered the small box. "Betray me, will you?" Morryn shouted to the two men. He had heard of the power of wizards to control the minds of men, and Morryn didn't understand how their spell was broken. Now all he wanted to do was leave the underground chamber.

He started back toward the staircase. Again, the sense of watchful eyes penetrated his perception and made his flesh crawl. He looked around with the skill of an experienced hunter, but all he saw was thick darkness beyond his pale light. Careful to avoid the fallen debris, Morryn stepped over various broken objects and drew closer to the stairs. The cold air of the cavern hung heavy with moisture, musty and stale. He found the wall and navigated the circumference of the room until he arrived at the open hole of the stone stairway.

The passage was steep, and he climbed with deliberate steps. But the fearful sense of some unseen menace lurking in the shadows behind him forced him to climb faster. Morryn wished he could run, but the precarious nature of the stairs prevented any rapid ascent. His panic continued to grow to the point that it overwhelmed his thoughts. He considered a sprint to the exit.

A breath of wind began to blow from the deep, and it carried what he thought was a low groan. Morryn trembled with panic, unable to outrace the fear that chased him up the stairwell. Ahead in the distance, a ruddy light outlined the exit. *The campfire*! Yet fear gained on him, no matter how fast he attempted to outrun it to the cavern's entrance.

Morryn panicked as the dread of some unseen adversary overwhelmed his senses. He stumbled and tripped along the stairs. Terror propelled him until the entrance was in full view. In a desperate attempt to outrun the fear, Morryn fell through the mouth of the cave and tumbled onto the ground.

The soldiers at the encampment jumped back in surprise. Morryn stood and panted with exhaustion as he moved toward the fire. He searched through the small band of soldiers until he spotted Lorik talking with three others. "Sergeant!" Morryn shouted. His voice trembled in unrestrained panic. "We must leave now!" he ordered. "Everyone mount up. Leave the gear. Leave the fire. We must get out of here now!" He ran to his horse, ignoring the questions and the bewildered looks that followed him. Morryn tightened the straps on his mount and rode off as a great shriek sounded all around them.

In a sudden rush of movement, a horde of massive creatures cascaded over the surrounding cliffs. Trolls! Large, dark beasts with knobby clubs in their huge fists fell upon the unwary soldiers. The men were surrounded on every side. Panic filled the eyes of each remaining soldier. With dust still rising from Morryn's unexpected and hasty departure, Lorik knew he'd have to rally the men. There was no time for retreat.

A veteran of many battles, he commanded the men to form a line of defense. "Stand strong!" he called. "We stand together, no one fears, no one flees!" He stood at the head of the unit, sword drawn; his heart pounded like a hammer in his chest. The men marshaled to his courage and followed his lead to hold their ground.

The creatures were on them. Huge monsters, nine

feet tall, with grey, leathery skin and faces a hideous mix of human and animal, came at the unit with the ferocity of wild beasts. They hit the line of men, swords against clubs, and for a moment the soldiers threw them back. Steel swords flashed in the firelight and reflected upon the rocks while the shouts of battle reverberated in the small hollow. Monsters growled and roared in agony as many fell, sliced and pierced by the skill of the soldiers. Yet many more of the massive beasts poured over the walls of stone, violent, unrestrained, like a flood over the Shattered Hills that broke upon the soldiers, wave after wave.

In the darkness the men had no idea the number of their adversaries. To Lorik, it seemed endless. One beast after another rampaged over the hills to attack the small band. Swords deflected clubs, skill fought strength, but the small cluster of men began to waiver. Then a troll landed a blow to the head of one young soldier who fell in a heap. The sergeant knew the men's strength began to dim, and their line soon must fail. They had to retreat. "Into the cave!" he shouted, "into the cave!" Those closest to the cave began to shift toward the entrance, but found no quarter given from the hoard against them. Before they could enter, two more soldiers were gone.

Only three soldiers remained with Lorik. The horses were scattered, and he assumed they fled in terror down the path. One large troll rose up before him, and Lorik spun then thrust his sword deep into the heart of the creature. Two more came up behind the first and lunged at Lorik. He ducked the swing of the first, slashed at the second, and realized he was behind the line of creatures. Lorik attacked and dropped both trolls in their tracks. He gasped for air, exhausted. Silence filled the hollow. No more enemies approached. The small cul-de-sac was deathly quiet.

Bodies lay scattered around, soldiers as well as beasts, their red blood mingled on the rock floor of the campsite. Dozens had fallen by the sword. He gazed over the piled carcasses. He was the lone survivor. Every soldier lay dead, crushed under the weight of the attack. Lorik knew to remain was certain death, so he gathered up what food he found, wrapped an extra cloak around his shoulders, and took to the path that led out of the Shattered Hills. Darkness had settled in. The cold winter air tried to rob him of his strength, but he knew he must keep going, keep moving, and keep warm.

He hurried past the location of the guard post and saw two more dead soldiers, ambushed by the beasts. To his fortune, a lone horse remained just a few yards down the trail. It shivered as Lorik rubbed its neck. The mount seemed glad to have found a survivor. It nuzzled up against his shoulder. Lorik grabbed the reigns and threw himself into the saddle. Alone, it didn't take long to navigate the path back the way they came and his mount seemed just as eager to leave. Behind him, the howls of the creatures echoed through the hills. He tried not to imagine what the beasts did to the bodies of the men who had fallen. Grief stricken, Lorik had no time and little strength. So, he pressed his mount through the night.

"What happened?" he asked himself. "And where is the lieutenant?" He had never seen a man in such terror, and had never seen a soldier of Morryn's skill flee the scene of a battle. He had no answers and too many questions. He needed to get away, find the lieutenant, and get some answers.

5

Madness and Mysteries

Morryn spurred his horse back down the dark, cold crevice and took no thought for danger. Behind him, the noise of battle echoed through the pass. The cries and screams of his soldiers mingled with the howls of the ferocious beasts and shattered the stillness of the night. He knew the beasts; trolls were fierce, brute animals. He continued through the ravine and ignored the desperate plight of his men. He rushed past the place where the two guards had been posted. In the dim moonlight, Morryn spied two massive trolls as they dragged the limp, fallen bodies of the soldiers. With sword drawn, he spurred his horse into a run. Man and beast, with breath like smoke from a dragon's mouth, rushed toward the two trolls with reckless ferocity. He passed between them and struck the nearest troll. The monster howled in pain—a sound that seemed to shatter the night. The trolls made no effort to give chase, and Morryn disappeared around a corner and vanished into the night.

Several miles of rough, cold stone passed beneath him, and his mount began to show signs of fatigue. He slowed the steed to a walk as the cold air took its toll. Morryn ached in every joint and shivered with uncontrollable spasms. The snow on the ground, stirred by a frigid breeze, blew against him like frozen needles. Several drifts had accumulated along the path like white barricades and made his journey out of the Shattered Hills even more difficult. Yet Morryn warmed himself with the knowledge that he had outwitted the two wizards in the catacombs and now possessed both artifacts.

His men were doomed, but he'd never wanted them to come in the first place. Aaron had caused the slaughter. Morryn pressed on through the night and kept to the path that brought him into the hills. The pale moon continued its slow passage through the sky; its ghostly light shone upon the narrow path that meandered through the barren rock, back to the encampment. A sense of relief washed over his thoughts as he began to understand that no one else knew of his purpose in the hills. Morryn intended to keep it that way. He smiled, self-satisfied, as he rode through the cold, bitter night.

The moon disappeared behind a casual cloud that drifted in slow motion across the velvet night sky and cast the world in darkness. Miles passed beneath him as his horse plodded along the trail. As the breeze continued to blow, Morryn wrapped his cloak tighter around him and pulled his hood lower to cover his face and ward off the effects of the winter night. Without the light of the moon, the impenetrable shadow of darkness prevented him from seeing the path. He had to trust the horse and his instincts to find his way.

Underneath him, the stallion shivered, the penetrating cold biting both horse and rider to the core. Time seemed irrelevant in the frigid air, and Morryn had no idea how far he had traveled. But knew he must keep moving just to keep warm and alive.

He climbed a small elevation and peered into the

valley beneath him. In the distance, an orange glow stood out like a beacon against the deep darkness. It was the encampment. Though distant, he rejoiced to see the flicker of the campfire as it blazed like a warm invitation. Even from a distance, through the crisp, chill air, Morryn heard the muffled voices of soldiers. He hurried his poor, cold mount, and found even his horse seemed eager to arrive at the warmth of the fire.

"A rider!" one of the guards shouted. "A rider approaches!" All those around the fire came at once as the two guards drew their swords. Morryn slumped over in his saddle, his cloak and gear covered in frost. They hurried to his side, gathered him off his mount and rushed to the campfire. Several others collected more wood. Embers exploded into the night as they threw the extra fuel onto the fire.

Another young soldier brought the lieutenant a warm cup of broth along with the remnants of supper. Morryn shivered, and he sat near the blaze to draw every ounce of warmth from it. The young guard removed Morryn's frozen cloak and draped a heavy wool blanket around the lieutenant's shoulders.

A tall, thin soldier sat next to Morryn. His eyes reflected the flicker of the firelight and revealed a genuine anxiety. "Sir," the young man asked, "what happened out there? We didn't expect anyone back before tomorrow and now you've returned alone?"

Morryn's teeth chattered as he responded. "Y-y-yes, I-I know." Morryn tried to gather himself, to speak with clarity. "No... one... else... survived. We were attacked. Trolls ambushed us... another creature...unseen." Morryn shook with uncontrollable spasms as the effects of exhaustion set in.

Thankfully, the young soldier in charge held off

any more questions and ordered another blanket and more hot broth prepared, for which Morryn was grateful. He also ordered a doubling of the guard, saying the sound of trolls on the prowl did not set well in his thoughts.

A palpable tension filled the camp. Conversations filled the air of an imminent attack from beasts out of the Shattered Hills. Swords were drawn in anticipation of the potential threat.

Morryn was escorted to his tent as clouds drifted across the luminescent moon. Bathed in pale moonlight, the peaks of the hills shimmered in the incandescent glow, filled with an impenetrable darkness. Even the continual campfire brought no comfort as the men awaited dawn.

****

Morryn roused from his sleep. Covered in heavy wool blankets, he finally felt warm. He listened to the voices of the men outside his tent.

"Half the men are dead in those accursed hills!" A soldier hissed. "Do we just sit here and wait for our own death?"

"No," said the one who had taken charge, "we don't. But we can't leave yet, not with the lieutenant in his condition. I fear this trip to the Shattered Hills was a fool's errand."

Morryn moved to the tent flap and peeked out to see the man who had taken charge.

The young soldier reached his hands out to warm them with the fire. "We'll wait till morning and then we head south. Lieutenant Morryn, I'm sure, will agree to that." The soldier looked up and signaled to three others, posting them at the corners of their camp. "You will each take watch and cry out if you see anything coming. Your relief will come in three hours. Don't hesitate to sound the alarm if you suspect trouble!" The three guardsmen, not much younger than the first, slowly walked toward their posts.

Morryn wanted to make a hasty departure and checked his gear to ensure his treasures remained hidden and secure. Then he left his tent to sit beside the fire.

The young soldier still sat by the fire, head in his hands. Morryn stood behind the thoughtful soldier, looming over the unaware young man. "Soldier," Morryn said.

Startled by Morryn's appearance, the young man stood and saluted his commander. "My apologies sir!" he said. "I didn't see you there."

"At ease Bran... Brin..." Morryn started.

"Brendal, sir!" the young guard replied.

"Well, Brendal," Morryn continued, "you've done well to keep the men in line and post guards around the camp. You are to be commended."

"Thank you, sir," Brendal said and took his seat again next to the fire. "Lieutenant," he asked, "what happened out there?"

Morryn sat down and reached his hands toward the flames. "We were ambushed, set upon by a horde of trolls that took us by surprise." Morryn gave careful thought to his words. He didn't want to arouse any suspicion.

"Sir," Brendal said, "trolls aren't known to band together. They normally attack alone, and rarely against armed men."

"You seem to have some knowledge of this. How

do you know so much about trolls?" The lieutenant tried to cover his apprehension.

"Well, sir," Brendal replied, "I grew up on a farm near North Village, and my father had his share of encounters with a marauding troll. You get to know them after a time."

"These trolls seem well organized," Morryn continued. "I think they had a leader over them. There was an unseen assailant which let out such a cry that froze the marrow in my bones." Morryn shuddered as he remembered the horrific sound. "Trolls seemed to come from everywhere, and when it was over, I alone survived."

"You're fortunate to be alive." Brendal's voice quivered. "I just wish the others were as fortunate as you."

"Buck up, soldier," Morryn attempted to sound hopeful. "They didn't give up, and the mission was accomplished. You can be proud to have served with them."

"But, sir...what mission was so important that it was worth the sacrifice of nine men?" Brendal's trembling voice echoed his troubled thoughts.

"That, soldier, is a question that must be left unanswered. It concerns the emperor, and only the emperor. Just know that your fellow guardsmen died for a greater good, for the good of the empire." He hoped to dissuade Brendal from any more conversation. "Now," Morryn continued, "I need to rest some more." He stood to stretch his tight, cold muscles. "Just one more thing... where's my horse?"

"Oh, yes," Brendal replied, "we've taken him and secured him with the others. He's been rubbed down and given warm water as well as an ample supply of food. He'll be just fine, sir… just a bit chilled and very tired. I suspect that in a couple of days your horse will be fit to travel again."

"Very well," Morryn said. "Keep the perimeter secure and watch out for any movement coming from the hills. If you sight anything, and I mean *anything* alert me at once and be ready for it—it will be trolls." Morryn turned toward his tent, his gate stiff and body sore. He was tired, every muscle ached and his head pounded. High above, a dark shadow passed in front of the moon. Tensing, he remembered the creature at North Village and looked up, but all he saw was a lazy cloud caressed by the moonlight.

Once back in his tent he wished to collapse upon his mat, but Morryn knew he needed to leave the encampment before dawn. As the night deepened into rich darkness, the moon fell below the horizon, and he slipped from his tent with a satchel slung over his shoulder. He moved with stealth to the horses and nestled alongside the stallion. Morryn secured his pack to the saddle and mounted the steed. He departed without a sound and carefully avoided the men put on the watch. The three guards on duty were on the other side of the compound and gave little attention to any movement in his location.

He spurred his horse to a slow walk, desperate not to disturb the other animals, and slipped into the woods. Morryn rode west in a direct line away from the camp. As time passed, and he realized that no one followed, he turned and rode south. Branches reached for him in the dark like gnarled fingers, as if they tried to thwart his purpose. The darkness intensified as he ventured deeper into the forest, but he continued. The moon had long settled beyond the horizon and Morryn knew that dawn neared.

He rode with haste, as swift as the grasping trees allowed, and put as much distance between himself and his men as possible. Erratic as he swerved and weaved his way through the trees, Morryn continued south. In the east, a faint glimmer of light crested the horizon as sunrise neared.

Then a sudden dread fell upon him, the same fear that had gripped him in the cavern. He looked around with growing fear and knew he was being watched. He sensed it, eyes that glared at him from the darkness. Morryn spurred his horse to try and move faster, to outrun the unseen hunter.

Then he heard a sound that chilled his blood. Carried on the cold air, far behind him. The faint sounds of battle rang through the forest. The clash of swords and screams of agony resonated through the sparse trees and mingled with the distinctive howls of trolls. Morryn stopped. He wanted to return to his men in a valiant attempt to save them. He turned his stallion around and listened. With his hand resting on the hilt of his sword, he shook his head, and left his men to their fate.

****

Lorik rode through the night. With the keen eye of a veteran soldier, he pressed on. The rugged terrain gave no quarter for carelessness, but Lorik navigated the path with skill. The moon, hidden behind a thin layer of clouds, peeked out to shine upon the earth for brief, unexpected moments. He was tired and his horse showed increased signs of weariness as she hung her head and continued with slow, laborious steps along the stone path. He knew he and his mount needed rest if they were to make their way back to the base camp.

After several miles along the path, he had to dismount. He found a small alcove of rock, a formation just large enough for him and his horse, and settled in to wait out the night. Some wood remained on the mare's pack, enough for Lorik to build a small fire and fight off the chill night air. It wasn't much, but it provided sufficient warmth for Lorik and his mount, and in the little alcove, his fire was small enough so that even from the main path it was hidden.

He found some dried beef and bread wafers in the saddlebag and ate a solitary meal. The night passed as Lorik dozed on and off in fits of sleep, miserable in the cramped stone alcove. His horse lay beside him, close to the fire as if it tried to capture as much of the warmth the small blaze provided.

Lorik woke with a start, and found his small fire spent to ashes. Darkness surrounded him, and the air felt thick with cold and heavy with moisture. His bones ached and body shivered as he stood to stretch. He was still several hours from the base camp where he hoped to reunite with his men. He needed to get moving as a sliver of dawn broke over the eastern horizon.

In the dim, pale light of the early morning sun Lorik checked his mount for any injury. He didn't have the time or inclination the night before, but was glad to see that the horse showed no wounds of any kind. He strapped on the saddlebag, checked to make sure all was secure, threw snow on the fire to douse the last embers, and mounted the steed. He took to the path and navigated his horse through the rocky canyon, careful to stay true to the trail that had led them into the hills.

The night's events still played on his mind as he thought about the battle. Why did Lieutenant Morryn panic like that? What brought the trolls? What was that scream? He had no answers. The sun crested the horizon and illuminated the fractured terrain.

Lorik took a moment to investigate his surroundings and noticed the clear evidence of a horse's hoof prints in the snow. He dismounted and examined the tracks. From the space between footfalls, Lorik knew that someone had driven the animal in a mad dash along the narrow path back toward the western border of the Shattered Hills. There was no doubt in Lorik's mind that the rider was Morryn. He felt his heart skip a beat when he saw the obvious tracks of trolls moving westward, out of the Shattered Hills.

Lorik mounted his horse and took flight, desperate to prevent a disaster at the base camp. He had to reach the men and try to avert another tragedy.

Lorik pressed his horse as fast as he dared even as the chill air bit his extremities and froze every breath into a heavy vapor. He crested a small hill and looked out upon the entire valley before him. From his vantage point, Lorik saw the edge of the piney forest. The trees stood tall and reflected the morning sun with their white, snowy coat. In a clearing on the edge of the forest, he recognized the camp; tents were formed in a circle and wisps of smoke rose into the air from the center. However, he saw no movement and Lorik's desperation rose like gall in his throat.

Had it been abandoned? He wondered. "Well, there's just one way to find out," he said as he stroked the neck of his horse. "Let's get down there." He started down the hill, and small rocks tumbled as his horse dislodged them from the pathway. When he arrived at the camp the sun neared mid-day, but still he saw no signs of activity.

On the edge of the camp, just behind his own tent, Lorik dismounted and secured his horse to one of the tent's ropes. He quietly drew his sword from its scabbard. His heart pounded in his ears as he prepared his mind for conflict. He was cautious as he peered around the tent to ascertain the situation. No guards, no lieutenant, no troops, only an eerie quiet that worked to amplify the sound of his own heartbeat. However, the inner circle of the tents was obscured from his view, so Lorik slipped between two tents and ventured toward the center of camp. He took a deep breath and stepped out between the tents, slow and guarded.

Lorik's eyes widened in horror and grief as at every turn soldiers lay dead. The fire, trampled and dislodged from the center of the camp, left charred embers scattered throughout the grounds. Once a brilliant white blanket that covered the earth, snow now mingled with ash and blood to form a putrid slush. Even the horses were slaughtered; their carcasses stripped of flesh and left to the bitter cold. A dozen trolls also lay among the dead, their bodies slashed and punctured with wounds from the soldiers' swords. Lorik fell to his knees. He was a veteran of many battles, but this was more than he expected.

His heart sank, and he dropped his sword to the ground. Anger and sorrow flared up in his mind, anger at Morryn for leading the men to such a bitter end and anger at himself for his failure to prevent the foolhardiness of the lieutenant. As he gazed upon the death that surrounded him, he knew that his duty was clear: find Morryn! But first he needed to check the bodies, count the dead, and find any who might be left alive. Lorik mustered his will, stood again on his feet, and retrieved his sword from the ground. With stoic determination, the sergeant searched each tent but held little hope of finding survivors.

When Lorik finished his sweep of the tents and campsite only one man was missing—Morryn. *Where was the lieutenant? No body, no horse, where did he go? The lieutenant is mixed up in all of this... I need to find out why!* He investigated the surrounding landscape. The ground was covered with tracks: *large bare feet—those must be the trolls, smaller booted feet—those were the soldiers.* Lorik widened his examination of the terrain, like a bloodhound desperate to find the trail of his prey.

He ventured into the sparse forest about twenty yards in an effort to discover the direction Morryn had fled. It wasn't long before he found what he needed, the distinctive print of a shod horse moving with speed through the woods. The prints led southwest away from the camp. The trail was clear, and Lorik needed to follow it. In his heart he mourned for his fallen companions, but he resolved to find the truth and bring justice on the one who did this.

****

The night scattered as dawn forced its light upon the world. Morryn looked to his left and watched as the sky ignited in flame when the sun crested the horizon. The world was flooded with shades of red mingled with pale blue as the golden orb burned in the sky. He sighed, his thoughts mingled with relief and apprehension at the sight, and continued on his journey. The quiet whispers of the forest were now his only companions. Either he had traveled beyond the reach of the sounds of battle or the battle was over, but now the silence echoed in his heart. He was alone and told himself that if he was successful in wresting power from the emperor then their sacrifice was worth it.

The sun shone full and bright above the horizon, delivering its warm, yellow glow over the terrain. The snow, covered by a thin layer of ice, glittered like broken bits of glass and crunched with each step. Morryn felt weighted with exhaustion, tired and sore from the extended ride. A quiet glade came into view, no more than twenty yards ahead. He decided to take the time to rest, care for his steed, and examine his treasures. A massive evergreen served as a fragrant escape from the snow, like an island of pine needles in an ocean of white. He tied his horse to a branch and settled down to enjoy a quick bite of dried beef and cheese. From his satchel, he retrieved the book and the small box.

The lid of the small, jeweled container was secured by a gold clasp. No lock, no security device of any kind protected the contents within. He looked over the box and pondered the possibility that some magical trap waited for him to open it. Cautiously Morryn unlatched the lid. He peered inside—the box was empty! All his work, all his plans, the death of all his men, and all he obtained was an empty box! He glared into the jeweled case, incredulous as he continued to think about what happened.

As his anger burned, he delighted even more he had killed the wizards. *Power indeed*, he thought to himself. *The power of an empty box*! He took the box and threw it like a stone into the field. The choices he made now rested in his heart like the weight of an anvil. All that he sacrificed for the promise of power filtered like sand through his fingers. Now there was nothing... no power, no glory, no conquest!

Unless...this book has some power to it. He gripped the leather-bound tome and wondered what magic might reside in its pages, magic enough to prompt the interest of wizards. He was no wizard and despised those who practiced the dark arts, but he had worked too long and lost too much to come away empty handed. The emperor desperately wanted the book returned. Perhaps, the Book of Aleth contained some hidden source of power. He held it up and examined the strange markings emblazoned on the cover. The gold symbols shone with a dim, pale glow as it reflected the sunlight, symbols that he had no means to interpret or had ever seen before. He opened the book to look upon the pages, but the words were made of such strange markings that they remained a mystery to him.

Truly, this must be an ancient book, he thought as he examined the crisp pages. He had heard many old storytellers regale children with tales of the Elder Days, how the ancients used strange weapons and powerful magic in some Great War, power that his modern world had never known. Now, he wondered, if those myths and legends had any truth to them and if the book he possessed contained some great magic—magic enough to overthrow the emperor.

Morryn left the shelter of the tree and walked aimlessly in the field. He tapped the cover of the book and ran his fingers along its design as he thought about who he might trust to try and interpret its words. He'd probably killed those who might have been able to translate the tome—the man in the mountain cottage and the two wizards. *But, if the emperor fears this book, then perhaps I can use it to my advantage!* He continued to wander through the meadow and stare at the strange writing. He flipped through the pages, and he tried to discern some way to unlock the mysteries it contained.

The sun rose to midday, bright and warm. A shadow passed overhead. Morryn glanced up and his eyes widened as a large, winged creature descended into the meadow. It landed fifty yards from him and steam rose where the creature stood in the snow. Massive, muscular, and dark skinned with large, leathery wings that protruded from its back, it walked on two legs like a man, with huge, sinewy arms and hands that ended in strong, sharp talons. It stood nearly ten feet tall and walked with slow determination toward Morryn. Each step left a mark of melted snow. He began to tremble. It was the same creature that he saw at North Village.

Morryn fixed his gaze upon the creature's eyes which burned like orbs of crimson flames. The monster glared from under heavy brows with a fierce hatred that pierced his thoughts. Fear iced his blood. Step by step, the creature continued toward him, in its hand a great, double-edged sword as black as midnight, and so massive no man could have wielded it. The monster snarled as it approached.

"You have it!" The creature growled, its voice low and powerful.

Morryn rejected the fear that had taken him and shouted, "Leave me, foul beast!" His courage was slow to return as he unsheathed his sword. He held the book in one hand, his sword in the other, and stood in defiance of the creature. Still the beast stepped closer; its long strides closed the gap between them.

Again the creature growled. Its thunderous voice sent waves in the air to make even the trees tremble in fear. "I have tracked you for three days, and now I will take it!" The creature raised its black sword over its head, ready to strike.

Morryn, desperate for any escape, looked around but knew there was no place to run. He had wandered too far from his horse to try and outrun the beast; all that was left was to fight. Morryn didn't wait for the beast to attack. He dropped the tome, took his sword in both hands and rushed toward the monster. With a shout, he engaged the daemon. His sword flashed with brilliance in the bright daylight. He slashed and thrust at the creature with the skill of an expert warrior, but the creature moved with lightning quickness. It easily dodged his sword and attacked with its mighty weapon.

Minutes felt like an eternity to Morryn. Weariness began to tell in his movements. He was outmatched and exhausted as he tried to gain advantage over his opponent. He fought for his life. Morryn parried and deflected every strike as the creature pressed its attack.

He redirected blow after blow, then Morryn's sword snapped with an agonizing ring. The beast backhanded Morryn and he fell, his broken sword thrown from his grasp. The creature laughed as it loomed over him. Its resonant voice echoed across the glen.

"Now you will die." The creature raised its mammoth weapon over its head and brought it down in a swift, final strike.

6

Forest Encounters

Aaron awoke to the clatter of people in the common room. Dawn broke upon the land, and a bright, clear day shone through the frosted window of his small chamber. He was alone and still in his clothes. His body ached, and his head felt as if it swam in an ocean of pain. Mingled with his throbbing headache was his own confusion over the bizarre visions he'd experienced. Much of what Aaron remembered still hung in that haze between sleep and consciousness, with dream-like shadows that clung to his thoughts. The images he witnessed in his vision churned through his mind and perplexed him to distraction.

Never before had Aaron encountered a device as the fire orb or seen such people as he saw in his vision. He recalled stories from his childhood, tales of ancient warrior races that existed before the birth of the empire. Aaron had always considered those stories to be mere myths and fables. As his head cleared, he started to wonder if the vision he saw was just some illusion, a trick of the fire mingled with exhaustion that caused his mind to drift into fantastic imaginations. Aaron stretched out the stiffness he felt in his entire body. The strain of the past few days caused him to feel as if he had endured a forced march. Despite his confusion, he did know this: he needed to get started on his journey. He sat up in his bed, placed his feet upon the cold, wood floor, and rubbed the haze of sleep from his eyes.

Aaron moved to the window and wiped the glass to remove the frost that veiled his view of the world outside. The day shone bright, the clearest morning he had seen since he arrived in the northern reaches of Celedon. A scintillating blue sky canopied snow-covered trees which glistened with a display that dazzled his eyes. Aaron enjoyed the moment of serenity. Then he heaved a sigh—he needed to get about his business.

A rattle shook the door, and Rayn entered with a startled, jovial expression. "Good morning sir," he said, a lighthearted lilt in his voice. "I see that you've finally decided to wake up!"

"Yes," Aaron replied. He did not share the cheerful disposition of his private. "I'm up. How long have I been asleep?"

"Well, Captain," Rayn hesitated. "It's been almost two days."

"Two days! How can that be?" His eyes widened with bewilderment. Aaron rubbed his face and felt the two days of stubble.

"Oh, yes sir. It's been two days. Kaylan said that you might; he said that these orbs will take a lot out of a man. Apparently, you can't just go sticking your nose into one without paying the price. But, if you're up to it, our host told me to have you come down for breakfast. You need to eat and regain your strength."

"Tell Kaylan that I'll be down momentarily. Bring up a wash basin and a shaving knife." Aaron again stroked the two day's growth of stubble on his face. "Afterward, I'll be down for breakfast. By the way, what time of day is it?"

"It's just past dawn, perhaps an hour," Rayn replied.

"Good, we'll need to leave soon after we have both breakfasted. Have our horses ready, and make sure we're fully supplied. We leave in an hour." Aaron dismissed the private. Uncertainty hounded him. He needed to find Morryn, to find the Book of Aleth. The vision of the strange men still hung heavy upon his mind. He did not know if his vision was trustworthy, but had no other lead to follow. His only other option was to return to Celedon and face the anger of the emperor.

Rayn returned with a basin of warm water, towel, and razor then hurried out the door. Aaron, loath to be unkempt, was careful to groom and prepare for the day. His cloak and sword hung on the bedpost. Aaron donned the items and left the room.

The common room buzzed like a hive of activity. Several men sat at the table and enjoyed the hospitality of their host. Laughter filled the room and all seemed quite at ease in the old man's lodge. Others stood near the fire to warm themselves. The fire in the hearth blazed with light and warmed the room like the multitude of jovial conversations warmed the air. A cast iron pot simmered over the fire, a breakfast treasure hidden within. Several decanters were scattered on the main table and steam issued from them like miniature volcanoes while good-humored men poured the hot drink into their cups.

Kaylan seemed to be everywhere at once. He came and went through the door under the stairwell, and as he moved about the table, he delivered plates piled with a variety of food. The din of voices rose like a chorus, jumbled and cheerful. Aaron stepped to the staircase and descended into the swirl of activity.

Kaylan moved through the crowd of people with great agility. He bustled to and fro, brought in cakes and biscuits, bowls, cups, and an assortment of utensils. The men around the table welcomed the additional food and wares as they offered cheers to their host. As Aaron descended the stairs one man at the table, brawny and rugged with a dark, bushy beard and eyebrows to match, nodded his way.

The rugged stranger welcomed Aaron to breakfast. "Come, good sir! Come and sit down for a bite!" His rich accent and the deep warmth of his voice filled the room. The greeting started a cascade of welcomes and "good mornings" from the men in the hall. Another man, seated next to the first, stood from his place at the table and offered him the vacated spot. Aaron didn't have the heart to refuse such munificence and took the emptied chair.

A bowl of porridge was scooped from the cook-pot and placed before Aaron as he sat, along with a cup and decanter of coffee. Aaron poured himself some of the warm liquid, rich and dark, and enjoyed the hearty meal. Since he slept through two entire days, he was famished and welcomed the food with eagerness.

As Aaron ate, Rayn entered the room and came to stand immediately at his side. "Sir," he said, "I have secured our horses; we are ready to go. All we need now is our personal gear and we can be off. I see you have met the rest of Kaylan's guests." Rayn smiled as he gestured to the other men at the table.

"Aye, lad, he has." The bearded man replied in his rich baritone, a grin on his face. The stranger looked to Aaron. "Your young private, here, has been good company while you slept. He's entertained us with tales that had us amazed, and I'll be bound that you might bring many more details to light."

"Well," Aaron said as he shot a look of disapproval at his private, "I am sorry he's troubled you with his tales."

"Ah, now, there's no trouble for a bit of conversation! Don't be too rough on the lad. I'm sure that he didn't share your secrets. His talk was of journeys and adventures." The jovial disposition of the new guest added an air of warmth to the conversation and settled Aaron's mood toward Rayn.

"Indeed," Aaron replied as he finished a biscuit that dripped with honey. "Now that I've overcome my hunger, perhaps you will tell me a bit about yourself."

"Not much to tell, we're just travelers—a troupe of performers for the most part. We have a swordsman," he gestured to the man across the table from him, "but, for the most part we're actors. We were caught unprepared on the road when that winter storm fell on us from the mountains. We wandered through the woods and stumbled upon this house. Aye, what luck that was! There are twelve of us, and our host has been mighty busy to keep us fed. You'll not find a better table set in these parts!"

Cheers rang out from the men who sat around the common room along with a toast for Kaylan. Then the storyteller continued, "We are on the road to Hamilton and will make our way to the capital. We hope to have an audience with the emperor himself. Your private gave us quite a story that we hope to use in a new play."

"I see," Aaron said. "I'd like to know what he shared with you."

"Aye," said the man. "He told us of a great hunt that you and your men were party to, a pursuit that ended in the mountains north of here. The lad said your game gave quite a chase, but that you are again on the hunt, in pursuit of a quarry more dangerous than the first. It makes for a fantastic tale, the captain of the guard and his young soldier against the odds and the elements to protect the nation." The burly man smiled. "We are always on the lookout for a chance to add to our collection of plays. Yours will be a wonderful addition."

A voice spoke from behind them. "Don't be premature with that performance." Kaylan entered from the hallway under the staircase and approached the table.

"Ah, Kaylan!" interjected the bearded man, "come join us at the table. We have had very little time with you on this fine morning, and you must join us so we can enjoy your company as well as your food!"

"Indeed, I will." Kaylan sat at the table as several men excused themselves to prepare for the troupe's departure. "You must not tell his story, not yet Master Bruhn. He has yet to live the full story, and what is to come might be of greater interest than what is past."

"Aye, now… you have piqued my interest!" The performer slapped the table and rattled the dishes. "Give me this tale, and I will see that every performer from Shepherd's Peak to the southern coast hears of this great adventure!"

"Don't worry, my dear performer," Kaylan said. "I believe you will have more of a tale than is contained in all the history of Celedon. Now," he said, as he turned to Aaron, "we have much to discuss, and our time is limited."

"Indeed," Aaron rejoined. "I have many questions and hope you will provide me some answers."

"I will endeavor to do so, as well as offer some information that may be of help to you," Kaylan said. "Let me tend to my other guests and then we will have that talk."

The other gentleman, Bruhn, looked at Aaron with renewed anticipation. "So, your story continues! I'll be eager to hear the entire tale if we meet again. But, now, I must be off and tend to my troupe. They are eager and want to leave as soon as we're ready. So, Captain, I bid you farewell." He stood and offered his hand to Aaron who took it in his own. Then Bruhn departed through the main door into the brilliant, sunlit morning.

With Bruhn and his companions gone, the common room fell silent. Aaron enjoyed the quiet moment as he sipped his coffee and ate some of the corn biscuits that remained. He smiled as he considered the energetic performer. Bruhn looked more like a woodcutter.

Several minutes passed before Kaylan returned with Rayn close on his heels. They both sat at the table, Rayn's expression showed an eagerness to hear more from their host.

Kaylan poured himself a steaming cup of coffee and turned to face Aaron who began to feel a bit uncomfortable as the wizened host fixed his eyes upon him. He hoped Kaylan's information might help him piece together the riddle of his experience with the fire orb.

"Now," began Kaylan, "let's discuss what happened two days ago. I'm sure that you have questions for me, and I know I have a few for you. Perhaps together, we can discover all that needs to be understood." He sipped on his drink and leaned back in his chair as he waited for Aaron to begin.

"Well," Aaron hesitated, "my first question is who are you?"

"I am Kaylan," replied the old man. "That is who I am. But, I think your question is more about *what* I am rather than *who*." Aaron nodded in agreement. "I am from days long ago and have dwelt among the races of this world for ages beyond count. I am Kaylan the Elder, and I am here to aid you in your task."

"Your words are riddles to me," Aaron spoke in frustration. "My task is to retrieve the Book of Aleth and return it to its rightful place." Aaron pushed away from the table and moved to the fire. He leaned against the hearth and stared into the flames as they moved in chaotic patterns upon the wood. "How can you be of any help in that?"

"You don't understand, Captain. Your quest to regain the Book of Aleth is more than you realize. You have not come to my door by chance or circumstance, nor did a snowstorm guide you to my steps. You were meant to come to me, and I have waited for you; I knew of your arrival long before you showed up on my doorstep. And now I need to help guide you to the right course." Kaylan's voice took on a more serious tone.

"The right course?" Aaron exclaimed. "My orders tell me the right course! I've been sent to find this book that has vanished into the wild. My course hasn't changed. I am a soldier of Celedon and will do my duty."

"Kaylan," Rayn interjected. "I don't think you know what you're talking about. This book belongs to the emperor, and we are vowed to keep his commands. If you have any knowledge of its whereabouts, let us know, otherwise we need to leave."

"Patience, Rayn," Kaylan said, "Your captain has a destiny before him, a destiny far greater than he can begin to imagine. Don't assume that I brought you into my house and entertained you for the sole purpose of passing the time. It is given to me to provide your captain with what he needs in order to begin his true quest."

"Well, then," Aaron said. "Tell me plainly what this is all about."

"To do this, you must recall for me what you witnessed. Very few are able to look unaided into the fire orb, and yet you did so not two nights ago. That in itself is worthy of discussion, but we haven't the time. I need to know the vision you saw." Kaylan sat up and focused his gaze on Aaron.

Aaron took a deep breath, leaned against the hearth, and shared his vision with Kaylan. He spoke of the cavernous hall in which the bearded lord sat enthroned. He described the people he saw, smaller than anyone he had ever seen yet strong and warrior-like. He told how he watched another look into an orb, not unlike Kaylan's. He also told of the information the other spoke to his lord. When Aaron had given a complete account of his experience, he sat and waited for Kaylan to make sense of it.

Kaylan sighed and fixed his eyes on Aaron. The intensity in his gaze took Aaron by surprise. "What I will tell you"—Kaylan began—"you may not be ready to hear. But I will attempt to explain all that you have experienced so far. Explanations are difficult to understand when you look at them from a lack of experience. You cannot understand the tapestry before all the threads are woven together. What I hope to provide you is knowledge of the threads that are attached to you." He took a deep breath, "Please, be patient Captain, and together we will find some answers."

Kaylan continued. "You are caught up in the conclusion of a story, one that spans a thousand years and has filled the land with ancient legends. It began when, under the power of his dark craft, a creature of great evil entered Celedon and deceived the nation. This brought about the rebellion which led to the Great War. Our realm was once ruled by a King, one of great power and wisdom, and though he had the power to cast down the rebellious people, his great love for them prevented this. Instead, he allowed his enemy to triumph. But the King promised that Celedon would be released from the usurper's control. To that end, he set in motion a series of events to restore the nation. However, it all depends on the Book of Aleth.

"Races of many kinds lived in the land at the height of the King's glory. Some you have seen already in your vision—you're description of the warrior-race, those are dwarves. Others, those who lived under the King's banner, you have dismissed as tales and legends, but they are real. Those whom we now call elves—though they referred to themselves by another name—are lost to the kingdom, but they once roamed the lands freely. The usurper had no power over these races, and they were not deceived by his craft.

"So the usurper appointed himself as emperor and

tolerated no one who refused his authority. He made war against them and forced them into exile. All reference to the King and all instruction that concerned the glory days of Celedon were destroyed, which left the truth to fall into the realm of myth and legend.

"The emperor appointed those who were loyal to him and of his same evil nature to govern over the realm and gave them power to act on his behalf. This power came with one provision, however, that the usurper alone ruled supreme and that any dissension spelled doom for the rebel. So, through fear and deception, the usurper maintains his supremacy and keeps the nation in darkness.

"The Book of Aleth is the key to the restoration. In that book, the King placed his wisdom. The King imbued it with his own power and proclaimed that a protector would walk out of obscurity and, with the Book of Aleth, break the power of the deceiver. The Protector alone has the capacity to use the book which is why the emperor wants to keep it hidden, never to reveal its location. The Book of Aleth is the power that the emperor fears."

Aaron listened with intense fascination at the tale woven by the old man before them. He was already familiar with some of the stories, most of which he heard on the streets or in the orphanages, stories told to keep children from bad behavior. Aaron remembered one story from his childhood, that if he didn't obey the orphan-master, the great despot would come in the night, take him from his bed and force him into slavery.

Aaron shook his head in disbelief. "The educated don't hold to such nonsense. It's ludicrous to believe in some man, king or otherwise, who wields such power."

"Kaylan, *only a fool* holds to such nonsense!" Rayn scoffed at the notion. "So, you're telling us that this book we're after contains magic enough to destroy the emperor!"

Aaron, however, did not feel the same as Rayn. He considered Kaylan's words with greater patience and was not so quick to challenge all that Kaylan had to say. "Rayn," Aaron said, "don't dismiss Kaylan's words so quickly... all legends have their foundation in some truth. Through the years, the tales grow and get distorted until they become myth." Aaron felt there was more at stake than he first imagined—more than he understood. "Kaylan," he said, "I can understand what you're trying to say, but I am not so quick to believe the ancient myths are true. Even with some of the strange experiences that we've had, I can't believe your words. You sound like an advocate of rebellion against the emperor."

"Let me ask you a question, Captain." Kaylan's words were gentle but as hard as flint. "Who are you loyal to, Celedon or the emperor?"

"What kind of foolish question is that? I am loyal to the oath I swore to uphold the law and defend the nation." Aaron's voice carried a note of agitation.

"Let me ask, then," Kaylan continued, calm and direct. "If you knew that the emperor himself was a danger to the nation, would you oppose him?"

"Captain!" Rayn again protested. "We can't just sit here and listen to this man ramble on against the emperor. He's spoken enough for us to take him into custody for dissension."

"Rayn," he said, his voice filled with frustration as he chastised his overzealous private. "I don't think

Kaylan is about to incite the entire nation to overthrow the emperor, or that this is an attempt to convince us to do it. A man still has the right to speak about his own heart-felt convictions without fear of arrest." Aaron sighed with resignation.

"But, Captain!" Rayn persisted. "If everyone has the right to speak against the empire it promotes anarchy!"

"I don't think we're in the presence of an anarchist, Private," Aaron said. "Kaylan, please continue. I want to know what this has to do with me."

Kaylan looked at Aaron; the wizened man's eyes spoke his silent concern. "Captain," he said, "you are the one who has been given the responsibility… you are the one who is meant to recover the book. You are the," Kaylan hesitated. "You are the Protector of Celedon."

"But," protested Aaron, "my duty is to recover the book and take it back to the emperor. I am a loyal soldier. I won't betray my oath."

"No, Captain, I don't believe you will." Kaylan gave a slight grin. "But I do believe you will discover that the oath you took will lead you to make decisions far different than you can imagine right now."

Aaron shook his head in disbelief and frustration. "Kaylan," he said, "you may have aspirations to change the nation based upon ancient fables, but all I will do when I recover this book is take it back to the archives in Celedon and leave it there." Aaron sighed as he returned to his chair. "I'm sorry. I am no answer to your fanciful hopes; I'm just a soldier of the empire."

Kaylan leaned closer. "It was not mere chance that brought you to this place. It was not chance that put you in a position to seek the book. There are forces that swirl around you that will guide your steps, even if you can't see it or won't believe it."

"You still speak in riddles. I am charged to defend the empire against all who want destroy it. This book, from what you say, holds great potential to inflict chaos on the nation and turn people against the emperor. Rayn is right, you speak like a dissenter. This story of yours is just a myth told to children, a fairytale. I stopped believing in fairytales a long time ago." Aaron's words were hard but his thoughts were filled with the possibility that somehow Kaylan spoke the truth.

"What if I told you that the emperor you serve is the same usurper who has deceived the nation? He has cast a shadow of lies and has blinded the people to the truth. He has tried to destroy all those who oppose him and now has set his desire to eliminate any remnants of the ancient truths. Without that book, the nation will never again know the truth—and you are the one sent to find it. You see, you are meant to find the book, but not for the emperor, for the nation. If that book returns to the emperor, there will be no one left to set right the wrongs that he has brought about," Kaylan said.

Aaron returned Kaylan's steady gaze and looked upon the ancient man with strong doubts and suspicions. He believed what he saw in his vision was real, yet he was unable to resolve his recent experiences with what he had always believed. "Tell me, then," Aaron continued, "if what you say is true, and the emperor has ruled for over a thousand years, what's to say that his rule is any less valid than a supposed king who gave up on his nation?"

"I can't give you those answers; it will come from others you have yet to meet. All I can do is start your journey and weave my portion of your tapestry. Don't try to view the full picture; let the tapestry come together, and you will begin to understand the path that is yours to take." Kaylan stood from the table with a sigh of resignation. "This home will be open to you when needed. I trust that you will find the path that will lead you to the truth." He turned and walked down the hall and disappeared beyond the view of the two men.

Aaron stared into his drink as he contemplated all their host had said. The fire crackled and sparked in the hearth beside them and the gentle whisper of a slight breeze rustled through the trees. Seconds passed like hours, as if time stood frozen in a single moment of indecision. He remained motionless.

"Sir," Rayn broke the silence. "You don't believe what that old man had to say? He speaks of the emperor with nothing but hostility and malice. We ought to send a squad to this house and take that old man into custody!"

"Private," Aaron said, "one old man's rant of ancient rhetoric is no threat to the empire. There is no basis for truth in what he said; it is all fanciful myth, nothing more." Aaron sighed, as his unvoiced thoughts argued with his words. He wished the empire was as Kaylan had described: a realm of peace and not the continual disputes and strife that incessantly plagued the land.

His mind rushed back to his childhood when he imagined himself as a great warrior who led the nation in a mighty contest against overwhelming odds and brought peace to the land. He chuckled at the thought of how far his dreams had fallen, how he had risen so fast in the ranks of the Royal Guard only to discover that at each level he was little more than a tool in the emperor's hand. After years of service, he resigned himself to the fact that he was a mere soldier, trained and positioned to squelch any squabble the emperor deemed a threat to his rule. The story Kaylan told stirred old, childhood fantasies that slept in the recesses of his mind, thoughts that had slumbered for years.

Aaron turned to Rayn and looked squarely at the young private. Then he tried to speak with resolution. "I will not give myself to believe these myths. We've had some strange encounters, and experiences I can't explain, but it does not validate what Kaylan said. What I've seen tells me that we need to find Morryn and the book he stole. Beyond that, I will decide later. Now, back to our business...you've readied the horses so let's get our gear and go." Aaron finished the last of his coffee, stood, and walked up the stairs to his room. Rayn followed and both men retrieved their gear, their saddlebags and packs, and went back downstairs to leave.

Kaylan was nowhere to be seen; so without any farewell, the two men left the house.

The day was bright and cold. Aaron's conversation with Kaylan had spent the morning hours and now the sun had risen to almost midday. The brilliant yellow sphere illuminated the world. No clouds broke up the blue sky, and the snow which had fallen two nights before sparkled like crystals scattered across the earth. The horses were tied to the rail on the front deck and waited for their riders. They looked good, well groomed and fed. They pawed at the ground, eager to be on the move.

Aaron thought about their direction and the

quickest way to the Shattered Hills. "We will have to go north," he said, "take to the road again, and turn east through the woods when the trees thin out a bit. The Shattered Hills are not far, and we may make it through the forest before nightfall."

"Sir, if you believe that the book is with Morryn, why not let him take it back to the emperor himself?"

"Because I don't believe that the lieutenant intends to. He stole the book and is riding toward the Shattered Hills, not toward the capital." Aaron stared into the distance as he spoke. "No, we need to catch up with him and recover the book ourselves."

"Then, Captain, why don't I ride to the emperor and inform him of what we've discovered? Surely he needs to know. I can ride south and you can pursue the lieutenant in the north."

"No," Aaron said. "We will stay together."

"But, Captain—"

"Private," Aaron said with deep authority. "We ride together."

"Yes, sir," Rayn said with reluctance as he mounted his steed, a chestnut mare, strong and sturdy.

Aaron mounted up and spurred his horse to motion.

Under the bright noon sun, the men rode north in silence. The most recent snowfall hindered their horses with its deep, frozen drifts. Tracks of various creatures, some deer and rabbits, dotted the path. Aaron even noticed the large prints of some hound. Yet, their journey was undisturbed, except by a gentle breeze that drifted through the boughs and brushed snow off the trees.

After an hour, the two men left the main road and entered into the forest as they made their way east toward the Shattered Hills. At the point where they entered, the forest had thinned and provided the best possibility of passage. Despite the sparse growth, however, the journey through the woods was bogged down by heavy drifts that piled up between the trees.

Aaron's thoughts drifted to Morryn. What drove the lieutenant to abandon his position and turn against his command? He recalled the night before they left, how Morryn talked with two strange men. Aaron didn't recognize them and believed they were involved in Morryn's decision. *Perhaps, Morryn was given orders contrary to my own, and was just following some new directive?* He quickly dismissed that thought as foolishness. Whatever the reason, Aaron was determined to find him.

"Captain, what will we do when we find the lieutenant?" Rayn broke the silence after they had traveled for several miles. "He's said to be one of the best swordsmen in the country and...well...I'm concerned that we might be put to it, if you know what I mean."

"Yes, I do know what you mean." The very same concern had touched Aaron's thoughts, and he did not relish a confrontation with such a formidable adversary. "We'll do what we must, Rayn. The sword is no foreigner to my hand as well. Besides, if he's alone and decides to put up a fight, then it's two against one."

The sun had settled against the western horizon when Aaron stopped under a large bundle of trees which had twisted and grown together. Gnarled branches wove themselves like a thatch roof in the circle and formed a natural shelter. The ground beneath the braches was free of snow and littered with pine needles. Aaron was glad to have a dry, if not warm, location to rest. Rayn tied their horses to a nearby branch and kicked away the snow to give their mounts a chance at the grass beneath. Afterward, they settled down for a cold, hearty meal.

Aaron, reluctant to waste more daylight than necessary, ate his meal with haste. "Rayn," he said, "let's try to make the eastern edge of these woods before nightfall."

The two soldiers again set out to follow what appeared to be a trail that led northeast through the pine forest. It was an easy path, likely made by other travelers and various animals as a road through the forest. Far to the west, the sun hovered over the mountains and cast long shadows that mingled with shafts of light through the trees. A gentle breeze picked up, and the air grew colder as the light failed. Aaron signaled it was time to set up camp. Their northeast journey kept them in the forest longer than he anticipated.

The cold deepened and shadows lengthened in the fading light. They noticed what appeared to be a clearing in the distance, where Aaron saw a flicker of light, like the gleam of the sun reflected off some object in the midst of the glen. The distinctive ring of metal on metal echoed through the still twilight air, and Aaron grew cautious, unsure what lay before them. "Rayn," he whispered for fear of discovery. "Let's dismount. Tie the horses here, and we'll walk to that clearing. Be as quiet as you can. I thought I saw movement, and we must not draw any attention to ourselves."

They crept toward the open field. The rapid clang of metal resonated through the cold air, as if two hammers struck each other in synchronous rhythm—or two swords. Now, closer, Aaron noticed movement within the glade. A large figure like a man moved about with another, smaller figure. Aaron crouched down and crawled closer, hidden in the underbrush that surrounded the field. Behind him, Rayn kept close. Aaron stayed low and hoped the undergrowth was sufficient to hide their approach.

Slow and cautious, Aaron crawled toward the clearing, anxious and unsure what he might discover. He drew nearer and it was obvious to Aaron who battled in the field—the beast from the mountain cottage and a valiant man, dwarfed by his adversary. Aaron watched in horror. The two were locked in combat and fought with the ferocity of two timber wolves in a death match. They wielded their weapons with expert skill until the man was thrown down. The creature raised its tremendous black sword and in one swift stroke, crushed his opponent.

Aaron stifled a gasp as they witnessed the incredible scene. Then the creature began to search the snow-covered field. It turned over the body of the dead man and brushed his great claws through the snow. The monster's head darted back and forth, until it found an object that lay near the fallen man—a book! The creature picked it up and sent a roar into the air that punctured Aaron's heart. The reverberations caused a shower of snow all through the forest as even the trees seemed to quiver at the fierceness of the beast.

Aaron's attention was fixed on the man who lay dead on the ground. Blood pooled around the body and mixed with the snow to form a crimson slush. Even from Aaron's vantage point, he clearly saw the gold insignia on the fallen man's cloak—a man of the

Royal Guard. He was sure the man was Morryn.

In a flash of awareness, Aaron remembered his terrible dream. It returned in a flood of memories like a waking nightmare. The realization filled him with dread and chilled him more than the icy snow he knelt in. The scene unfolded, and panic filled Aaron's thoughts, along with a desperate desire to flee. The creature lifted its head and fixed its gaze toward them. Its eyes blazed with red fire. Aaron felt his heart melt in fear from the presence of the vile creature. Rayn clutched at Aaron's arm, and he could feel the young soldier tremble. He gave a quick glance back and witnessed the terror in Rayn's eyes.

Step after step the creature stalked toward them. Steam rose from every footfall and left a bare patch where snow had lain. Aaron listened as the beast voiced a low, guttural growl that rumbled across the glen. Behind Aaron a branch snapped, and he glanced back to watch their horses bolt in a mad dash to flee from the monster. In moments the beast would be upon them. Aaron feared that his nightmare had come true.

He slipped his sword from its scabbard, careful and silent, desperate not to make any noise. Rayn followed suit and took his sword from its sheath. Aaron turned and motioned to Rayn to follow his lead and not make any sudden move. He waited like a spring, holding his coil until the last possible moment. He was a soldier and refused to let fear decide his actions.

The creature stepped closer. Aaron heard its low, deep breaths as it approached. In every place where the beast stepped, the snow melted in the monster's heat. Red eyes burned under heavy brows. Aaron prepared to strike first and strike fast. *Surprise,* he thought, *is our only chance.* With Rayn behind him, waiting on his signal, Aaron bided his time. His heart raced and the tension in his muscles ached as he waited for the creature.

One step...two steps. Aaron leapt from his crouched position, Rayn close on his heels. Both men flashed their swords in the diminished sunlight and shouted a battle cry as they charged at the monster. In that moment the creature stopped, looked around to the north and unfolded its massive, leathery wings. With a strength and agility that amazed Aaron, the creature leaped into the air and flew over the two soldiers. They both stood, dumbfounded, as they watched the malevolent creature vanish from their view.

"Now," said Rayn, trembling and out of breath, "I hope you're as relieved as I am. I couldn't believe that you decided to attack that thing!"

"If I thought there was another option," replied Aaron, breathless, "I would have welcomed the suggestion." He paused as he looked back at Rayn. "I didn't think we had the speed to outrun it, even in these woods, and I doubt that the beast would have accepted our surrender." Aaron paused as he looked over toward the body. "We had the advantage, two against one. But I don't think our fate would have been much better," he said and pointed to the man who lay dead.

"Well, we've been fortunate twice with that thing. I hope that we don't have to be fortunate like that again." Rayn sheathed his sword. Aaron, as well, returned his sword to its scabbard and went to the fallen soldier.

Morryn's body lay broken and crushed; his chest was caved in and blood still dripped from a massive wound. Within one crawl, the lieutenant's sword lay notched and broken, useless now to its former owner. Aaron shook his head as he looked with sorrow upon the body. He had too many questions and no answers. He had no idea what might have driven the lieutenant to this end, and now the book that he sought rested in the claws of the beast. All Aaron could do was watch it fly into the darkness of night.

As Aaron hovered around the body of his slain comrade, a noise rustled from the woods, as if a herd of creatures traveled through the undergrowth. He dismissed the sound as the breeze. He was more intent on Morryn and searching for clues than the woods around him.

But when an eerie sense of being watched grabbed Aaron's perception, he looked up. Dozens of small, bearded men walked toward them, stout and fierce. The diminutive warriors wielded spears and battle-axes and surrounded them so Aaron and Rayn had no escape. Rayn remained transfixed on Morryn's body but when Aaron tapped him on the shoulder he looked up, and his eyes widened as he took in the scene.

"You will come with us!" A gruff, harsh voice commanded. The stocky speaker stood no more than four and a half feet tall but brandished his axe with great confidence and skill. He was well dressed, with gold cord woven into his long, red beard. Upon his head he wore a circlet of gold, and his chest and arms were covered in a ringed, mail shirt.

"And who are you?" demanded Aaron, though he immediately recognized the men from his vision—dwarves.

"We are your captors. Come with us or die with your companion. The choice is yours." The stout figure gave no quarter to Aaron and Rayn.

"You may find us more than you can handle." Rayn spoke with bravado as he unsheathed his sword.

"Brave words, young one—but you will discover that a spear can be cast through your chest before you have a chance to prove your mettle."

Aaron gripped Rayn's arm and held back the young private from any further discussion. "We're surrounded, private. Now's not the time for heroism." Aaron fixed his eyes on the gruff commander. "We surrender," he said, and yielded his sword. Rayn was not so eager to be taken captive but gave over his own weapon with a scowl.

"You are now the prisoners of Lord Dunstan, ruler and sovereign of Brekken-Dahl." The dwarf bound Aaron and Rayn's hands and gave their weapons to two others. Then they forced Aaron and Rayn into the woods and moved with marked agility through the trees. They traveled north and left behind the fallen body of Morryn. Then night fell upon the world.

7

The Road to Brekken-Dahl

An hour passed, and the sun departed over the peaks of the Shadow Mountains. Darkness covered the world. A chill wind blew through forest and bit at Aaron's skin. The dwarves moved undeterred by the darkness or cold as they continued with great speed through the woods, forcing Aaron and Rayn to try and keep pace. He marveled at the inexhaustible endurance of the dwarves. His amazement grew when, despite the darkness, the dwarves did not falter. Without torches or any other source of light, the brigade didn't slow for a moment and navigated through the brush and trees as if it were daylight. Aaron struggled as he stumbled along and found it difficult to cope with the dwarves' rapid pace. From the noise behind him, he knew Rayn struggled as well.

As night deepened a crescent moon ascended over the tops of the trees to cast its pallid light down through the branches stroked by the wind. The silver glow gave some slight help to the two soldiers as they labored to keep up with their captors. The air continued to grow colder as they marched. The frigid temperature froze extremities and shot pain up Aaron's legs with every step. The leather straps which bound his hands dug deep into Aaron's skin.

Exhausted, he continued, swift and unseen, always north and always within the confines of the trees. Aaron had no notion where they were but imagined it was far from help.

The hours passed with no indication the dwarves intended to stop. Although fatigued and hungry Aaron kept pace with his captors, but the stress of the forced march proved too much for Rayn, and he fell to the ground. With his hands tied, he crashed through the brush and struck his head against a fallen log. Rayn tried to rise but collapsed again in a heap.

Aaron rushed to his side and bent down to care for him, but with his hands bound, he was powerless to help. Anger welled up in him, and he shouted at the nearest dwarf, "Get down here! He's hurt!" In the faded moonlight, Aaron saw blood flowing from a gash on Rayn's forehead.

Two of the dwarf soldiers grumbled, but came over to gather him up and braced the private against a tree. Though alive, Rayn's breathing was shallow and quick. He slipped in and out of consciousness and trembled in uncontrolled spasms. His cloak and shirt were torn and revealed long red welts and a host of abrasions on his arms and torso. Aaron sat next to him and tried to administer some aid despite his bound hands.

One dwarf, older, with a long grey beard, came to Rayn with a leather bag slung around his shoulders. He pulled out several vials and some cloth then began to clean the wounds. The dwarf dabbed some liquid from a brown vial—its aroma nearly made Aaron gag—into the deepest gash on Rayn's forehead. Rayn winced in pain from the pungent solution.

"What is that?" Aaron demanded.

"Medicine," was the dwarf's curt response. "And you'll do good to leave me alone and let me work!" The dwarf continued to grumble as he put away the vial. Even as the old dwarf spoke, the liquid began to work. The blood stopped, and a wax-like seal formed over the wound.

"There," said the grey dwarf, "good as new. It'll heal in a day or so and then that patch will fall away."

Rayn began to revive and lifted his bound hands to feel the place where the gash had been. Just as the old dwarf had said, the wound was covered and the bleeding stopped.

The dwarf commander pushed through the crowd that had formed around Rayn and stood before the two soldiers. A tall, powerful figure in comparison to his companions, he stood over four and a half feet tall and wielded a large double-bladed battle axe, honed to a razor's edge. His long, dark-red beard, braided with gold woven twine, gave the man the appearance of some form of royalty. The dwarf carried himself with a confidence that bordered on arrogance. His companions parted to let him pass.

The dwarf commander stood over Aaron and Rayn as they sat on the frozen log. He looked down at the two soldiers with a hard expression on his face.

"Who are you… and what do you want with us?" Aaron spoke first and anger filled his words.

"I am Kaurn, commander of the warriors of Brekken-Dahl. You are our prisoners and will be handed over to Lord Dunstan where your fate will be determined." His voice, strong and rough, carried a hint of disdain toward Aaron and Rayn.

"By what right do you take us captive?" Aaron challenged his captor. "You have no authority in

Celedon, and I've never heard of your land. You will do well to release us now for the emperor will not sit by while citizens of the empire are abducted." Aaron's spoke with stern authority, his composure tempered by years of service.

Undaunted, the dwarf commander looked Aaron up and down, a grim expression on his bearded face. "I know of you and your emperor." The dwarf leader spoke with a note of finality. "You will be brought before Dunstan to stand trial for the atrocities you've committed. There you will learn your fate, both you and your companion." The dwarf turned and hoisted his axe over his shoulder. "Give them some of the draught!" Kaurn barked his order to the older dwarf as he walked away.

Aaron and Rayn were given warm, thick liquid that tasted of licorice. Then, with little regard for dignity, two guards forced Aaron and Rayn to their feet and pushed them to continue the march. Aaron was afraid Rayn might collapse again, but discovered the elixir had an unusual effect. It coursed down his throat and radiated warmth to the very tips of his fingers. Exhaustion from the long journey through the cold winter night faded in the warmth of the drink. Aaron felt refreshed and noticed the private also gained a renewed vigor.

Mile after mile they continued through the darkness. Aaron wondered if the dwarves intended on carrying the forced march through the woods all night. He was right. The hours passed in a blur of shadows when the morning light broke over the eastern horizon. Aaron believed they traveled farther north than the village where their adventure began.

The dawn shone red and illuminated a hazy mist

nestled in a valley before them. Carried along on the morning air, the pounding rumble of a river echoed through the mist. Their road, a narrow passage, overgrown and treacherous to navigate, descended along the side of the ravine through the dense forest, and meandered back and forth down switch-backs into the mist-shrouded valley. Far to the east, the sun crested the horizon and shone its glorious brilliance upon the band of travelers and reflected like stars in the snow. No clouds, just a brilliant blue sky heralded the arrival of a crisp, bright winter day.

As they made their way down the trail, the noise of the river grew louder and filled the forest with its rhythm. The drink that Aaron imbibed hours before had worn off, and his joints ached with each step. He looked at Rayn, concerned for his young private, and realized Rayn's strength began to fail him as well. Several times Aaron stumbled, half asleep even as he walked, his muscles burned with weariness but he forced himself to press on. He didn't understand how the dwarves endured such a long, forceful pace, but Aaron willed himself to suffer through the pain and not give his captors the satisfaction of seeing him collapse.

Rayn, however, did not fare as well as his captain. The young soldier had grown increasingly worse and often needed to lean on Aaron to traverse the precipitous valley wall. Together, however, they navigated the terrain without any aid from their dwarf guards.

"Halt!" Kaurn barked, and a collective sigh of relief resounded among the party. "Keep those two men together and get them some food! I'll not have them fighting hunger when they have to climb the mountain."

They stopped at a thick enclosure of trees and brush. The ground was bare; the winter snows never penetrated the canopy of branches that shrouded their encampment. The forest, however, displayed a dazzling frost from the mist that swirled off the nearby river. Aaron listened to the violent flow, its roar echoed through the woods like thunder.

Aaron pressed close enough to Rayn to be heard over the din of the river. "Rayn," he whispered, "we must be near the northern border of Celedon." He paused as he looked around. "Yes, we are definitely at the most northern border." Troubled, Aaron wondered if his captors meant to try and cross the massive torrent that roared in the distance.

"Captain," Rayn whispered, "where do you think they'll take us?"

"I don't know. We're too far north," Aaron replied. "As far as I know, everything beyond this is just mountains and wasteland."

As if on cue, the dwarf commander returned to speak with Aaron. "Soon we will cross the river and enter our realm. Soon, you and your companion will travel blindfolded. No one but the inhabitants of Brekken-Dahl are permitted to know its entrance."

"You expect us to continue at the pace you've set, and then you take our sight? How are we to navigate a river blindfolded?" Aaron spoke up, agitated at the prospect.

"I expect you to, yes." The commander's voice came across stern and left no room for debate. "You will not be given the opportunity to know the secret entrance to our realm. You will be blindfolded or you will be blinded, either way you will not see the passage that leads to our home." His words ended the debate, and Kaurn walked away. Aaron let the matter drop.

"Sir, the night we spent at Kaylan's... your vision, wasn't it about these very people?" Rayn leaned over to speak.

"I don't know." Aaron seethed with anger at his circumstances. Yet his mind reeled at the fact that he and Rayn were captured by a race of people he thought were a mere myth. What he saw with his eyes fought against what he thought was the truth. He struggled against the fact that all around him stood the very evidence that defied what he had long been taught and believed. Ancient stories leapt through his mind as he considered the reality of his situation, and he wondered if any more fairytales might jump out of the mists of legend and reveal themselves. His eyes gazed at the ground. "I just don't know," he spoke, almost to himself. Tired from the march, Aaron regressed to introspection.

After an hour the sun rode high over the canopy of trees that sheltered Aaron and Rayn, its yellow light brilliant in the ice blue sky. Noon had come and despite his captivity, he marveled at the beauty of the day, painted in colors of green and white. Tall pine trees reached toward the heavens. Shafts of filtered light broke through the intertwined branches and illuminated the mist.

To Aaron's relief, the steep descent leveled off. Now, however, the roar of the river filled the air. Mist swirled just beyond the tree line, churned up by the turbulent waters. The icy waters flowed swift over massive boulders, worn smooth. From Aaron's vantage point, the river flowed southwest and raged along its channel for miles. The river stood as an impasse, a barrier too wide to cross, which rolled with the deadly fury of a violent storm.

On the opposite side of the river, as if grown out of the very edge of the torrent, the Shadow Mountains rose in stark contrast to the vibrant colors of the forest. Large, sharp monstrous mountains, grey and dismal, stood like a granite bulwark. In the clear light of day, Aaron looked up to the very peaks where enormous glaciers filled massive cracks and valleys at the higher elevations.

The forced march brought them to the riverbank and there they stopped. The cold mist generated by the maelstrom again covered trees and rocks along the edge of the river with a thick layer of frost. Even the dwarves' beards seemed to have turned white from the spray off the river. Icicles hung like spears on various trees, and branches too weak to bear the weight were cast down like severed limbs on the ground. He saw no possible means of crossing the river and only a fool would dare to swim in such a turbulent wash.

Aaron knew the river that raged before them, it was the Hoppe River, a torrent that cut its channel along the entire length of Celedon's northern regions, ultimately pouring all its force into the great Inland Sea. He also knew the rumor that no one who ever tried to cross into the mountains beyond ever returned to speak of it. Aaron turned to see Rayn staring in disbelief at the fury of the river.

"Captain," Rayn exclaimed, "there is no way to cross this!"

"Perhaps," Kaurn said as he approached, "we dwarves have some means to cross the river that you're ignorant of." The dwarf leader held two squares of cloth in his gloved hands. "Here is where you must be blindfolded. We do not allow strangers to enter our realm, and all prisoners are forbidden to know the secrets which allow entrance. You will be blindfolded until we pass through the gateway to our land."

Rayn was blindfolded first, and then Kaurn wrapped and tied the cloth over Aaron's eyes and took pains to ensure that he was unable to see.

The men were made to stand and led blindfolded toward the river. Aaron feared for Rayn's safety as the sound of the river grew louder in his ears. The icy mist stung his face, and he stumbled on the frozen ground. His dwarf guard, however, proved stronger than Aaron surmised, and the steel grip on his arm prevented him from falling. Then his guard stopped him.

"Captain!" Rayn shouted over roar from the river. "Captain, these dwarves mean to throw us into the river!"

Aaron listened as Rayn struggled against his captors. "That's enough, Private!" Aaron barked. "Control yourself!" The commotion ended, and Aaron took some small comfort in the silence.

Suddenly, the noise of the river was overpowered by the sound of massive rocks grating against iron, slow with reverberations that felt like a minor earthquake. Then, as Aaron listened, the sound of the river changed. The rhythmic pounding of the water took on a new sound, as if it rushed over a fall and crashed back to earth. Then the river's tone changed again and became a hollow roar like water in a mad rush through a large tunnel.

The cold air and frozen vapors of the river chilled Aaron to the bone. He shivered uncontrollably in the grip of his captor as he waited for the dwarves to make another move. A few minutes passed that seemed like hours to Aaron when Kaurn gave the order to move out. "Make sure these two keep their feet! We'll not let Lord Dunstan's prisoners escape in the river." The dwarf commander laughed, echoed by his squad as Aaron was forced to move forward.

Held in the iron grip of his dwarf escort, Aaron was led across a rough stone walk. All around him the river rumbled its thunderous voice. The ground beneath him shook, but with each step, he felt more secure his captors meant to keep him from a disastrous fall. Soon he stood on a solid ground, and the roar of the river dimmed.

Aaron's guard propped him against a cold stone wall. The same grating sound resonated like the working of a massive machine and the river regained its former voice, that of a rushing torrent. "Rayn," Aaron shouted over the noise of the river.

"Yes, Captain, I'm here," Rayn said.

Relieved, Aaron again found himself in the grip of his escort.

****

Lorik gathered the necessary equipment for his campaign to find Lieutenant Morryn. He dismantled a small tent, not much more than a lean-to used to keep firewood dry. He took some food, dry wood for a fire, and two heavy wool blankets. By the time he was ready to go, it was past noon, and the sense of urgency nagged at his thoughts. Lorik took one last look around. He heaved a sigh of resignation and left the scene behind. *These men deserve better*, he thought, *but I have no time to spare and cannot take any to give each one a proper burial*. He swung his leg over the saddle and spurred the mare to follow the trail through the woods.

The tracks were not difficult to follow. "Morryn didn't bother to cover his trail," Lorik spoke aloud. He rode through the woods as swift as possible but took care not to miss Morryn's tracks. The forest was wrapped in a serene beauty as light filtered through the trees and snow-dressed branches shimmered in dazzling display.

The woods that he rode through reminded him of the forests he enjoyed as a boy, full of mystery. Now, however, it was more than just boyhood adventures that captivated his life, more than just childhood games. The mystery before him was grim, and Lorik grew increasingly cautious, unsure of what he might find at the end of the trail.

Morryn's tracks continued southwest and weaved through the forest to disappear in the distance. To Lorik it seemed endless. As he continued to follow the tracks, the sun fell close to the western horizon and filled the sky with a ruddy glow as it descended beyond the Shadow Mountains. Shafts of light glimmered through the trees and reflected off the carpet of snow.

Clouds from the north trailed a slow path across the sky with their grim reminder that winter was still in full command. He had to decide, follow the trail or make camp and run the risk of losing the path to a new snowfall. Lorik stopped a moment, dismounted and examined the hoof prints of Morryn's horse. The tracks continued southwest and drew close to the Hoppe River. He took a bite of beef and gave his horse time to rest, but he decided to continue the pursuit until the last possible moment.

It didn't take long until he came to a wide glen, a meadow covered in snow. The dim light of dusk cast voluminous shadows across the frozen glade. From a distance, Lorik spied a horse, black and large that wandered near the edge of the glen. He dismounted, anxious over what he might find, and tied his horse several yards beyond the meadow. Keeping to the trees, he made his way to the stray horse. He knew, even before he laid his hand upon the animal, that it belonged to Morryn. The mount looked in good condition as he examined it, no injury or sign of trauma. Lorik was comforted to know that the horse was well. But the lieutenant was still lost.

He stepped through the trees, drew his sword, and moved closer to what looked like a man lying motionless in the center of the field. The snow was trampled all about as if a mighty host of soldiers marched across its breadth. Lorik gazed over the circumference of the glade and, with no sign of an adversary, rushed to the fallen man. His heart fell when he saw the man's face. It was Lieutenant Morryn.

The lieutenant lay in a pool of his own blood. His chest was crushed by some massive weapon. His sword lay several feet away, out of reach and of no use—it had been broken. Tracks unknown to the sergeant ranged all over the glen along with the obvious prints of the lieutenant. Intermingled with Morryn's steps were deep prints like cavities of melted snow. Lorik judged by the size of the footprints that Morryn's assailant must have been over eight feet tall. There were several places where the snow had been melted to the ground and the grass beneath seemed charred. Lorik scratched his head, puzzled over what type of creature could leave such tracks.

The twilight deepened, and Lorik paused to consider his next move. He didn't want to remain in the glen for fear that Morryn's adversary might return, but he needed to piece together the strange circumstances that destroyed his entire squad and left Morryn dead in a lonely field. To try and find some answers, Lorik began to search the surrounding environment.

The snow all about the field was littered with tracks. Some Lorik easily identified, others remained a mystery. Some animals, perhaps deer and elk, had crossed through less than an hour before he arrived. In the western side of the meadow, he discovered the tracks of two other men, both booted. He followed the tracks to some brush on the edge of the field and noticed that two men must have lain on the ground and used the brush to hide.

From the north, however, Lorik discovered the greatest mystery of all. Dozens of prints from booted feet, small and heavy, covered the ground. The prints were too small to be that of men, certainly not soldiers. They were the same size of adolescent children, but made much deeper impressions, much like that of grown men. From what Lorik surmised, a group came into the glen, wandered about for a moment, gathered into a two-column formation and left again. What surprised him was that the same tracks he had seen at the western edge of the glen joined with the smaller prints and left the field northward.

It appeared, from what Lorik observed in the dim twilight, that the smaller prints had scattered all around the meadow. There were several places where the snow had been brushed away as if someone had searched the field for something lost. All the evidence around him left him with more questions than answers, but he was a soldier not a sage, and all he knew to do was to follow the tracks that headed north. Night started to envelop the region, and he needed to set camp. The tracks were fresh, and there were plenty to follow so he didn't fear losing the trail even if it snowed. From all that Lorik determined, whoever belonged to the tracks took no pains to hide their passage through the forest.

He returned to where he had tied his horse. Morryn's stallion stood with it. Lorik relieved the lieutenant's horse of its burdens and let it roam free in the wild. He would follow the new tracks until he found the answers to all the mysteries. Alone and unaided, Lorik determined to stay on the trail until he came to its end, no matter where it led. With less than an hour of light, he mounted his horse and turned north.

He departed the glade and followed the tracks into the forest. He surmised that his quarry traveled with haste, and with little regard for secrecy. Branches and undergrowth were snapped and broken, and a multitude of footprints scraped across the snow. Of the score of smaller prints, there remained two sets larger than the rest. He didn't know who the larger tracks belonged to but, with the lieutenant dead, he assumed the two were somehow associated with Morryn and taken captive.

By the light of a pale crescent moon, Lorik continued to follow the tracks. Being mounted, he hoped that he might overtake them. Frost and snow glistened in the soft moonlight, and the frigid night chilled his skin. But he burned with the memory of his slaughtered men, and those images forced him to press on. He wished that he had defied the lieutenant's orders, challenged his authority, but Lorik refused to dwell on regrets. Now his singular obsession was the possible rescue of two comrades. His imagination failed to conjure any idea of who ran before him, but he was determined to find out. Lorik held onto hope—the hope that if he caught up with them he might find some answers.

Night wore on and weariness crept into his bones. Even his mount showed signs of exhaustion as it took one labored step after another. Lorik, worn out, knew he and his horse needed to rest, so he stopped and dismounted in a small clearing. The trail of footprints continued north and disappeared in the dense forest. The clear night, with stars that shimmered in the cold dark sky, showed no signs of snow. Lorik did not fear he might lose the trail. His own weariness weighed him down like an anchor around his neck. He rubbed his eyes to try to stave off sleep, but with each passing moment, his eyelids grew heavier. Lorik forced himself to assemble his small shelter and clear a place on the ground for a campfire.

The frigid night wore on as he gathered scraps of wood. He set the wood, along with the kindling he carried, into a pile and struck his flint. With a brilliant spark, the wood ignited, and a warm campfire came to life. The warmth was welcome. He held out his cold hands to gather in the heat as the fire radiated its welcome glow all around the clearing. It was enough for Lorik to enjoy a comfortable night.

Lorik sat on the cold ground under the shelter of his canopy. He melted snow in a small cook-pot and boiled some dried beef into a warm broth. He sipped at the warm potage, and enjoyed the savory taste, though insufficient to satisfy his appetite. He needed to sleep; his eyes felt like some unseen agent had thrown sand in them. *Well, there's nothing to it,* he thought, *I'll just roll up in my blankets and trust my night to good fortune.* Wrapped with his blankets, he collapsed to the ground and fell asleep.

****

Lorik woke to a bright and cold morning. His blankets were covered in frost, though within them he felt warm and protected from the elements. His horse stood nearby grazing on scrub grass that grew through the snow. He stood and stretched his stiff, weary muscles in the frigid air. The campfire had died, and he stirred the coals only to scatter the ash that remained.

"Well," he said to no one in particular. "I better get moving if I intend to catch my quarry." Lorik quickly dismantled his makeshift shelter and tied it to the back of his saddle. Then he foraged for more small sticks of wood, suitable for the next campfire. *Always better to have dry wood,* he thought. As he gathered the small sticks, he noticed an object. Under a fallen log, half buried was a torn piece of cloth, its color and fabric resembled a piece from a guardsman's cloak. Where the cloth had settled, a large spatter of blood had stained the snow. With a renewed purpose that warmed his thoughts, Lorik placed the torn swatch in his saddlebag and resolved to press on with greater determination.

Lorik bundled the wood he gathered and secured it to the saddlebag, mounted his horse, and continued north. Broken branches and trampled grass provided a clear trail to follow. Those he pursued were ahead by several hours, but he was determined to catch them. With the tenacity of a bloodhound, he spurred his horse and traveled through the forest as swift as the terrain allowed.

Hours passed, and Lorik pressed on. He came to a large valley which descended into thick trees and heavy undergrowth. Still the tracks continued, following a narrow path that switched back and forth down the wall of the ravine. In the distance, Lorik heard the reverberations of a raging river as it rolled and crashed along at the bottom of the valley. The trail he followed vanished down the embankment and disappeared into the thick foliage of the valley before him. Without hesitation, Lorik spurred his mount down the ravine.

The noise of the river grew louder as he followed the trail into the valley. Damp air clung to his clothes like an icy film and cold penetrated his flesh. Vapors coursed from the horse's nostrils as its warm breath mingled with frozen air. Lorik guided his mount through the twilight of the dense forest. Winter snows failed to penetrate with any force, and the ground beneath him was bare and brown.

Within the grove of trees, crushed grass gave evidence to the passage of many feet. Those followed must have taken rest within the grove's protective shelter. He dismounted, searched the area, and found the direction of the tracks. The heavy sound of a mighty torrent indicated he was very near the river. Lorik left his horse in the copse of trees and proceeded on foot, careful to follow the trail left by his quarry.

As he passed through the foliage, he heard what sounded like a detachment of men shouting over the din of the river. Lorik crept through the brush and drew near to the water taking extreme caution not to be seen or heard. He peered through the dense undergrowth.

At the edge of a raging river stood a score or more of small, stout men dressed in leather and mail shirts. They wielded large battle axes and waited in a clearing at the edge of the river. Through the crowd he noticed two others who sat together, blindfolded and hands bound. As he watched, he caught a glint of gold on the cloak of one of the men, the insignia of the Royal Guard! He was right; two had survived somehow and were captured by these diminutive soldiers.

Then, a change came over the river. The water took on a hollow, resonant tone. A rough, stone structure started to rise from beneath the water. It was slow, yet it continued to crawl from the depths of the torrent. Then, as if it had always dwelt in that very spot, a stone bridge stood over the white water. He had never seen such machinery, or perhaps this was magic. He didn't know.

Once the bridge had reached its full height, and the river flowed beneath it, the stout soldiers crossed over. The two men of Celedon were forced to stand. Then horror stuck through his heart. One of the soldiers was his own captain.

He almost gave his position away but squelched the desire to gasp aloud at the incredulous circumstances that unfolded before him. His mind raced to understand how or why the captain and, he assumed—Private Rayn, were taken captive. He wanted to free them but knew that a direct assault on the group of soldiers was pointless. "If the captain was captured," Lorik whispered to himself, but let the thought trail off. He decided to remain concealed and wait for a time to rescue his commander.

As the last soldier crossed the bridge, it sunk back into the river and vanished beneath the rapids as mysteriously as it had appeared. He continued to keep his attention on the diminutive warriors as they marched up the narrow pass in a column of two until they disappeared into the spires and rocky crags.

Lorik crawled from the foliage. "There must be some way to activate that bridge hidden around here," he murmured. *I must find a way to cross this river and rescue the captain.*

****

"We travel swift; we must make the door before nightfall," Kaurn shouted over the noise of the torrent. The stone path was slick with ice and frost. Aaron and Rayn stumbled along, blindfolded and guided by a dwarf. The steep climb and rapid walk exhausted Aaron, but still he marched. Below them, the sound of the river dimmed.

Aaron lost track of time in their cold, uphill march. Soon each footfall became a weary grind, and it forced the dwarves to slow their desperate pace.

The dwarf commander berated Aaron and Rayn and cursed their diminished strength. "Give them some more draught! We can't delay in these mountains for long!" Grateful, Aaron accepted some of the potent drink. It warmed his tired muscles and renewed his strength.

It wasn't long, though, before the dwarves stopped again. The wind whipped and howled through the peaks of the Shadow Mountains. Aaron listened as even the dwarves complained about the frigid conditions. From the sounds around him, he could tell the entire contingent huddled together. He could only surmise they took shelter behind a rock formation of some sort that offered protection from the bitter wind.

"Commander!" shouted the dwarf who guided Aaron. "We must take care and start a fire. Most of our men will be frozen before we reach safety!" Aaron heard the desperation in his guide's voice.

Kaurn shouted back, "Very well! Get a fire started and bring the prisoners."

The rattle of wood sounded as a dwarf unbundled brands for a fire. Footfalls shuffled all around as dwarves moved about the small campsite. Soon, Aaron heard a small crackle and felt the warm radiance of a campfire.

Aaron's escort sat him near the fire with Rayn at his side. He remained blindfolded and bound. Despite their situation, Aaron was grateful for the warmth of the flames. Several others gathered near them. Two dwarves who sat close by enjoyed a spirited conversation.

"No," said one gruff dwarf in his rich baritone voice, "I don't think that we'll be home before a week. It is a long way through the passage, and with these two blindfolded it'll slow us down."

"You're right," said the other dwarf as he spoke between bites of food. "I wonder what Lord Dunstan will do with these two? Lock them up to keep them out of trouble I suppose."

"He may just interrogate them and return them to the other side of the river. I don't think that they will pose much of a threat... we took them captive easy enough!" The dwarves laughed.

"So much for that Royal Guard," mocked the second dwarf, "there's not much fight in them."

Aaron was handed a strip of dried beef and blindly he ate, thankful for the bite of food.

"We will enter the passage in two hours. When it's time to go, make sure nothing remains; remove all signs of our journey." Kaurn addressed his men.

The first dwarf spoke in a low tone under his breath to his companion, "Two hours...do you think *they'll* show up?" Aaron could hear the fear in his voice.

"I don't know... we've seen no sign of the horros, but they might be hidden in the crags above." The second dwarf said, his voice anxious.

He felt Rayn lean over and press against his shoulder. "Sir," Rayn whispered, "do you know what a *horros* is?"

"No," he whispered in return, "But if these dwarves are concerned, I imagine that we don't want to meet one."

The dwarf guard closest to Aaron overheard their conversation and responded to the captain's concern. "You don't want to meet one!" His harsh, deep voice resounded in the hollow alcove. "A horros is a fierce, bloodthirsty beast that lives in these mountains. They travel in packs and are predators of the worst kind. They possess jaws that can crush a dwarf and claws that rip flesh from the bone. They feed on the wild animals of the mountains, bears and mountain goats. But in these winter months, they will attack an entire legion of dwarf warriors." These words chilled Aaron worse than the frozen air. "Don't fret, we are nearly safe. Just a little longer and the way will be open and we can enter the passage. One thing is certain," the dwarf continued, "you don't want to be in these mountains by yourself. No one ever survives here alone."

"It's time," Kaurn ordered. "Get these prisoners up and move out. The way is open and the passage clear for travel." The company of dwarves rose and words of gratitude washed through the group like a wave at the announcement.

They had traveled a few hundred yards when a howl echoed through the mountains. The dwarves froze in their tracks, and a chill rushed down Aaron's spine. It was loud, like the cry of a wolf mingled with the roar of a bear, and it reverberated up the canyon behind them. Above another howl answered back—the malicious call of a hungry beast. The dwarves began to murmur among themselves. A sudden dread came upon Aaron. Blindfolded, he still sensed the presence of the predators and knew they closed in on the small band of warriors. From the passage ahead, Aaron heard the sound of claws clicking the stony path. The dwarves hurried their pace up the narrow ledge.

"Captain," Rayn said, his voice trembling, "at this rate we're going to stumble off this mountain."

Aaron had the same concern. "Rayn," he said, "try to keep near the rock face."

At the head of the party, Kaurn shouted orders. "Move! Keep your heads. Faster!" The howls behind them grew louder, closer, and were answered by guttural growls ahead.

"The horros are upon us! The horros are upon us!" Shrill shouts were heard from ahead, followed by the clang of metal; the sounds of battle rang out loud across the ridge. Dwarves shouted and screamed as they fought against their assailants. Kaurn's voice boomed over the din as he gave orders and directed his men in the fight.

The two dwarf guards who led Aaron and Rayn abandoned them and joined in the fray. Aaron, bound and blindfolded, groped along the sheer rock wall until he found Rayn. With some careful maneuvering they helped each other remove the blindfolds and leather straps that bound them.

Dusk shone upon the narrow passage with an eerie orange light. It illuminated a horrific scene and filled Aaron's heart with dread. Large, dog-like beasts leapt down from above. Their dark, massive bodies might have been mistaken for small horses with hair that grew matted and long. They possessed long, powerful claws and massive jaws. Aaron knew the creatures indeed had the power to rip through flesh and bite off a man's leg, though armored head to toe. Four horros leapt from the mountain cliff and three more stalked down from the passage ahead. Behind, at least four more of the beasts advanced up the path.

"We have to get out of here!" Rayn's voice quivered.

Aaron looked toward the dwarves. He had never abandoned a people in such desperation, and he wouldn't start now. "We can't leave, but we can help fend off these creatures." Aaron stood tall, his sense of duty clear. He spied their swords, cast aside with the other equipment when the battle began. "Follow me," he ordered.

The two soldiers rushed forward, unseen by the dwarves who fought for their lives ahead of them. Aaron unsheathed his sword and faced the predators. The two soldiers stood their ground against the horros.

The narrow ledge provided just enough room for them to stand abreast, with little space to maneuver. But they stood their ground and waited for the attack.

The horros leapt upon them with surprising speed and lashed at Aaron and Rayn with their long, razor-sharp claws. The beasts snarled and growled like rabid animals. Aaron weaved and parried, desperate to hold his ground against the predators. Two horros fell immediately as Aaron struck with lightning quickness. The other horros growled at each other and clawed for the remains of the fallen beast. Distracted only for a moment with the carnage, the beasts turned back to Aaron and Rayn.

Again the horros lunged and forced the soldiers to step back against the assault. Aaron refused to yield, and Rayn held his own alongside him. Against every attack, Aaron and Rayn fought the horros with expert skill. They slashed through the creatures and struck at them, forcing the beasts to back off. They worked in unison, a deadly display of grace and agility, rejecting all fear. Two more horros fell. Though Aaron and Rayn dispatched the first creatures, several more approached from the passage behind them.

As Aaron fought, he caught a glimpse of the dwarves as they stood firm against the horde of beasts. One dwarf had fallen, but the others held their ground as axes swirled in coordinated motion. The two dwarves who had guarded Aaron and Rayn rushed to their aid and joined the soldiers in the fray. They leapt over the two men with an agility that took Aaron by surprise.

The dwarves sprung over the battle and landed on their feet with a thud. Now, behind the remaining horros, the pair of dwarves raised their weapons against their adversaries. They wielded their battle axes with impressive skill and struck with a ferocity that Aaron had never seen. The two dwarves fought like berserkers against the ferocious creatures and pressed their advantage. With renewed momentum, Aaron and Rayn continued their attack, filled with an improved hope they might survive the onslaught.

In a matter of minutes the battle was over, dead horros lay strewn across the path while others had fallen to their death over the precipice. Two dwarves were killed in the melee. Exhausted, each person stopped to take in the scene. Aaron breathed a sigh of relief, grateful to have survived. The dwarf commander stumbled to him.

Kaurn was injured. He nursed multiple wounds to his arms and one large gash across his face. Blood trickled down his features and matted his beard. He walked with a limp and used his axe as a crutch. Still he looked the two men up and down as he wiped blood and sweat from his eyes, and shook his head in disbelief. The hostility in his expression was gone.

"So, you *are* warriors… hmm," Kaurn pondered. Aaron held his sword, stained with the blood of the horros, a defiant expression on his face. "I see that you are familiar with battle." Kaurn continued. "I assumed you would try to flee from here, and I would have branded you as cowards. But now… now I must acknowledge that you fought with us." Kaurn took a deep breath and rubbed his matted beard. "In our realm, courage is honored above all other virtues." He paused and gauged Aaron and Rayn. "You've earned my respect. I will allow you to carry your weapons; but our laws demand that you are blindfolded again to keep from learning our secrets." He ordered the two guards who had joined Aaron and Rayn in the battle to blindfold them once again. However, Kaurn permitted Aaron and Rayn to walk with their hands free and their weapons at their side.

The brigade continued up the path. Aaron kept close to the mountain's face as they navigated the icy precipice. The day had passed swiftly and, with the setting sun, a slight breeze began to blow. The cold, biting air chilled Aaron to the bone.

Higher and higher they walked; snow swirled around them. Through the many canyons, the blowing wind howled and sent frightful reminders of the call of the horros. It wasn't long, however, before Kaurn again halted the group and ordered two others to his side. Aaron didn't hear what was discussed, but after a quick word from the commander, he heard the two dwarf warriors run up the mountain pass until the sound of their steps disappeared.

The commander returned to Aaron and Rayn. "We will wait until our scouts return. When they do, we will enter the realm of Brekken-Dahl."

"Oh, and then what?" Rayn no longer held his peace. "Another long weary march, another fight for our lives against monsters unheard of, is that what we can expect in this realm of yours?"

"Private!" Aaron snapped. "Hold your tongue."

"It's all right," Kaurn returned. "You both have been pressed beyond your endurance, and I am surprised you didn't break under the strain. There are few who are as hearty as a dwarf!" He exhaled a boisterous laugh. "As for what will come... when we enter the presence of Lord Dunstan you will give account of yourself, and I will tell him of your courage as you fought the horros with us." The commander paused as he thought. "Perhaps he will show you leniency." Kaurn walked away and left Aaron and Rayn to blindly listen as the wind continued its relentless howl through the mountains.

When the scouts returned, Aaron heard the others begin to stir and felt that it was good news which the scouts brought back. Once again he and Rayn were led to stand and follow their guides. The path pressed higher up the mountain, but the steep climb gave way to a gentler slope.

They rounded a corner, and Aaron felt the gentle breath of warm air against his face. Grateful for the touch of warmth, he tried to surmise what it meant. They walked into this warm draft, a welcome sensation, but he wondered where it came from. The stone upon which they walked seemed to echo, hollow and dull, but an echo nonetheless. The voices of their captors echoed as well, as if they stood in a hollow tube—or tunnel. He jumped when a tremulous grating sound of stone on stone silenced all other voices. The rumble ended with a heavy, dull thud.

Kaurn removed their blindfolds, and Aaron's eyes were pierced with a brilliant, white light that emanated from crystalline formations. They stood in a tunnel, long and wide. Aaron marveled at the workmanship of the passage, with walls made to resemble smooth, dressed stone and a level, cobbled floor. The tunnel continued ahead of them for hundreds of yards and passed beyond eyesight. It was illuminated with brilliant crystal-like stones, imbedded in the wall every fifty feet, which gave off a radiant white light.

The stout Kaurn approached, still limping from his encounter with the horros. Proud and unassailable, like a living representation of the mighty statues that

Aaron had witnessed in his vision. "Welcome," he said, "to the realm of Brekken-Dahl!"

8

Through the Shadow Mountains

Lorik looked out over the wide torrent as it coursed through the channel and knew that the bridge was hidden somewhere under the surface. The river poured down the ravine in massive white-capped rapids and cascaded over the rocks as it rushed along. A heavy mist drifted through the air, churned up from the turbulent wash, to cover the landscape with a thick layer of frost.

Across the river, mountains ascended in sharp spires with a narrow ledge that wound through the rugged terrain. The pass disappeared into the heights. Lorik searched for a mechanism to trigger the unseen causeway. He paced up and down the bank of the river but found no means of raising the bridge.

"I don't even know what I'm looking for!" He shouted his exasperation. Lorik stared at the massive trees that stood near the river with the thought that he might fall one over the rapids. But there stood no tree tall enough to cross the expanse, and he had no means to cut one down. In frustration, he returned up the hill to the place where he had left his horse. Lorik guided the animal down near the edge of the river and then started building a small campsite.

He refused to quit, but he had to be ready for the

cold night that approached. The mist off the river shrouded the world in a frosty-white coat, and Lorik was now very thankful to have brought his own firewood. He set his lean-to on the southwest edge of a small clearing near the river, but near enough to the trees to gain their added protection from the wind. Lorik piled his dry wood at the front of his small tent and struck his flint. A spark dashed off the stone and ignited the wood.

Confident the fire was of sufficient strength to keep burning, Lorik left his campsite to gather more fuel. He did not look forward to the prospect of a long, cold night. He added the extra fuel and the blaze intensified—a welcome companion in the frigid conditions. However, Lorik still needed to discover the secret of crossing the river. Night slowly encroached upon the world as the sun touched the tips of the Shadow Mountains, but he determined to use every possible moment to investigate.

He remembered several of the diminutive men had wandered away from the river. Lorik hoped their tracks might lead him to the secret of the bridge. With little time, he hoisted his cloak around his shoulders and began to scour the area.

Lorik scratched at the heavy, thick whiskers which covered his face. Methodically he looked about the clearing and examined the frozen terrain with great care as he searched for footprints in the snow. It had crusted over with a thin layer of ice which crunched under his feet and left his mark upon the environment. The smallish men he had seen also left impressions in the snowpack as they meandered all about the glade. Two sets of prints, however, wandered away from the river to the east, away from the main party.

Lorik moved all about the small field and, like a dog on a hunt, searched for any evidence to release the bridge. He stooped low on occasion to peer close to the ground, and then stood again to scan the panorama of his surroundings. Slow and systematic, Lorik explored every possible indent and depression in the cold, icy surface.

He arrived at the eastern edge of the glen and found two sets of prints. With a sigh of hope, despite the failing light, Lorik followed the tracks away from the river.

The prints ventured into a heavily wooded area about two hundred yards from where he had seen the bridge rise from the water. He was several hundred yards away from his campsite and looked back to see his fire, bright in the final glow of dusk. The prints stopped near a large grey boulder. It was massive, almost eight feet in height, with a circumference large enough to hold at least thirty men. Lorik had no notion why the tracks he followed led him to the massive rock, but somehow he knew the stone was linked to the causeway hidden beneath the river. However, the day had grown too dark to examine the stone with any thoroughness, so he returned to his campsite to await the dawn.

With little to do but wait, the sergeant sat near the fire and huddled under his makeshift shelter, facing the warmth of the flames. His shoulders sagged under the weight of his circumstances. Night had fallen on the world as he brooded over his meager meal. He thought of the men of the Royal Guard who were now no more than memories and mourned their loss in the cold, quiet darkness. The solitude left little for him to do but wait for the break of dawn.

Lorik was a man of action and to brood in the night grated against his sense of responsibility. Lost in the haze of his murky thoughts, the sergeant rose to care for his horse. She was warm with plenty of dry, cold grass to eat. He brushed her mane and groomed the mare with careful skill. A trained and disciplined military mount, the horse shivered in the cold, yet stood still as her master provided the necessary care. Again Lorik's thoughts drifted to the events of the past several days. He wondered if, somehow, he might have prevented the tragedies and stopped the brutal course that he and his men had followed.

Though the night was young, Lorik felt the weariness of the day overwhelm his strength. *Get an early start*, he thought, *and I'll find a way to cross that river.* Wrapped in his cloak, and with his head shrouded by blankets, the sergeant took one large yawn, and closed his eyes.

****

Lorik woke with a start. Something moved in the trees beyond his sight, or so he thought. White, cloud-like mist drifted in currents through the trees. The fog which flooded the forest in the night was thicker still, and prevented Lorik from seeing more than ten feet beyond his camp. His fire was out, but it was clear that the morning had dawned and the sun had crested the horizon. He hunkered down in his shelter; reached for his sword which lay beside him and quietly unsheathed the weapon, waiting for the mysterious traveler to appear from the mist.

A twig snapped and again Lorik heard the sound of some unseen creature approach, closer now and to his right. His muscles tensed in the cold, and every one of his senses came alive, heightened by the anxiety of the moment. He smelled the burned remains of his campfire, heard the gentle breath of his horse and felt the cold steel in his grip. In front of him, across from where the fire had dwindled to embers, his horse stood unaffected by the approaching mystery. Beyond his sight the river raged on, the noise of its passage dulled in his ears by constant exposure. He tuned it out, and fixed his concentration on the anonymous visitor.

Snap! Snap!

Nearer now, he noticed a vague shadow, large and ominous, wandering through the trees to his right. It approached with such casual motion that Lorik became convinced the creature was unaware of his presence. The fog was his advantage as he watched the shadow move toward him. He gripped his sword in his right hand, ready to strike. The strange visitor moved slowly as it approached. Then it came out of the hazy fog into view and looked directly at the sergeant. A deer! Large brown eyes gazed at the place where Lorik crouched on the ground. By its appearance, it was a young buck, with two small spikes protruding from the top of its head and a thick brown coat of hair grown for the winter. Lorik exhaled a sigh of relief and his horse whinnied in recognition of a fellow creature. The sergeant stood from the place where he lay and the deer bolted out of sight to disappear in the fog.

"I'm getting too old for this," he spoke to the less than congenial fog that hung in the trees. Lorik gathered his gear, stirred the small embers that remained of his fire and coaxed a flame from the ashes. He threw some dry brush and sticks on it and it grew into a friendly, warm blaze that he used to heat some water and cook a small breakfast. As his meal cooked, he ate some dried bread and cheese and began to make his way back to the boulder that he'd discovered the night before.

The sun climbed in patient motion and burned away the layers of mist that blanketed the valley. He found the rock in a thick cluster of alder trees, a bulwark of stone in stark contrast to its surroundings. He saw his own footprints from the previous day and the smaller prints of the two others were evident along the frozen ground. The two sets of prints meandered all around the granite boulder.

The stone itself was nondescript and showed no clear marks. To Lorik, it was an ordinary boulder, misplaced in the copse of trees. His instincts, however, told him that the stone was more. It possessed a smooth surface, worn down with countless years of weather and showed not one jagged edge on its exterior. No crack existed on its surface, not one fissure, which Lorik noted as unusual. In fact, it seemed to Lorik that such a stone was out of place.

With that thought, he forgot about the breakfast that waited for him on the campfire and continued to examine the boulder for evidence or clues to help him discover the secrets of the bridge. *Somehow*, he thought, *this stone is the key*. He stroked his growing beard and wrapped himself tighter in his wool cloak, grateful for the protection it provided. He had no time for delay and feared that his captain was in great distress.

His initial examination of the stone gave him no clue how it related to the bridge. But, as he thought about the size of the captain's abductors, he began to examine the lower portions of the boulder. Nearer the ground, he observed a rounded indentation worn smooth, about the size of a large thumbprint. Near this, he began to examine the ground below the indentation and discovered an unusual patch of earth. Disguised to look like the ground, a small, square access door sat just beneath the indentation on the rock.

Lorik pried the small door open and, just six inches below the ground, was a set of three circular stone dials. Each dial seemed to be made of a hard, black marble stone, smooth and solid. They were inlaid with ten white symbols on each, thirty in all, and devised some form of combination sequence. He'd found the secret to the bridge. A small notch was carved into the stone faceplate to indicate the particular selection that each dial rested on.

Lorik scrutinized each of the dials. Some of the symbols seemed to represent forms of nature. The first three he identified: a mountain, river and tree. The next two were rather vague, a set of three wavy lines and a symbol that looked like a leaf of clover. Three more symbols he easily recognized: a sword, an axe, and a bow. The final two symbols didn't make any sense to Lorik, three circles interwoven and a triangle with a vertical and horizontal line that crossed each in the middle. He looked at the three dials and sighed in exasperation. Lorik knew that it might take days to stumble onto the right combination.

He stroked his beard and stood to stretch his legs; the cold morning and icy ground chilled him to the bone. He walked around the boulder and tried to keep himself warm as he thought through the variety of combinations the dials represented. In the distance the river rushed on, the one barrier that prevented him from reaching the captain. The thunderous rumble of the rapids mocked his efforts.

Casually he strode, his gaze always returning to the wide torrent that blocked his way and the sheer granite cliffs of the mountains beyond. The dial symbols rolled through his mind as he attempted to decipher their secret, desperate to find his way across. He decided the symbols were grouped into three categories: nature, weapons, and then the two which were unknown to him. *If each dial fell into one category*, he thought, *that narrows the choices.*

Lorik found himself at the place where he had seen the viaduct rise from the water. Again he looked over the area and hoped to find a sign or symbol to help him unravel the mystery. The river's edge kept its secrets. As he wandered, he followed his own tracks back to the large rock. He tried to put himself into the mentality of those who crossed the river, but to no avail. He had no knowledge about the strange, diminutive men and, try as he might, the mystery of the bridge eluded him.

Overhead, the sun climbed high in the sky and shone bright and warm. Trickles of melted snow flowed into the river, and Lorik appreciated the less-than-freezing air. He welcomed the brief warmth that fell upon his face, chapped from exposure to the cold and snow. Back at the boulder, he knelt at the hidden dials and decided to use the distinctions of the different categories as a guide. Lorik manipulated the dials into various combinations. The minutes passed as he tried different arrangements: river, sword, circle… no change; mountain, bow, triangle… still nothing. After an hour, he sat back in frustration. In the distance, his horse nuzzled her nose into the snow to get at the cold grass beneath. He heaved a sigh, irritated by the secrecy of the men who'd led his captain away.

"One more try." Lorik spoke as he leaned over the uncovered hole. He manipulated the dials, organizing them into various combinations, desperate to find the pattern that unlocked the secret bridge. The morning had long trailed away into late afternoon and the sun started its slow descent toward the Shadow Mountains. He was again about to surrender to the mystery of the dials when his last try issued forth a sound from within the boulder... *click*. He stopped, looked around to see what happened and checked to see if, perhaps the bridge began to rise out of the water—nothing.

Then Lorik examined the boulder again. He pressed upon the small indentation near the base of the stone and found that the rock moved. Lorik pushed on it and the rock opened to his left, revealing a hollow interior. Inside was an iron handle attached to a well-oiled set of gears.

The gears of smooth, polished agate, round and large, filled the cavity inside the boulder. He applied pressure to the handle which protruded from off-center of the vertical gear and found that, with some exertion, the device turned. It moved slowly and gave great resistance at first to his efforts, but he continued to turn the wheel. Undaunted, he pushed harder and the gears began to move more freely. He watched toward the river and, with each turn, the river began to change its shape, rushing over a stone partition that rose out of the torrent.

"The bridge!" Lorik shouted with delight. He redoubled his efforts and kept his eyes on the rising structure. Like a monolith, the rough stone conduit emerged from the flood to become a safe passage over the violence of the powerful waterway. Aaron was almost a day ahead of him, but Lorik felt hope restored with each turn of the crank. He continued to move the handle with all his might, and the bridge lifted. His mind failed to comprehend how such a conduit was manipulated by a device over two hundred yards away. Lorik dismissed the mystery, simply glad to have found the means to cross the river and pursue his captain.

The bridge at last had risen above the level of the river, forcing the water to flow through massive holes beneath the causeway. The water roared as it rushed under the bridge. Lorik moved quickly as he hoisted his cloak higher on his shoulders and ran back to his horse. His excitement was tempered by the realization that he faced the rugged, demanding environment alone. Lorik slowed and gathered several sticks of wood and bundled them together with his gear. He filled his leather flask with water from the river, cold and clear. Then, with a deep breath, he mounted his horse, patted her on the neck, and rode across the bridge into the mountains beyond.

The mountain pass was bleak and cold. It gained elevation quickly and followed a northwest direction. Lorik was amazed and grateful that the pass had little snow, and the passage proved wide enough for him to ride. The shod hooves of his horse clattered against the stone and sent echoes reverberating against the canyon walls.

The day had waxed into dusk and a cold wind howled through the ravine that the pass followed. Snowflakes swirled around him and stung his eyes. The changing condition forced Lorik to move much slower than he wanted. Far below, the river made its way south and west, on a journey that disappeared beyond his sight. He was high enough now that no sound from the river found its way up to his ears, and it appeared as little more than a ribbon of water spanned by the stone bridge which glistened in the fading sun.

Ahead, the passage wound through the jagged teeth of the mountains. In the cold, bitter wind, he needed to make shelter soon or die of exposure. He saw no rock or outcropping he could use and no cave or fissure to take cover from the wind. Instead, Lorik kept as close to the rock face as possible in a desperate effort to wrest from the mountain what little protection was available.

Beneath him, Lorik's horse shivered in the wintery exposure. There was very little comfort, as he, himself, found his own body shivering in an effort to keep warm. They trudged up the mountain; step by aching step. He wished his circumstances had never led him to such a miserable place. *Who could live here?* Still they continued, far more than a thousand feet above the canyon floor.

Darkness fell like a cold blanket, and Lorik decided to dismount. He led his steed up the passage with hope he might find some small crevice to take shelter.

Lorik rounded a bend in the pass and discovered a small alcove, little more than an indentation in the hard, cold rock, but enough for him and his mount to escape the howling wind. He unpacked his gear and arranged the firewood on the stone floor. No snow had ventured into the narrow shelter, and the dry wood caught fire with a flash, illuminating the recess with its yellow flames. Shadows danced across the walls as the fire flickered. Around him, cold shards of rock lay scattered on the ground.

To Lorik's surprise, several charred remnants of branches and wood littered the ground. Lorik picked a burnt piece and sniffed it. The wood had been burned not more than a day before. *Aaron's captors took refuge in this place.* Distinct footprints remained in the ash, reminiscent of the small prints he'd seen at the bridge site.

Lorik sat near the small fire, desperate for the warmth offered by the flames. The rock face provided some comfort as a protrusion over his head helped to capture the heat. An eerie sound, like the howling cry of a wolf, carried on the wind and sent a chill up Lorik's spine. He tried to dismiss the sound as the wail of the wind blowing through the cracks and crags of the mountains, but the noise persisted and began to grow louder. Wrapped in a cocoon of wool blankets, he huddled against the chill night air, but kept his sword within easy reach. Rationing his limited supply of wood, he kept the fire dim. *One more night in this desolation,* he thought, *and I'll have no choice but to abandon the pursuit.* Discouraged, he drew closer to the fire.

It was a bleak night, stark and cold. The fire, not more than a whisper of flame, struggled to dispel the chill air. Stars hung high above in the cold, black sky; a pale, waning moon continued its progress through the velvet blackness of night, its dim illumination only served to enhance the sense of cold. His hands felt frozen in their gloves and his feet, though covered with winter boots, sensed the bite of his frost-covered environment.

The sound of the wind changed, and sent a deeper chill to Lorik's already frozen bones. A howl carried on the wind conveyed malice and hunger, and it iced his blood more than the arctic air. Then, just beyond the fire, Lorik noticed two orbs reflected in the light—red eyes glaring back in his direction. They didn't move—malicious eyes just outside the circle of light that the small fire provided.

Panic welled up in Lorik's mind like a fountain, but years of discipline allowed him to dismiss fear and reach for his sword. He unsheathed the weapon and added another brand to the fire. As the flames grew, so did the light and Lorik saw the outline of some monstrous, wolf-like creature. Low growls rumbled from the darkness and in the distance, the howls of other creatures were carried on the wind. The sergeant stood and brandished his sword. He retrieved a burning branch from the fire. Then in one, sudden leap, the creature rushed into the circle of light and attacked. Lorik's horse reared up and bolted from the small alcove of rock.

Alone, Lorik faced the creature with his sword in one hand and a firebrand in the other. The creature growled and snapped its massive jaws as Lorik pivoted to avoid its attack. The hideous beast lunged at Lorik. But with the agility born of experience and desperation, the sergeant moved again and plunged his sword though the monster's breast. The beast howled, a sound that Lorik had never heard, filled with pain and malice, and lay on the cold rock as it quivered in the final throws of death, dark hair matted and bloody. Lorik pulled his sword from the carcass and wiped the steaming blood on the monster's coarse fur, he then cast the last pieces of wood onto the fire and it leapt up in a brilliant shower of embers. Lorik feared he faced the fight for his life and wanted to see whatever came next.

It didn't take long. From the darkness along the path, he heard the low growls and blood-chilling sounds of the wolf-like creatures approach. Four sets of eyes glowered in the distance, no more than twenty yards from his campfire. Guttural noises pronounced the creatures' awful intentions as they advanced with slow, cautious steps. The beasts growled and revealed long, sharp fangs. The huge, wolf-creatures stepped closer to the fire and sniffed at the air. Their eyes never left Lorik, and he heard the hunger in their ravenous tone. The fire stood between him and the beasts, its warmth and light blazed with brilliance in the cold night air. Lorik reached down and grabbed another brand from the fire, never taking his eyes off the predators.

He stood, sword in one hand, fire in the other. "If you want dinner," Lorik challenged the beasts, "it's going to cost you!"

The four beasts continued their slow, careful steps toward Lorik. Then one of the creatures stopped, its ears perked up as if it listened to the wind. It sniffed the air and gave a horrendous howl then sprung back to the path. The others followed the first into the darkness and back down the mountain trail. Lorik's shoulders slumped and he heaved a heavy sigh of relief, glad that the beasts were drawn away.

From the darkness, Lorik heard the ringing sounds of battle as shouts and cries echoed up the cold mountain pass. Lorik listened, concerned a greater threat approached from the dark. Again, unintelligible shouts mingled with the howls of the creatures and filled the night. With his makeshift torch and sword gripped tight in his fist, Lorik navigated the narrow path toward the sounds of battle.

In the darkness, a battle raged. The echoes grew louder, and Lorik now heard the shouts of voices: "Stand your ground... behind you!" Mingled with the shouts were the piercing howls of the ferocious beasts. Lorik moved through the dark, his torch flickered and shed very little light before him—just enough to prevent him from plummeting off the cliff. He had little doubt who else wandered the barren heights but guessed that it was another band of the rugged warriors.

The sounds grew louder as he approached. Just ahead and around a corner, the clang of steel and guttural bellow of the monsters set Lorik's heart racing. He slowed his pace and hugged the cliff wall, inching his way along to glance around the bend.

It was as he thought. The short men with their sturdy look and double-bladed axes fended off the assault of four monstrous beasts. The stout, diminutive warriors moved with great agility and surprised Lorik as they fended off the attack with remarkable skill. There were eight in all, two on each of the creatures, and they hacked and swung against their assailants until all four monsters were killed.

Panting with the exertion, one of the short men spoke. "Quickly now, we must hurry to find the intruder. Do not take time to dispatch the bodies of these horros, leave them to the mountain."

"Sir," replied another, "he must be dead; no one can survive alone."

"If he's dead," the first returned, "then he'll be easier to find. Now let's move out!"

Lorik knew that they meant him. He raced back up the mountain trail and hoped to outdistance himself from the others. He needed to give himself enough time to douse his fire and hide in the shadows until they passed. He arrived at his camp out of breath, his heartbeat ringing in his ears. The fire had diminished to orange embers and small, wispy flames. Lorik stamped the coals and flames to ash. Carried along on the wind, he heard the sounds of feet clamoring up the trail—*the patrol*, he thought. With the fire out, he gathered up his gear and ducked into a crack in the cliff wall to wait for them to pass.

They moved swifter than he anticipated and soon Lorik noticed the silhouette of small soldiers entering the alcove, twenty yards away. Lorik watched as one of the stout men drew close to his campsite. The man shouted back to his companions. "Over here!"

The others approached and noticed the dead beast, fresh blood still oozed from its fatal wound, and the defunct fire blew one final wisp of smoke. "He's gone." The first one noticed. Lorik held his breath as the band of warriors left the alcove.

"Let's move!" shouted the leader. "He must have continued up the mountain. If he knew about our bridge, he might know about the secret entrance to our realm. We must hurry!"

Lorik watched as the others disappeared up the path and beyond his sight. Slow and cautious, he stepped from his hiding place and listened for the sound of the patrol. The faint, rhythmic cadence sounded through the darkness. He retrieved his pack from the crevice and slung it over his shoulder. With sword in hand, Lorik wrapped his cloak tighter, hoping to gain any advantage over the frigid air, and followed the patrol through the darkness up the mountain pass.

He found it difficult to keep pace or to determine any sign of their passage. The one hope he had was the fact that with a large cliff on his left and a shear drop on his right, the pass was the only trail available. The wind howled and gusted all around him and prevented him from hearing anything more than his own footfalls. Lorik maneuvered along the stone ledge with stealth, anxious to remain undetected yet desperate to keep pace with the advancing guard. With no light except the thin sliver of the moon, his movements were slow.

Lorik stopped. Were those footsteps behind him? He listened—nothing. Turning slowly, with his sword clenched in his hand, Lorik peered down the dark trail. The quick glint of steel flashed in his eyes, and Lorik fell to the ground. He blinked and blinked again as the world around him spun out of control. A searing rush of pain wracked his head as blood dripped from his face. Lorik tried to stand but collapsed in a heap on the cold rock. His vision blurred as he gazed up at one of the short men standing over him, a battleaxe in his hands. Then all went dark.

****

Lorik woke in a corridor illuminated by large, white crystals imbedded in the rock wall. He was lying on a cobblestone floor in a wide, warm passage. The cold night air was gone and so were the stars as he stared at the smooth ceiling of a cavernous tunnel. His hands were bound with thin, but strong leather straps and his head throbbed with pain. Every heartbeat brought a new sensation of anguish as the world spun in dizzying disarray. He tried to gain his bearings but the illuminated environment was foreign to him. Lorik heard the sounds of muffled speech from somewhere beyond his line of sight. Then all went dark again.

Lorik next woke from the continued effort of one of the dwarves who alternatively slapped him across the face and splashed cool water on him. He tried to speak but the stabbing pain that filled his head prevented him from offering much more than a muffled, muted moan.

"Sir," shouted one of the dwarves, "the man is waking up!" The dwarf's voice hit Lorik's ears like a hammer against an anvil.

"Very well," said another. "Let's get him on his feet and move out. We've waited here too long."

Two of the dwarves stood over Lorik and hoisted him up. He collapsed in their arms as the world spun like a top. He grew nauseous and stumbled over his own feet. Yet the dwarves held him erect with each of Lorik's arms draped around the broad shoulders of his two guards. He was loathe to walk, but the strength of his captors denied him any quarter, so Lorik took one laborious step after another. Several times he almost fell as he stumbled through the dizzy effects of his head wound. He sensed the slow trickle of blood as it dripped down his face and matted his hair. With his head bowed, Lorik watched his own blood splatter on the cobblestone floor.

As they walked, he tried to determine their direction but had no means of knowing if they traveled north or south. One thing Lorik did know, they were on a steady descent, deep into the roots of the mountains. The miles passed beneath his feet one weary step at a time while his captors showed no signs of fatigue. Spaced along the wall, radiant crystals gave off soft, white light, providing ample illumination for the journey.

Lorik began to regain his equilibrium and moved more freely than before. His head pounded with pain, but he began to see with greater clarity as the dizziness subsided. Two stout warriors stayed by his side and allowed him to walk without support. He was grateful to stand erect without nausea overwhelming him.

"We'll stop here," the patrol commander ordered. "We've walked for several miles and will take a moment to rest. Besides," he continued, "now that our captive is conscious, he needs to answer some questions." The stout commander strolled over to Lorik and stood before him, arms crossed over his massive chest, glaring.

Lorik looked down at his captor. His head still throbbed with pain. "What is the meaning of this," Lorik stammered. "Who are you?" His speech was slurred and hesitant, and he struggled to keep his mind focused on the short man in front of him.

"Silence prisoner! I will ask the questions." The gruff voice of the commander rumbled in Lorik's ears and pounded against his skull. "Why have you invaded our land?" he demanded.

"Invasion?" Lorik questioned. "No, no invasion." His mind was still swimming in confusion as he tried to respond.

"Well," barked the dwarf, "if you're not here as an advanced scout for invasion, then why are you here? How did you find the way into our realm?" The leader of the patrol stood firm, his countenance like iron.

Though Lorik still felt dazed from the blow he suffered, he took a defiant, resilient tone. "I am a sergeant in the Royal Guard of Celedon," he said. "I am a soldier under the command of my captain and servant of the emperor." Lorik was clear-headed enough to conceal his actual purpose in the mountains.

"Very well *sergeant of the Royal Guard*," the patrol leader mocked, "you are now a prisoner of Lord Dunstan, and you will be brought before him to answer for your crime."

"What crime?" Lorik demanded.

"You have invaded our land. Either you're a terrorist or a precursor to war. Unwelcome intruders must face Lord Dunstan. Now march! We have a long road before we arrive in our capital." He ordered the two who stood near Lorik to act as his guards. The leader led them down the long, wide passageway deeper into the heart of the mountain.

They journeyed for days and kept to the same passage through the mountain, though there were several offshoots which meandered left and right from the main causeway. Lorik's wound healed enough so his eyes cleared, and he no longer struggled with double vision. The passage continued its descent, and to Lorik's best guess, they were several thousand feet beneath the surface, near the base of the mountains. On the fourth day, the passage ended and opened into a wide, spacious valley. They were still several hundred feet above the valley floor and stood on a large stone platform like a balcony overlooking a stage.

In the distance, he saw a massive, brilliant city. Its high walls sparkled as if adorned with thousands of gemstones. The day shone brilliant upon the ramparts, as if the sun rose in the sky just to cast its light upon the distant city. Behind him, the mountains loomed like giant bulwarks of stone. In front, the passage they followed became a wide road that meandered through large, well-tended fields and abundant groves of trees.

The city waited several miles away in the center of the valley, a shimmering ship in a golden sea. Stairs, carved into the solid rock face, descended to the valley floor. Lorik was led down these stairs, exhausted from the journey. But the sight of the rich valley and beautiful city electrified him with anticipation. They traveled through massive groves of trees, with leaves of gold and red occasionally falling in gentle motion. Amber fields of wheat shimmered in waves, stroked by a gentle breeze. In the fields many of the smallish people labored as they harvested the grain. Wagons pulled by mules and oxen navigated the broad road and passed Lorik and the patrol with little notice.

"What's happening out there?" Lorik asked the guard to his right as he pointed toward the fields.

"It's the final harvest," the dwarf said. "We had a late growing season, and they're trying to bring in the last crops."

"But the snows have fallen in Celedon," Lorik observed. "How is it that your valley is untouched?"

"This land was given to us by the ancient King, and it is sheltered from the harsh conditions of other regions," the dwarf said.

Three hours later, they entered the city. Colossal, ornate doors hung open, and the guards led Lorik through the arched gateway. Thousands of the diminutive people bustled about their business with no regard for Lorik though he stood a head taller than the entire population. Stone houses lined the streets, adorned with gold and silver decorations. He marveled at the wealth and craftsmanship displayed in the city's architecture.

All the people of the city, Lorik noticed, seemed of

the same stock as his captors. The men sported long, thick beards and many wore leather shirts with ringed mail and carried at least a small double-bladed axe. The women, however, were just the opposite. Small, slender forms weaved their way through the crowded streets, many of them with young children at their heels.

As they walked along the main thoroughfare of the city, his captors turned left and led Lorik down a side street. The passage narrowed so just three were able to walk abreast. At the end of the lane stood what looked like a standard barracks, square and unremarkable. The dwarf guard pushed Lorik through the door with little concern for gentleness. They entered a main hall, large, with barred windows. At the back of the room, a staircase descended into the unknown. Along the center of the room, large stone pillars held the roof in place. A younger guard, with a thin beard, hurried from the back of the room and stood at attention before the patrol leader.

"What orders, sir?" The young soldier seemed eager to please.

"Take this man to the cells and lock him up. Take care to keep a close eye on him; he took out a horros single handed!" The commander smiled as an expression of surprise and concern crossed the young guard's face.

"Yes sir!" With that, the younger one took Lorik by the forearm and led him away toward the stairs.

They followed the well-lit passage down one flight to the floor below. It was a damp basement, walled off in sections to provide various cells for incarceration. The guard took a key from a belt pouch that hung at his side and opened a wooden door into a cell. The door boasted one small square window with vertical bars at eye level and a metal flap at waist level to allow for food trays. It was into this dark chamber, damp and dismal, that the young dwarf escorted Lorik.

The door slammed shut, and Lorik's hopes fell. The guard opened the small metal flap and spoke to the sergeant. "Stick out your wrists!" Lorik did as he was ordered and the dwarf cut off the bindings. Grateful for the release of his hands, he rubbed his wrists to try and relieve the soreness. He leaned his head against the door in despair, while behind him he heard the sound of rustling in a pile of straw. He didn't give it much attention. *Just rats*, he thought as he leaned against the prison door.

"Well, well..." spoke a voice from behind him, "it seems that we have company!"

Startled, Lorik turned and looked at a familiar face. The grizzled appearance and untidy whiskers did not disguise who had spoken to him... it was his captain.

9

The City of Dwarves

For several minutes the captain just stared at him. He seemed bewildered and amazed Lorik stood before him. Rayn leaned against a wall in the corner, sullen and agitated as he sulked in the darker shadows of the small chamber. Lorik stood at the doorway, astonished at the sight of his captain.

The cramped quarters boasted no furniture and lacked any warmth. A large pile of straw filled the back right corner and it appeared that is what Aaron and Rayn had used for sleeping arrangements. Their cell was dark; the small window above Aaron's head and the light from the hall provided the only illumination. The smell of old, musty straw filled the room and made the chamber feel more like a stable than a prison cell.

Lorik felt beaten and tired. His eye was swollen shut and traces of blood still clung to his beard. "I…" Lorik stammered, "I thought I would never find you. And here you are—both of you."

"What are *you* doing here?" Aaron stared with marked astonishment as he spoke.

"Well, sir," he said hesitantly, "I've come to rescue you."

"And a fine rescue it is!" Rayn quipped as he

began to pace. "Well done!"

"Hold your place, Private," Aaron commanded. He returned his attention to Lorik. "But, how did you get here? You and the others were supposed to be on your way back to the capital."

Lorik took a deep breath. "There is much I must tell you," he said as he stepped away from the door and sank beside the captain on the pile of straw. He began to relax, scratched at his beard, and started to tell Aaron his story. "Sir," Lorik hesitated. "Captain...we were betrayed by...by Morryn.

"For some reason the lieutenant led us into the Shattered Hills." Lorik continued to recount his tale. "I should have seen it. Morryn was on edge and distracted, even distant from the company...more so than usual. He was anxious and in a hurry to arrive at the hills.

"Once we arrived, Morryn took half of us about a day's ride into that dreadful place, to some ancient cavern. He ordered us to make camp and wait. It seemed like we waited in those accursed hills for hours when Morryn appeared from out of nowhere, mounted his horse and fled down the path, screaming like a madman. I've never seen a man so...well, so desperate...especially a man with Morryn's skills.

"On the heels of his escape we were ambushed by a horde of trolls. They attacked from every side, and the men fought for their lives...no one else survived. I found a horse and rode for the men that we had left behind. They were also attacked, and when I arrived at the camp, there was no one left alive." Lorik's grief began to overwhelm him as tears of anger and remorse filled his eyes.

"We found Morryn in a small clearing in the

woods," Aaron said. "We saw him fight against a hideous beast, but we were too late to save him." Aaron shook his head, despair and anger on his face.

Lorik nodded in acknowledgement, and told the captain how he discovered the tracks which led him to the river. "It was at the river," the sergeant said, "I discovered I was tracking you and Rayn." He smiled as he recounted the image. "I was hidden under the brush on the hill above the river and watched as the two of you were bound and blindfolded. Then the most startling thing happened… a bridge rose right up out of the water." Lorik paused as he remembered the details of his ordeal. "It took some time, but I discovered the means of raising the bridge, and then I began climbing the mountain.

"On the mountain," Lorik continued, "I was attacked by some monstrous dog-like beast. After that, I heard a patrol behind me so I hid in a crack in the mountain wall. I thought I had fooled them because they passed me by. But these dwarves are clever, and I think they can see better at night than I gave them credit. They must have known I was hidden and waited for me. It wasn't long, not far up the mountain pass, when they struck me from behind. With one blow, I went down and here I am. I can only guess that my journey afterward was long, but much of it is just a blur to me." He rubbed the swollen bruise left by the axe that struck his face, painful with every touch.

"You are right… it is a long journey. It took us four days to walk through the passage under the mountains to this valley." Aaron stood and began to pace the floor of their cell. "I must tell you of our journey and arrival here. Perhaps that will better explain what's happened and the situation that we're in." He began to unfold the tale of his and Rayn's journey.

****

Aaron knew that Lorik was aware of the book they hunted. Now he told Lorik why the book was of such importance to the emperor and why they needed to find it. He spoke of his meeting with the governor at North Village and of the emissary that came from the emperor. He told of the encounter with Kaylan and his experience with the fire orb and explained how he had already known that Morryn betrayed them and that their captors were the very dwarves that he had seen.

"It feels," Aaron continued, "as if we are in the midst of a dilemma that might shake the very foundations of Celedon."

Rayn continued to pace. "Sir, what are we going to do? We're stuck here and these dwarves don't seem in too much of a hurry to let us go!" Irritation poured out with every word as the private moved in their small cell.

"I'm not sure," Aaron replied, "we have to wait and see what these dwarves will do next."

As if on cue, the metal plate on the cell door snapped open. "Come and get your dinner!" a guard ordered gruffly. Through the opening, a hefty, rotund dwarf pushed a tray laden with food. Outside in the hall a cart waited, piled high with trays.

They went to the door and retrieved their dinner. Aaron was astonished at the amount of food offered to prisoners, a loaf of grain bread, an ample supply of vegetables and fruits as well as a large decanter of cool water. The portions were generous, and it seemed their guards meant to feed them well. All three men sat in silence as they ate. The guard barked out his command to the next cell.

After they ate, Aaron spoke with Lorik. "This might be of some interest… The troop commander who brought us here seemed to hold a better view of us when we helped fight off those mountain beasts. Perhaps we can use it to our advantage. If we have found some favor with him, we may be able to persuade the lord of this realm to release us back to our own land." Aaron paused as he continued pondering over their situation. "In any event, one of us must get free and make it back to our country. The emperor will need to know about what happened and that these dwarves are after the Book of Aleth as well."

"With all due respect, captain, splitting up might be a bad idea. Our best chance of recovering the book is if we stay together." Lorik said

Rayn stopped in his tracks and shot a look of anger toward Lorik. "Are you mad?" He started pacing again, behaving like a caged animal. "Find the book! That winged beast must have it across the continent by now. No, we abandon our mission and one of us tries to escape. Two of us can keep these dwarves occupied long enough for the other to find a way out of this valley."

Aaron listened to the two men as he sipped at a cool cup of water. "Lorik, why try to find the book?" He was puzzled at his friend's suggestion, though Aaron longed to find the Book of Aleth as well.

"Captain," the sergeant said, "from what you've told us, there are hostile forces who want the book. If this book is so important, then recovering it is our highest priority. It is in our best interest and the interest of Celedon that we find it before it can be used against the nation."

"You may be right, Lorik," Aaron answered, "but we don't know where it is and our captors have given us no indication that we will ever be released." Aaron stroked his growing beard thoughtfully. "Unless our circumstances change so that we all can escape together, when one of us has a chance to get out of here, we take it."

"You mean *if* we get that chance, don't you Captain?" Rayn retorted. "It doesn't seem that we will have an opportunity for any of us to escape. The rest of the men are dead, and we're trapped in a dungeon somewhere in a realm that none of us ever heard of before. For all we know, these dwarves planned this whole thing!"

"That's not helpful, Private," Lorik responded. "We will escape this place; it's just a matter of time and opportunity. It is our duty to be ready when the time comes."

"The sergeant's right, we will find a way to escape… it is just a matter of time. I believe that we are to have an audience with the lord of this realm. We will reevaluate our situation after that." Aaron spoke as Rayn continued to pace the cell; the young private's frustration filled his eyes with glaring anger. Aaron wanted to try and alleviate Rayn's distress but had no means to do so. Instead, he focused on their environment. "Sergeant, when you came through the mountain passage, did you notice another way out?"

"No," Lorik said, "I was disoriented from the blow I received. All I remember is that it seemed we steadily walked downhill. From what I recall, we encountered no one else. I do remember it was well lit and took several days."

Aaron nodded his head, "I noticed the same thing," he replied. "Several passages led away from the tunnel, but we never strayed from the main road. The other passages might lead to other dwellings. If we can get to the main passage, we might be able to lose any pursuer down another corridor. Anyway, it's late. Let us ponder our fate in the morning."

****

Aaron woke to the sound of a guard in the corridor. Loud and obnoxious, the guard beat against the cell doors to wake the occupants. All through the jail, the reverberations of clashing metal and groans of unsuspecting prisoners mingled with the clatter of a wooden cart that moved through the hall.

The guard arrived at the cell and rapped on the door with a fist like a hammer. "Wake up!" the guard shouted into the room. "Breakfast ain't gonna wait!"

Lorik roused, groggy and half asleep, but stumbled to the door and retrieved three wooden plates passed to him. He woke Rayn and together the three men enjoyed a breakfast of crisp bacon, toast with jam, and assorted fruits. The morning passed in quiet contemplation. Aaron sat, propped against the wall, and watched the light of the sun penetrate through the small window and move the shadows in the room, Rayn took to his agitated pacing, and Lorik occasionally peered through the cell door.

The day crawled along, a slow procession to afternoon. Afternoon dragged into evening with little to disrupt the passage of time, when the sound of steps echoed through the hallway. The noise stopped at their door, a key was thrust into the lock and the door creaked as it swung open. In the corridor stood a group of six stern dwarves, malice filled their hard expressions. All six dwarves wielded double-bladed battleaxes and held them at the ready. Each was dressed in leather armor fitted with iron rings and grey, wool cloaks draped their shoulders with a hammer-axe insignia on their left breast. Their beards were long and braided, and they carried themselves with stern confidence, like warriors accustomed to trouble. "Come with us," said the leader, his red beard and hair looked like fire on the dwarf's grizzled features.

"Where are we going?" Aaron demanded.

"You are to stand before Lord Dunstan. Now come with us!" Two dwarves stood by each man and took them by the arm.

They were led from the cell and into the streets of Brekken-Dahl. Their guards escorted them up the same narrow road they had walked when they first arrived. The day waxed late as the sun sat low upon the western horizon. Streaks of orange and purple ignited the sky.

The city around them buzzed with activity. They entered into the main thoroughfare and hundreds of dwarves filled the street. Heavy-laden, wooden carts pulled by mules maneuvered along the cobbled passages, led by their dwarf masters to some unknown destination. Small dwarf children scurried along the streets as they played any number of assorted games. To their right, a broad road led back to the main gate of the city and to the left, towering in grandeur, stood a castle with four turrets and a high stone wall.

The streets were lined with large, opulent

buildings, a display of magnificent designs. The entire city appeared to be made of stone, from the cobbled streets to the majestic stonework of the structures along the main road. The people of the city moved about with the concern of their own business, giving little heed to the three men escorted by the dwarf guards.

As the sun continued to descend beyond the western mountains, and the shadows of the buildings grew long in the waning light, Aaron noticed the street began to glow. Large, white stones, each a foot in diameter, lined the thoroughfare like lamps upon pillars. Evenly spaced, they gave the entire city a mystical, almost magical appearance. As night fell, the stones grew brighter and illuminated the city with their iridescent light.

The dwarf guards led them toward a towering castle in the distance. They passed many shops, booths, homes and other places unknown. Each structure was a testimony of craftsmanship, designs Aaron had never seen. Many were adorned with gold or silver decoration that shimmered with the reflected light from the stones.

Lorik, too, marveled at the exquisite design of such common buildings. "Captain," he whispered, "have you ever seen such a place as this? We don't have anything like this in all of Celedon."

Many structures were decorated with mountain motifs. Some seemed to have engineered their dwellings to resemble the rough, natural stone of the mountains that lay to the east. In all, the entire city was a festival to the eyes, beautiful and wonderful.

Behind them high mountains stood like majestic sentinels, their peaks enflamed in the sunset. The setting sun showered the mountains in colors of purple and orange, making the snow-covered summits look like a fountain of light. The effect lasted a few, brief minutes, but imprinted a lasting memory on Aaron as he marveled at the incredible grandeur that surrounded the hidden city of dwarves.

His guards prodded him forward, toward the large citadel. As they continued through the streets, it looked to Aaron as if the city itself was an extension of the mountains, beautifully crafted to display the magnificence of the peaks beyond.

Aaron noticed the city was entirely surrounded by mountains! In every direction he looked, spires and cliffs rose up as fortifications, thousands of feet high and provided a formidable barrier to protect the inhabitants from the world beyond.

They arrived at the castle, a veritable fortification of stone. The walls towered like a bastion of masonry that appeared seamless. High atop the wall, dwarf sentinels kept watch over the entrance to Lord Dunstan's stronghold. The main entrance to the palace was across a wide walkway which spanned over a moat of sorts, more like a lake that surrounded two thirds of the citadel. The escorts led them across in swift procession and the lead dwarf gave some form of hand signal which drew an immediate response. The tall, twin doors of the castle swung outward, and Aaron and his men were ushered in.

The tall doors, when closed, possessed the same seamless design as that of the stonework. Stairs led up either side of the inner wall of the castle, and each ended at a small wooden door. Before them, a long, magnificent hall waited.

Aaron gasped in recognition; it was the same hall that he witnessed in his vision. The floor was made of shimmering marble, specked with gold and silver flakes. Two great rows of granite columns supported a vaulted ceiling. Statues of dwarf warriors kept silent vigil at the base of each pillar. All around the room hung spectacular tapestries that depicted scenes of great battles—dwarf warriors in epic endeavors. Wall sconces held glowing stones and far down the center isle of the great hall, atop a dais, sat a marble throne. Two great cauldrons of burning liquid heated the room, belching dark smoke that escaped through a small vent in the ceiling.

The men were escorted to the throne. "You'll wait here until Lord Dunstan arrives. Bring in some chairs for these men." The commander of the dwarf squad barked out the orders as three others ducked behind the dais and returned with chairs.

Just as the men took their seats, a procession of dwarf soldiers entered into the room and took positions around the hall. Several stood along the wall; two on each side of the throne and two more by the entrance door. The dwarf guards who entered were dressed with far greater pageantry than the six who stood vigil. They wore large metal breastplates, polished like mirrors, and carried sturdy, double-bladed axes with long shafts that were plated in gold. Their heavy beards were long and braided, and each dwarf warrior was garbed in a crimson cloak.

Then the dwarf lord entered into the room. He was large in comparison to the other dwarves in the room, muscular and stern. His beard was long and deep red, dusted with streaks of grey and braided with slender gold thread. Upon his brow he wore a circlet of gold, decorated with diamonds and emeralds. He, too, was garbed with a crimson cloak and a single-piece breastplate inlaid with gold in the form of an axe and hammer crossed above a large silver mountain. As he walked up the dais to the throne, all the soldiers in the hall knelt in honor. He sat and the guards all rose to their feet and stood silent around the room.

The dwarf leader's face was set like chiseled stone, hard and unyielding. He looked with scorn at Aaron and his men seated in the chairs. "Welcome to Hidden Valley and the city of Brekken-Dahl." His tone carried no hint of welcome, and his countenance revealed a strong animosity.

Aaron spoke up, his own disposition one of calm defiance. "Who are you and why have you taken us against our will!?"

"I am Dunstan, lord of Brekken-Dahl and regent over the ancient mountain provinces." Adamant and hard as flint, the dwarf lord directed all his attention toward Aaron. "You are here for you have murdered one who was servant of the Great King and friend to all who remain loyal to His Royal Majesty!"

Rayn opened his mouth, but Aaron restrained him, and then spoke again. "We have not heard of any king, nor have we committed any crimes against your people. You have no just reason to hold us for we are true servants of Celedon and the emperor."

"Do you deny that in the mountains south of here you trapped and murdered a man when you set his cottage to flame? You, Captain, killed him." Dunstan's accusation shot like an arrow.

"He stole a book from the archives of the emperor, and I was ordered to recover it by any means necessary." Aaron tried to sound confident, but the memories of his time in the mountains still haunted him.

Dunstan began to grow fierce with anger. "That book rightfully belongs to those who still serve the ancient King. Your emperor is the one who stole the Book of Aleth!"

"Lord Dunstan," replied the captain as he attempted to remain calm. "I do not know what you're talking about."

"No, of course you do not!" raged Dunstan. "You, Captain, have no idea what is going on at all, or what trouble you've caused!" Dunstan rose from his throne; fury filled his features as he paced across the dais. The dwarf lord glared at Aaron and shouted, "Tell me where the Book of Aleth is! You were the one who murdered its keeper."

Rayn refused to be held back any longer. "We have no idea where the emperor's book is!"

"Private!" Aaron commanded.

Rayn looked at his commander. "Captain, this man is talking nonsense!"

"Be still, Private!" Aaron's voice trembled with agitation at Rayn's tirade. He returned his attention to the dwarf leader and took a deep breath to regain a sense of composure. "We do not know where the book is." Aaron was reluctant to reveal too many details. "It was taken by one who betrayed me. When I found him the book was already gone, and he was dead. After that, we were taken captive by your soldiers and brought here against our will. But what is it to you?" Aaron wanted to press the matter further. "This book has no value to anyone else."

"Then you're a fool!" Dunstan waived his hand, dismissing Aaron's remark. "If you think that this book is of no great worth, why did your precious emperor send his esteemed Royal Guard to recover it? This book is the key to unlocking all that was and that will be again. The Book of Aleth is the hope of the restoration and the one weapon your great emperor fears the most," Dunstan said.

Aaron replied, "How can you know all that?"

"How can I know?" Dunstan roared in amazement. "Has your nation been flung so far into darkness that every shred of truth is lost?" The dwarf lord paced as he spoke. "How can I know; that answer is easy. A thousand years ago, during the time you call the Elder Days, my grandfather was lord-regent of Brekken-Dahl when your emperor waged war against the King. My grandfather told me all that took place. He told me that my people stood with the King in the Great War while your nation rebelled and betrayed him, joining instead with your emperor. By the King's command, we were sent beyond the river and into the mountains to wait for the time of restoration.

"Now, dear Captain," Dunstan continued, "I want you to tell me exactly what happened in the field where we captured you! Speak the truth, for you and your men will have no other end but death if you lie."

Dunstan returned to his throne and took his seat. His piercing glare fixed upon Aaron who occupied the center chair. The cold stare of the lord of dwarves never strayed. With Lorik on Aaron's left and Rayn on his right, Aaron considered how much information to share with the dwarf lord.

"May I stand?" Aaron asked. Dunstan nodded his permission, and Aaron stood and started to slowly pace in front of the dais. He thought through the options that were presented to him. "I will tell you what happened, but first I ask that you at least release my sergeant. He was not with us in the clearing and has nothing to do with what you ask."

"No." Dunstan's voice was resolute. "Your sergeant was found trespassing in our realm and had discovered the secret to the hidden bridge. He will not be released, ever." Lorik's shoulders fell as he heard the dwarf lord, but showed no other emotion.

Aaron stroked at his beard and looked at Lorik with concern. Then he began, "Very well, I was ordered to take a regiment of the third order of the Royal Guard to track down and neutralize a man who was considered a dissident and threat to the empire. I was also told he possessed a book, stolen from the archives of the royal library, and that I was to retrieve the book at any cost and return it to the emperor. We tracked leads and hints of the whereabouts of the man's location and finally discovered that he lived in North Village, near to the northern most reaches of Celedon.

"I sent one of my soldiers to investigate, and it was reported to me the man had returned. When I arrived, he fled into the mountains and barricaded himself inside a small cottage. He refused to surrender, so we burned the cottage to the ground. I returned the next morning to retrieve the book, or its remains, and found it was gone. I soon discovered it was stolen by one of my own men, and I went in search of him. This brought us to the glen where you found us, and you know the rest of the story."

Aaron took his seat while the dwarf lord stood. Dunstan contemplated Aaron's testimony as he stroked his long, crimson beard. The dwarf-lord paced upon the dais. "You haven't told me the entire story. You are withholding information, and I want to know what it is."

Aaron's frustration burst out and overwhelmed his self-restraint. "If you know that I have more to say, tell me what it is! Have your spies spoken to you about my movements and activities? There is nothing more that I will say!"

An almost imperceptible smile crossed Dunstan's face but it was there. "I will give you time to reconsider that decision." Dunstan turned his attention to the six guards who waited behind the three soldiers. "Take them back to their cell until this captain is ready to reveal everything."

"On your feet," barked the guard behind Aaron. As the men reached the massive wooden doors, the echo of another door resonated across the room. Aaron turned to look back toward the throne and saw an older dwarf, with a grey beard, enter from behind the throne. The older dwarf had a harrowed look upon his face. The dwarf rushed around from behind the dais and knelt in respect before his liege. He talked in muffled tones. Aaron didn't hear the conversation that ensued between Dunstan and the other dwarf but a look of frustration filled Dunstan's eyes. Just before Aaron left the throne room, the older dwarf looked straight at him, perplexity in his features. Aaron pondered what it meant as a sense of foreboding flooded his thoughts.

The guards led them through the city streets back toward the barracks and their cell. Darkness filled the sky and no trace remained of the beautiful display on the mountain slopes. As they walked, dwarves shuffled about with torches and glowing stones to illuminate their steps. One ruddy young dwarf, carefree as he played along the ancient streets, did not pay attention to his surroundings and collided with

Lorik and almost knocked the sergeant off his feet. The young dwarf fell. His wide, young eyes looked up at the tall, bearded soldier, an expression of wonder and disbelief crossed the young boy's face. Lorik reached down to help the boy to his feet. With a smile, the young dwarf accepted his hand and then bolted off in the dark.

At the barracks, they were led again down the corridor and back to their cell where they sat in silence. Sometime after their return, Aaron heard the dinner cart rattle through the corridor. The three men went to the cell door and quietly retrieved the trays. They ate with no conversation. Aaron, more than the others, was deeply troubled by their circumstances, and his expression conveyed great anxiety.

"Captain, it's obvious you're holding back." Lorik spoke, his voice filled with the warmth of friendship. "With all due respect, what are you brooding over?"

Aaron hated circumstances beyond his control, and his current dilemma engulfed his thoughts and crashed through his mind like a torrential storm. "Lorik, I can't help but feel that there are forces around us far beyond anything we've ever encountered. I've believed from my youth that the stories of the Elder Days are only myth and legend, that there is nothing to them but simple childhood fantasy. From the days that I spent on the streets to the time I graduated university, I have always believed those stories were foolish. Now everything I believe is being challenged right in front of my eyes! Is there some truth in what Dunstan said? We can't deny any longer that there is some legitimacy to these stories... the proof is right before our eyes."

"I don't know," replied Lorik. "Those days are so far in the past that the truth is sure to have been lost over time. But it does seem that these people have stepped out of myth into reality. That doesn't make their claims to be anymore valid. It does, however, force us to consider the credibility of their statements. You're right about this: there is more going on than we can begin to understand. Our regiment was killed, and we've been captured all because of this Book of Aleth."

"What we need to do is to get our hands on that book and find out for ourselves," Aaron said.

"What?" Rayn stood and began to pace in their small chamber. "We need to get out of here and get back to Celedon! We must get back and tell the emperor what these dwarves mean to do!"

Aaron looked at the young soldier. "And what is it that they mean to do, Private?"

"It's obvious that they mean to try and invade our nation and overthrow the empire." Rayn looked at Aaron with frustration and anger. "Once we get the chance, we make a break for it and get back to the capital. One of us is bound to make it."

"Well," returned Aaron, as he thought about what Rayn had said, "you may be right, but I am still captain and the final decision will be mine."

Rayn was about to continue but one look from Aaron silenced him.

"Sir," Lorik asked, "what do you think we must do?"

Aaron stood and paced the floor. He casually stroked his beard and contemplated their situation. Calmness washed over his countenance. "Lorik, I agree with you. We need to recover the book. We leave together. Either we find a way to convince the lord of this land to release us, or escape when an opportunity arrives, but we will have a better chance if we stay together."

"But Captain!" Rayn interjected.

Lorik interrupted Rayn with a stern rebuke. "Be still, Private. He is your captain, and we will follow his orders." Lorik turned to Aaron and asked, "Sir, what do you have in mind?"

Aaron began to think out loud. "The key is this Lord Dunstan. He wants to find the book as much as anyone. I can only imagine that he wants it for the power he thinks it has. There have been many attempts to overthrow the emperor in the past. By his own testimony, Dunstan is certain the emperor is evil. It stands to reason, if he believes this book will provide him the power necessary to overthrow the emperor, then he will want to find it. That hideous creature Rayn and I saw must be the creature that now possesses the book. If we can track its location, we might be able to recover it."

As the night outside deepened, Aaron watched the evening stars shine in the velvet blackness through the small window. The moon slipped above the horizon and sent its shimmering light into their chamber, providing pale illumination. Rayn sat dejected while Lorik continued his conversation with Aaron. "It sounds good, sir, but how are we going to begin?"

Aaron stopped pacing and sat on the bed of straw. "I'm not sure," he said, "but an opportunity will come."

****

Two weeks of confinement took its toll on their nerves. The center of the barracks where they were quartered had a small, outdoor square used as a common area for the prisoners. Once a day they were allowed to enter the grassy plaza for recreation. To alleviate the boredom, Lorik took advantage of it. A small guard room housed a solitary dwarf who kept an eye on the prisoners in the square.

Often he was alone. But on one particular day Lorik encountered another prisoner in the square, a dwarf. He was older; his long beard was streaked with grey and unkempt. Several scars marked his features, but unlike the other dwarves that Lorik had encountered, this dwarf seemed to possess a humility that bordered on timidity.

The dwarf walked with a slight limp as he approached Lorik. The sergeant was about to stand but the elderly dwarf waved him off and insisted he remain seated. "No need to stand on ceremony for a dwarf like me." His gravelly voice spoke with clarity and a hint of liveliness. Large, brown eyes sparkled under his heavy brows and conveyed a lighthearted and cheerful disposition.

The dwarf sat down next to Lorik, crossed his legs in front of him and reclined back on his hands. The newcomer looked Lorik up and down as if he evaluated him. "Well now, with that beard I might have mistaken you for some giant of a dwarf!" Then he chuckled, his face filled with a smile. "So you're one of the Celedon soldiers, brought here to waste away? Hmm. Well, you know, there's no leaving this hole… You're here to stay."

Lorik's heart was gripped by the dwarf's words, but he held his expression in check as he spoke with the newcomer. "So, friend, who might you be?"

"Me, well, I'm not anyone in particular. Braden's my name. I got arrested years ago and have been here ever since. Not much to say about the accommodations, but the food is plentiful! I'm just a troll to my kinsmen, little more than a waste of skin." Braden absentmindedly picked at the grass and tossed the torn blades into the air, watching them fall to the ground.

Lorik continued the conversation, pleased to speak with anyone other than Aaron or Rayn for the moment. "Braden, if you don't mind my asking, why are you here?"

Braden exhaled a sigh as he continued to pick at the grass. "Well, years ago I worked the mines in the Kanton Mountains, digging rock and hauling it out of the tunnel when I stumbled on a bit of a trap. I didn't know that the tunnel we worked led right into a cavern filled with trolls! I got scared and ran and left my companions to fight without me. Cowardice pays a heavy price among us dwarves, you see, and my cowardice cost me my freedom."

Lorik was shocked at such a measure laid against a mine worker. "You can't be serious!" exclaimed Lorik. "You're not a soldier. You can't be expected to have the same discipline as trained military. How long have you been locked up for this?"

"You need to understand, all dwarf men are considered soldiers. When we can first wield an axe and hammer we are trained in its use." He looked up at Lorik. "You may have noticed the dwarves with gold cords twisted in their beards."

Lorik nodded. "I thought it was some sign of royalty."

"No, my friend. When a dwarf comes of age and displays his courage he is given the right to wear threads of gold woven into his beard." Braden looked at the ground as he spoke. "I will never have that honor for I was a coward, and I deserve to pay the price for it. But no matter how much I want to make up for it, I'll never get the chance." Braden sat quiet for some time; his eyes downcast. "You see, I've been imprisoned for two hundred years."

Lorik's mouth dropped open, aghast at the statement.

"Oh, now, not all here mind you. I spent several decades locked in the dungeon of the dwarf hold in the Kanton Mountains. That is where I spent my first fifty years as a matter of fact. Until the deladrin invaded and we had to flee for our lives." Braden shuddered as he remembered.

"What are the *deladrin*?" Lorik looked puzzled as he questioned his companion.

"It's hard to describe the deladrin. They are of such evil that I imagine they survived even from the ancient times. They are large, winged creatures that stand, well, that are taller than you, with a fire that burns on the inside of them. They are black as coal and dwell in shadow. A handful of those beasts attacked our hold in the Kanton Mountains. One's enough to put fear into our hearts, and the entire population of dwarves fled back here to Brekken-Dahl." Braden trembled as he spoke of the creatures.

It was obvious to Lorik that Braden didn't want to continue talking about the deladrin, but he had heard enough to convince him that the captain needed to learn about them. Lorik changed the conversation, "So, if I may ask, how old are you?"

Braden brightened and his tone lifted, "Ah, yes, I am three hundred and fifty two years old! Middle age, by dwarf standards! My father lived to be over five hundred years, as his father before him. I guess I'm cursed to live out my days in this place, for cowardice carries a life sentence. But, enough about my troubles. Tell me about yours... you and your companions are here, and it is rare to find your kind in our realm."

Before Lorik began, a burly guard with little patience entered. "It's time to go. You and you," he said as he pointed to Lorik and Braden, "get up and go back to your cells."

Lorik contained his enthusiasm and his eagerness to tell Aaron the information he'd learned from Braden. He had stumbled upon a piece of news that provided them a direction to search for the book. With a sense of hope, despite their captivity, Lorik began to think they might find the means to escape and regain the Book of Aleth. With renewed confidence he walked back into his cell.

Aaron and Rayn waited on the pile of straw, passing the time. Lorik entered and the door locked behind him. With a slight smile on his face, Lorik stood over the two men.

"Captain, I have some interesting news."

Aaron and Rayn sat up as they listened to Lorik tell about his encounter with Braden. Aaron's eyes widened.

"Lorik, do you think this Braden will be in the square tomorrow?" Aaron was eager to meet the dwarf and hear the story for himself.

"Sir, I don't know. Come with me to the square. I suspect he will be there eventually." Lorik's eagerness poured out with every word.

"If what he says is true then all we need to do is concentrate on how to get out of this place. Do you think this dwarf will accompany us as a guide?" Aaron asked.

"I don't know. But to leave two hundred years of incarceration might be incentive enough for him to help us." Lorik replied.

"Then all we have to do is to wait until the moment comes for us to make our escape. If we have a dwarf working with us, we might be able to find our way out of this mess." Aaron paced in the cell again with a new, anxious hope as he stroked his beard. "I can feel it," Aaron said. "Somehow I know...our time is near."

10

A Friend Among Enemies

Aaron lay awake in the cramped cell watching snow fall in a soft, silent dance outside the window. His companions still slept as dawn broke upon the world. Some unknown person rattled a key in the lock and creaked open the door.

"On your feet, prisoners!" barked a rough, grizzled dwarf. Three stern dwarves stood with the first, axes hoisted on their shoulders. Their beards were braided, adorned with the woven threads that Aaron had come to expect, and they wore brilliant armor, polished to a mirror shine. There was no mistaking these dwarves, Dunstan's own, private guard. Large helmets of polished steel protected their heads, with the axe and hammer crest imprinted in gold just above the brow. Lorik and Rayn woke with a start,

Rayn spoke first. "I see our room service has taken a step up! What can we expect for breakfast today?"

Lorik chuckled at Rayn's sarcasm.

But Aaron lightly rebuked the young private for his comment. "Rayn, that is no way address our hosts. So" —he collected his thoughts and spoke with a more serious demeanor to the three dwarf soldiers who waited at the door—"to what do we owe the pleasure of your visit?"

"You will accompany us to Lord Dunstan." The lead dwarf, larger than his companions, spoke.

"All of us?" Aaron inquired.

"No, just you," said the dwarf as he pointed at the captain.

Aaron was reluctant, but he stood, donned his boots and cloak, brushed off the straw that had collected on his garments, and followed the dwarf soldiers out the door. They walked down the hall, past several other cells, then up the stairs to the main door of the barracks. From behind him, Rayn's voice echoed through the hall. "But what about breakfast?"

Aaron shook his head and chuckled at his boisterous private. The guards led him, again, through the crowded, busy streets of the city. It was just after sunrise, and the crisp air was a refreshing change from the cloistered conditions of their musty cell. Snow had fallen upon the city and covered the cobbled streets in a shimmering blanket of clean, white powder. Sunlight streaked across the sky like ribbons tethered to the Shadow Mountains. Aaron breathed deep and enjoyed the sensation of fresh, cold air filling his lungs. With the point of their axes his guards encouraged him to continue toward the castle.

The city, though it was much as he had seen before, seemed alive with festivities. Young dwarf children piled snow into high walls as others bombarded them with a flurry of snowballs. Petite dwarf women, dressed in fine clothes hurried through the streets with scampering children in tow. Even the buildings, which Aaron still marveled at, were decked out with greater adornments than before. And lights, lights of every kind filled the windows of the shops and homes to displace all shadows in their radiance.

Soldiers, dressed in more ordinary attire, strolled through the streets and enjoyed the sights and sounds of the cheerful throng.

The guards escorted Aaron through the crowds. He felt like an object of curiosity as he stood over a head taller than any of the passers-by. Several of the dwarf children marveled at him as he passed and were barraged by an aerial assault of snow from their not-so-distracted companions.

As they approached the castle, the massive doors swung open, and Aaron was escorted once again into Dunstan's hall. This time, however, no other private guards entered and a single chair waited near the throne. Next to the chair sat a table adorned with food and drink. Dunstan waited on the throne, his gruff countenance tempered.

"Come, sit down Captain." He motioned for Aaron to take a seat. Dunstan waved off the guards who escorted Aaron into the hall. "You may leave us." Aaron sat and gazed at Dunstan with a sense of mistrust, uncertain what happened to change the dwarf ruler's disposition.

"Captain," began Dunstan, "our laws state that you and your men are subject to execution." The reserved tone made it clear that Dunstan was disquieted by such a possibility. Aaron wanted to use the moment to try and persuade him otherwise.

"Sir," Aaron returned, "I don't know your laws, but it is hard to believe that your society, with such beauty and refinement, possesses regulations that condemn men to death without a full examination of the facts."

Dunstan paused and breathed a heavy sigh. "I didn't call you to discuss the logic of our laws; I want to give you another opportunity to tell all that you know and all that you've experienced since you first pursued Derrick and the book that he possessed." Dunstan paused and motioned to the table. "Feel free to eat, Captain. I know that you were brought here before the morning meal."

Aaron thanked Dunstan and began to eat some of the food on the plate. The breakfast consisted of several selections of fruit, salted pork, grain bread, and a large decanter of water. A carafe of coffee was also available which Aaron drank with gratitude. He tossed down two glasses of water and enjoyed the rich, sweet fruit. Aaron looked up from his tray and noticed the dwarf lord enjoyed a hearty breakfast as well.

"Well, Captain, I am glad to see that your appetite hasn't suffered." Dunstan set his entire attention on Aaron. "Now, I want you to tell me all that you know."

Aaron fixed his eyes upon the dwarf lord, the intensity of his gaze matched by his captor. Like two mighty warriors locked in an effort to break the will of his opponent Aaron would not look away from Dunstan's stare.

"I was, as I told you before, following the orders of my emperor," Aaron said. I was given the assignment to track down a man who posed a threat to the empire and regain the Book of Aleth for the emperor. I'm not sure what more it is that you want."

"What I want to know is who has the book now? I believe you know and are keeping that secret to yourself!" Dunstan's tone resonated with authority as he shifted again to that of a gruff, stern ruler. His heavy brows furrowed with frustration as he glared at Aaron.

"Then, Lord Dunstan, tell me something," Aaron

said. "What is so great about this book? What does it contain?" Aaron spoke with great sincerity.

"You don't know?" Dunstan asked, incredulous at the thought.

"No, I don't. It seems to me a tremendous waste of time, and I have suffered an appalling loss of men because of a book the emperor needed to just throw in a fire." Aaron was perturbed and desperate for some answers.

Dunstan looked Aaron over with a hint of suspicion in his eyes. "Well, Captain, this is a surprise!" He stood and motioned for Aaron to follow him. "Come with me, for it seems I must teach you the severity of what you've fallen into. Throw it into the fire. Ha! The fires of Mount Sonna cannot harm that book!" Dunstan circled the dais; Aaron followed close behind.

The dwarf ruler led Aaron behind the throne and through a door that looked like a seamless stone wall. The secret door opened into a large antechamber filled with exquisite treasures. Mounted on wall brackets, numerous stones glowed with a pale-white radiance and illuminated the room. Bronze and stone statues depicted ancient heroes and lined the walls like a silent army of warriors. Marble pillars supported a high, vaulted ceiling.

Aaron followed Dunstan to the left where several paintings hung on the wall. Aaron marveled at the stunning artistry. He had no grasp of the value of the treasures in the room but believed that he looked upon priceless works of art depicting magnificent scenes of ages long past. One particular picture caught Aaron's eye.

He stopped to gaze at a canvas that illustrated a

panoramic view of tree-covered mountains and rich, fertile valleys. The image was dramatic and so realistic that Aaron imagined he looked through a window into a world that possessed unimaginable beauty and tranquility. He felt as if he watched the shimmering ocean crash against the distant shore, while a castle, with tall alabaster spires stood on a remote hillside, golden banners waving in the gentle breeze. The castle looked down upon an expansive harbor with tall-mast ships pushing out to sea. Quaint cottages and a small village garnished the terrain around the castle. The entire scene took Aaron's breath away. As he stared at the painting, a strange familiarity washed over his thoughts.

"Ah, yes," remarked Dunstan. "That particular work was done by one of our greatest artisans."

"This scene is familiar to me, but I don't remember ever seeing such a painting in my life." Aaron said as he continued to explore the image.

"You recognize that scene, Captain? It is your capital city more than a thousand years ago." Dunstan looked upon the panorama.

"That's impossible. The capital was built only three centuries ago... this cannot be the same place." Aaron argued.

"Captain, look upon the scene. The two rivers flowing into the bay, the hillsides and distant mountains, all the terrain is the same... this is your city before the Fall, before the usurper came. It was a place of wondrous beauty, magical and filled with splendor. One of our master artisans painted this portrait just ten years before the usurper came into the realm and led your people to disown the King."

"You're right, of course...the scene does resemble

the landscape around my city, but the artist must have taken liberty to depict it with a generous helping of imagination. Nothing this fantastic has ever existed in Celedon." Aaron dismissed the painting, but the image stuck in his mind.

"Young captain, I brought you into this hall to look upon this very picture, the image of what was once a jewel in your realm. You cannot so lightly dismiss this image; it represents how your country used to be. Given the circumstances you're in, you must have begun to question what you thought you knew. The power of your emperor is in his ability to deceive, and that is what happened to your realm. But his power fails in those who truly want to know the truth. What you've always considered true is the cloak of deception forced upon your people by the deceiver." Dunstan's voice grew louder as he pressed his words against Aaron's perception.

"Perhaps, Lord Dunstan, but if you say this image is over a thousand years old, and that your king has been gone for that long, what is to say that the growth and prosperity of our realm is not the natural course of events. Besides, if this king of yours was so mighty, how did he let someone slip in and turn his entire nation against him? You say he had the power, but of what value is that power if it is unused against an adversary?" Aaron became more vocal as he fought against a growing disquiet in his own thoughts. He didn't want to accept what the dwarf lord said, yet he had no reason to deny the evidence that stood before him.

"Captain, to rule with fear is to do no better than your emperor," Dunstan said. "The King ruled with power but not by force. He possessed the might to rule with unrestrained domination, but he wanted a nation to follow him, not out of terror but out of love. The people were deceived by the usurper and began to believe that they needed to cast off all allegiance to the King. It took several of your generations, but the twisted lies of the usurper finally destroyed the people's love for the King."

"But what about you and your people?" Aaron continued. "If you claim that Therion is so adept at deception, why haven't you been fooled?"

"Dwarves are long lived," Dunstan replied, "so the memory of the King's glory and his work among my people remained fresh and alive. Elves are the eldest of the races and even now, there must be those who possess firsthand knowledge of the King. Your race however seemed quick to forget. With each successive generation, loyalty dimmed and rebellion increased. Until, finally, the usurper had the strength he needed and the Great War began."

As Dunstan spoke, he led Aaron to another painting. The scene displayed a great city, large and immaculate. The surrounding countryside in the picture was small in comparison to the city. Massive towers and walls surrounded one great central tower that stood above all the others. High atop the central tower stood the figure of a man. He held aloft a sword that shone with brilliance, as if streams of light pierced the sky in every direction.

The picture displayed a massive horde of men and beasts, some Aaron recognized and others he had never seen, advancing against the gates of the city. At the gate, a legion of warriors stood ready to defend the city. He recognized an army of dwarves, and they fought side by side with men, along with another race—elves, he imagined. Leading the defenders was another solitary figure who brandished a weapon of great power. Green light surrounded the figure as he stood his ground against the advancing army.

Dunstan motioned toward the large painting. "Dwarves and elves sided with the King, along with a great many of your kind. In fact, all those loyal to him took up arms to defend the last stronghold of truth. Our forces were outnumbered, and the King ordered us to abandon the war and flee to the safety of our realms.

"Alone, the King sacrificed himself for his people. The new emperor divided up the nation like a thief dividing the plunder and gave authority to those who were chief ambassadors to his purpose. Now your nation is fractured and decayed. Your emperor rules by fear, and your governors are his pets.

"Many of your people vowed to retain the knowledge of the truth and the glory of the King's realm. But, as the generations of men passed, the truth diminished into history, until it became lost, discarded as myth and legend. The book that you so diligently pursued was the key that had the power to free all of Celedon from the usurper's control. The man you killed had found the book in the deepest archives of the capital and attempted to bring it here. He knew the Book of Aleth was the hope of restoration. The emperor fears the book more than any other artifact and sent you and your men to kill the man who found it. Now the book is lost again, and the hope of restoration is lost with it."

Aaron listened to the story with rapt interest. The dwarf who stood before him told it as if he had witnessed every scene, as if he tried to transport Aaron there with his very words and make him see the unfolding of history firsthand. A fire of passion filled the dwarf's eyes and revealed the ruler's zeal for all that he spoke.

Aaron looked upon the leader of the ancient realm. "You say that the Book of Aleth is the key to restoring the nation. Despite all you've said and what you've shown me, I am hard pressed to believe any of it. Perhaps this book is some mysterious power that causes the emperor to fear. From what you say, if you speak the truth, the Book of Aleth is a grave threat to the empire…and I am sworn to defend the empire. You say that it will bring some type of restoration and an ancient peace will return to Celedon, but all I can see is the potential for chaos." However, his own words did not calm the inner turmoil as he tried to resolve in his mind all the issues that swirled around him. "Tell me, Lord Dunstan, what's in this book? Why is it so desperately sought?"

Dunstan looked up at Aaron, the dwarf lord's eyes set like stone. "The Book of Aleth was written by the King himself. In it, he poured his power and wisdom. It is the one artifact that can overcome the usurper's power to deceive. After the Great War, the book was lost and many of my people believed that it was taken by the King's enemy. Our fears were confirmed when it was discovered in the ancient archives. Word came to us, and we sought out those of your race who remained faithful to the King and had the courage to try and recover it. It was hard to find anyone who still believed the ancient truths. Derrick was one. There are others, but now that the book is lost again, the power to defeat the usurper is lost as well."

"So where did this *usurper* come from?" Aaron

asked.

"He is a creature from ancient times." Dunstan took a moment before he continued. "He came from outside the realm and, unable to defeat the King in direct combat, chose instead to lead the kingdom astray. The Book of Aleth was the one artifact that possessed the power to dispel the web of darkness cast by the usurper for it contained the words of the King himself. Now it's lost, and with it so is the hope of restoration."

Aaron watched as the dwarf ruler's shoulders slump under the weight of his own words. He sympathized for Dunstan but fought against the belief that what the dwarf had said was true. "Your tale is intriguing, but I cannot believe it. You show me a picture and tell me about circumstances that may have occurred an eon ago. You cannot expect me to be swayed by such a fantastic story." Aaron's thoughts, however, were beginning to change. He wanted, very much, to believe the story of the dwarf lord. He longed for a real peace in Celedon. He wondered if he found the Book of Aleth, would it reveal the truth behind all the swirling mysteries that now covered his world like a fog.

"All that I've told you is true; I had hoped to convince you. The time is near for the restoration to occur, and without the Book of Aleth, there is no way to overcome the power of the emperor. If the Book is not recovered and the time of restoration passes, the nation will forever be locked in darkness. The emperor will have won ultimate victory and no hope will remain. You, Captain, may have become for us the herald of doom." Dunstan, heavy with the burden, walked back toward the throne room with Aaron close behind.

The two entered from behind the dais and circled the throne to retake their empty seats. From the main entrance, the guards who had brought Aaron into the hall entered and took position behind the captain. Dunstan sat in his throne, and regained his firm countenance. He looked upon Aaron with a hardened expression, his eyes sharp like daggers. The dwarf's voice was low as he worked to control his anger, "Now, Captain, I will ask you one last time, tell me all that you know… who has the book now?"

Aaron saw the flash of anger in his captor's eyes, and determined to keep his knowledge to himself. "Lord Dunstan, I have told you all I am able and willing. I am in your power, and you will do with me in accordance with your own laws, so I see no reason to give you any more information."

"Indeed, Captain, you will keep your knowledge." The dwarf ruler clenched his teeth and pounded his fist against the throne. "It will follow you to the grave." Dunstan looked to the guards. "Return him to his cell."

The guards brandished their weapons and took charge of Aaron to escort him back to the barracks. As Aaron left, another dwarf entered from behind the throne and took a seat near Dunstan. It was the same elderly dwarf who had visited the throne room before. As Aaron exited the chamber he listened to the two dwarves speak in grave tones.

"Are you sure you want to do this?" the older dwarf asked.

"Yes, it's the only way," Dunstan replied.

****

Back in his cell, Aaron sat upon the straw pile alone. Lorik and Rayn were gone from the small chamber. The gravity of the situation weighed upon his mind like an anchor as he pondered all the words of the dwarf lord. For all the evidence shared by Dunstan, Aaron remained unconvinced and believed the dwarf lord sought to manipulate him. Yet somewhere in the depths of his mind, Aaron began to question his own understanding. He needed to know more and the only way was to escape and find the Book of Aleth. Like a spark that sets a forest ablaze, came a silent and disquieting thought into Aaron's mind: *what if Dunstan was right*? Without any means of escape, however, he and his companions faced lifelong imprisonment, or worse, execution.

An hour later, Rayn and Lorik returned. They had spent most of their day in the common area. Rayn talked with a dwarf guard as he entered the cell.

"No," quipped Rayn, "I don't think that the battle-axe is superior to the conventional sword!"

"Hah!" said their escort, a rugged dwarf with dark brown hair and an exceptionally long beard. "You can't compare 'em! I can hack apart a troll as easy as choppin' wood with this," he said as he patted his weapon. "Your puny swords are no match!" The dwarf laughed as he left. The cell door closed behind him with a dull thud. A quick rattle of keys sounded and the lock was snapped secure. Once the guard was out of earshot, Lorik and Rayn's conversation immediately turned to strategies of escape.

"We might try and escape when they take us to the square," Rayn said. "Or maybe we all fake an illness, and these dwarves might allow us to see a healer... oh, Captain," Rayn noticed Aaron atop the pile of straw. "I didn't know you had returned."

"Captain, what have you learned…anything helpful?" Lorik said as he reclined beneath the small window. Rayn propped himself against the wall.

"I learned nothing that bodes well for our escape," Aaron returned. He heaved a discouraged sigh, his heart heavy with the weight of their plight. "It seems that our end is planned for us. Dunstan means to either imprison us indefinitely or to"—Aaron paused with the dread of his thoughts—"to execute us."

Lorik and Rayn gasped with the severity of Aaron's words. Lorik stood motionless as Rayn began to pace the small room.

"Sir," Rayn interjected, "then let's find a way to escape. I'll not simply walk up to the executioner's block without a fight. I'll fight with bare hands rather than allow these dwarves to take us on a whim!" His tone elevated until he was speaking loud enough for the guards to hear.

"You're right…and if that is the case, we will fight to the last of our breath. But tell me, did you meet with the dwarf in the compound?" Aaron kept a dim glimmer of hope alive.

"As a matter of fact," Rayn said, "we did. He was there, and he told us more about the creatures that took the book. These…these, oh what did he call them?"

"Deladrin," Lorik added, "creatures of immense power and extreme evil."

"Yes… that's right," Rayn continued, "deladrin. Well, sir, the creature you and I both saw must be one of these deladrin. It must have taken the book to these mountains he spoke of."

"Did you ask this Braden if he will lead us to the mountain caves? We will need a guide in order to find our way to the old dwarf stronghold." Aaron kept his hopes centered on the expectation of escape, and he wanted his men to concentrate on that objective as well. "We will wait for an opportunity…at some point these dwarves will slip and we will have our chance."

"Yes," Lorik said, "he did mention he wanted to escape with us. He hopes to have the opportunity to redeem himself. His people have forsaken him and count him of no value…his great desire is to prove his courage, but he never will get another chance from his people. He sees us as his chance to leave this captivity." Lorik spoke with passion and seemed to sympathize with the imprisoned dwarf.

"Does he know that in helping us he may be siding against his own people?" Aaron did not completely trust the dwarf's desire for redemption.

"Sir," said Lorik, "he believes if he helps us to recover the Book of Aleth, it will bring about the restoration these dwarves have waited for."

"Fine, as long as he keeps thinking that way he'll be of use to us." Aaron turned his thoughts to escape.

When Aaron finally looked up at the window, he noticed the day had vanished into the glowing remnants of dusk. A knock at the door startled him and Aaron rose to his feet. It was time for dinner but for weeks, the guards bellowed out their call to the inmates. *Why no call tonight*? Lorik shot Aaron a glance, his brows furrowed at the change of protocol. A key rattled the lock then the door slowly opened, creaking against the rusted hinges.

An older dwarf with a long, grey beard entered and carried a large tray of food. He was not the guard they had come to expect. He wore elegant raiment, adorned with gold and studded with precious gems.

His braided beard was ornamented with gold strands and a gold-encrusted belt hung upon his waist. He wore no axe, and was cloaked and hooded. Under heavy brows, his piercing eyes looked upon the three soldiers with sharp awareness. As he entered, Rayn approached him and took the tray from his hands. Then Rayn returned to stand with his comrades.

"Who might you be?" Aaron inquired.

"I am your hope of escape." The stranger whispered as he glanced through the open door.

"You seem familiar to me," Aaron said, his voice waivered with mistrust. "Have I seen you before?"

"Yes, once. I entered into the throne room as the three of you were escorted out. My name is Garam, and I am Lord Dunstan's chief advisor. I have listened to your conversations with my lord and have been intrigued by your plight. However, Lord Dunstan will not follow my counsel in this matter. I advised him to spare your lives because I believe you have a destined role in our great hope. I urged him to allow you to seek the book. He refused, and you three are to be executed tomorrow morning." Garam spoke as if some spy lurked in the shadows, a hint of desperation in his voice.

"I don't trust you." Rayn spoke with a cold look on his face. "You say you're his counselor, but do dwarves abandon their associations so lightly?"

"I do not *abandon* my associations, and my actions here are in league with my loyalty to Dunstan. I was his father's counselor before he died, and I've been Lord Dunstan's counselor since he assumed his father's throne. For two hundred years I have offered my wisdom to the regents of this land, and you will do well to trust my purpose in this matter." Garam's voice betrayed his agitation with Rayn's comment. The aged counselor composed himself before continuing. "What I do in helping you is like the drop of a stone that begins an avalanche."

Aaron was befuddled with the dwarf's speech. "You don't make sense, Garam. How can helping us be an act of loyalty to Dunstan?"

"Has all prophecy fallen from your land?" Garam expressed his agitation. "I don't have time to explain, but it was spoken by the ancient King that restoration will come when men of your race begin to seek the Book of Aleth. I believe you are the ones spoken of in the prophecy. Dunstan does not. He believes Derrick, the man who had found the book in your realm, was the one. If I am right, you are the catalyst to the restoration. That is why I consider my actions to be in harmony with my loyalty to Dunstan...by helping you I will help to bring about the one great hope of our people."

Rayn was still not convinced. He turned to Aaron. "Captain, this must be some sort of trick. I don't trust him."

"You either can trust me now, or you can die tomorrow. The choice will be yours," Garam answered.

"I choose to trust," Lorik replied.

"Indeed, it seems we have little choice." Aaron turned to Garam and sized up his benefactor. "I don't know if you can be trusted, Garam, and I am sure that there is more that you are not saying. But, we will believe you for now."

Rayn began to protest but Aaron cut him off. "We can either die attempting escape or die waiting like animals to be slaughtered. We will choose escape, and, Private, that is an order." Aaron turned his attention back to Garam. "There is one other that must accompany us who is also a prisoner here. His name is Braden, and he is a member of your race. He must leave with us."

"We don't have time, Captain," protested Garam. "I need you to be ready at the change of guard. I will have a horse and wagon set to take us from here. Be ready…if you're not, you'll be left behind."

"You will have Braden here," Aaron was insistent, "for if he's not with you, I will shout to the world that you are a traitor!" Aaron spoke with finality.

"Very well, I will do what I can. Just be ready to leave when I come!" With that, Garam left the room and locked the door behind him. He gave a quick remark to a guard who had just walked in from outside and disappeared out the barracks door into the night.

"What do you think, Captain?" Lorik asked.

"I think that our opportunity has come. This may be our best hope to leave this place and find the book," Aaron replied.

"Well, I think it's a trap," Rayn huffed. "I don't trust this situation or these wretched dwarves! I think that they are trying to manipulate us, and they want to use us for some purpose of their own."

"One thing I've learned about this people," Aaron returned, "is that they are deeply entrenched with the hope of this restoration. If Garam thinks we are elements in that process then I believe that he speaks the truth. One way or another, however, we will be ready to leave when he comes."

"Captain, I still think that one of us must try and go back to Celedon and report all that has happened here! If we do escape, we need to warn the emperor about these dwarves," Rayn protested.

"No," Aaron snapped, agitated at his young soldier. "We will seek to recover the book. Those are your orders, and I expect that you will follow them," Aaron said, hard pressed to keep his voice down, desperate not to alert any guards who might be able to hear the conversation. "Lorik…"

"Yes sir," Lorik offered a slight grin as he replied.

Aaron paced back and forth in the small confinement. "After we eat we will take turns watching for Garam. We have a journey ahead of us and we must be well rested." Eagerness and hope echoed in his heart. "You take the first watch; wake me in three hours to relieve you." He turned his attentions to logistical concerns. "All of us will remain dressed and ready for flight. We don't want to have to waste time in the dark fumbling with our boots."

****

They ate their meal in silence. Aaron paced the floor, and Lorik knew the captain was anticipating their next step. When they had finished, Lorik took position near the door while Aaron and Rayn lay down on the straw for a brief, but much needed rest. Aaron slept without tossing for the first time since his abduction while Rayn didn't sleep at all. He sat up near Lorik and took watch with him.

"Sergeant," Rayn began, "I don't understand why the captain won't try and tell the emperor what we've seen. It seems reasonable to me that one of us ought to make our way back to the capital and bring this to his attention."

"Private," Lorik responded, "all we must do is to

follow the commands of our captain. In all my years of service, Aaron has been the best commander I have served. He is not rash or cruel like so many others, but considers all options in his decisions. You will do well to heed his orders. He's never led his men unwisely."

"But," Rayn protested, "where is the harm in sending one of us to the capital? And what sense is there in keeping us all together?"

"There's great harm in sending one man alone, this is a perilous region, and a lone soldier might find himself without help in some dire circumstance. There is also sufficient reason to keep us together, for in the pursuit of this artifact we might need each other before the end. No, Private, the captain knows what he is doing, and we must trust him." Lorik ended the conversation and turned his attention to the hall beyond the door, listening for any footsteps. Rayn sat quietly for a moment then returned to the straw bed.

****

Aaron thought he'd slept only a few minutes when Lorik woke him. He rubbed his eyes, and sat up brushing straw from his beard and hair. He stood and stretched his stiff limbs. After an exceptional yawn, Aaron asked, "How long?"

"Oh, about four hours, Captain," Lorik replied. "The guard was changed an hour ago and won't be changed again for three hours. I've not heard from our benefactor. I imagine he will come at the change of the second guard."

Aaron moved around the cell and rubbed his arms for warmth. "Seems a bit colder," he remarked. Aaron glanced down at Rayn who lay in the straw. The private moved in restless fits as he slept. He took Lorik's place at the door. "You get some sleep. I'll keep an eye on things."

"Captain," Lorik said, "I need to tell you something."

"What is it?" Aaron was concerned about the troubled look that crossed Lorik's face.

"Sir, it's about the young private here. He's not at all agreeable to the pursuit of this book. While you slept, he questioned your decision, and I get the distinct impression that he might become difficult." Lorik spoke in a cautious whisper.

"He's young, Lorik," Aaron sympathized. "He's never been in a situation like this... as a matter of fact neither have I, but you and I have both been in some dreadful circumstances. His inexperience shows, but I believe that he will prove true in the end. Remember, this is his very first mission with the guard. We've lost our men, seen creatures beyond our comprehension, been captured and sentenced to execution. It's a lot for a young soldier to handle." Aaron smiled at the incredulity of all they've been through. "Get some rest, my friend; I believe that we will be leaving soon."

Lorik lay down and fell fast asleep while Aaron sat quietly by the door. The sounds of the other prisoners gently echoed through the corridors. One door down Aaron listened to the generous snores of a noisy dwarf. Two hours into his watch the silence was disturbed by the rhythmic sounds of footsteps in the hall. He woke his companions and kept them calm as they both bolted upright in alarm. The door lock turned slowly, as if the holder of the key made a great effort to keep quiet. Aaron cringed to hear the rusty iron hinges creak. In the silence the sound of the door was almost thunderous. Garam stepped in. Hooded and cloaked, he carried several bundles under his arms. He tossed the bundles to the floor and motioned for the men to approach.

"Quickly," he whispered. "Put these cloaks on." The men fumbled in the dark with the knots and donned the raiment. "I have a cart and horse outside the barracks. The dwarf guards are on the other side of the building sleeping off a draught of ale." Garam moved to check the door. "We don't have much time for the potion will only last an hour. It will give us a good start, but we must be off before the guards are aware of your escape and come looking for us."

Aaron then realized Garam had come alone. "Where is Braden? I told you to have him with you!" He kept his voice down but anger filled his words.

"Be still, Captain!" Garam whispered harshly. "He's waiting in the cart, keeping the horses quiet!"

Aaron relaxed for a moment and checked on Lorik and Rayn's progress. They were ready; each adequately adjusted the dwarfish garments to hide their uniforms. Garam motioned for them to follow, and the three soldiers cautiously walked out the door into the hall.

The passage was dim, with small stones illuminating the way. With just enough light to see, the men crept along the corridor, up the stairs and toward the main exit. Their booted feet echoed against the bare stone floor as they navigated down the empty corridor. They stepped as quietly as possible, but to Aaron their footfalls might as well have been an alarm signal declaring their escape. Undaunted, they walked through the hall and exited into a snow-covered night.

Aaron heaved a sigh as his eyes searched the

darkness for any sign of pursuit or alarm—nothing. The night was still. A heavy mist filled the valley and shrouded their movements. The only sign of their passage was their footprints on the snow-covered ground mingled with hundreds of other prints, so he dismissed the issue from his thoughts. Above them the sky was dark, dotted with stars.

To the right, around the corner of the barracks, a two-wheeled cart waited with a dwarf perched on the driver's bench. Two horses were hitched to the wagon and pawed at the ground as Aaron approached. The three men crawled into the back of the cart and covered themselves with several heavy wool blankets stored there. Each man ducked below the height of the cart's sidewall, and lay in deathly silence. Garam mounted the front bench and sat with Braden, quietly speaking to the other and pointing in the direction he wanted Braden to drive.

As they moved, Aaron whispered to the one who rescued them. "What is your plan, Garam? Surely we can't just simply leave through the main mountain passage?"

"No," was Garam's quiet reply. "The tunnel is too well guarded, and we have no hope of escape that way. Besides, the horros prowl the eastern slopes of the mountains. Our only hope of leaving Hidden Valley undetected is to escape by the river."

Aaron heard Braden gasp, and wondered what that might indicate. "Garam, we saw no river that might serve as an exit out of these mountains."

"You're right, of course,"—was Garam's sarcastic reply—"but if you begin to trust me, you will discover that I might know my land better than you! There is an underground river that flows through the mountains and empties into the valley south and east of here. It is a dangerous way, and many dwarves have perished in the currents, but there is no other way for us to escape detection."

"How far," asked Lorik, "before we reach this river?"

"It is several miles before we come to the road that leads to the river. Be still, we will make it there," Garam offhandedly commented. "You'll find your weapons hidden under the straw. Also, you will find satchels of food and drink for the journey. Now be quiet and keep your heads down; we need to reach the river before dawn. Near the river is a small village, and we must pass through without attracting attention." Without another word, the company passed along the snow-covered roads of Brekken-Dahl, anxious to leave the city.

11

Escape from Hidden Valley

The wagon rattled along the cobbled street as Braden drove through the main gate of the city. With a wave from the tower guard, the five travelers rolled beyond the city wall and into the valley. As they passed through, Aaron peered over the edge of the wagon and hoped to gain some view of their location. It was dark. Stars shimmered in the cold night air as the crescent moon sent down its pale glow and illuminated the world with a ghostly light.

Crisp snow crackled beneath hoof and wheel as the captain looked back. The city of Brekken-Dahl, which diminished in the distance, radiated with a faint illumination. Aaron didn't know if it was some trick of the moonlight that reflected upon the white, stone walls, or if the fortification itself possessed its own, pale light. The entire valley seemed almost magical to his eyes, a glowing paradise hidden for centuries beyond the grasp of outsiders.

At Garam's direction, Braden veered right and took a narrow road that meandered through a large grove of assorted trees. Apple, chestnut, and pear trees filled the orchard. The leaves of the trees had long since fallen and left only the bare branches surrounded by the thick mist. Aaron's companions popped their heads up from under the blankets and watched the trees pass by as well.

As they journeyed, not even a slight breeze disrupted their passage through the grasping branches of the orchard. Aaron glanced up at the moon. Its slow decent to the horizon signaled dawn's approach. The mist that hung in the trees grew thick and became a fog, a welcomed cloak over the world around them. Silent and still, the two dwarves sat at the reins and guided the wagon through the night.

Lorik tried to talk in a whisper, but his voice sounded amplified in the still silence. "It looks like we are heading a bit south and west, Captain. It's hard to say in this fog, but I don't think that we're traveling toward the tunnel that brought us here."

"You're right, of course," spoke Garam. "We are heading for a small village about five miles southwest of Brekken-Dahl. We will be through the village by daybreak. There is a glacial lake beyond that in the mountains which feeds a river that flows out of our realm. Our big concern will be the journey downstream; it is a perilous ride through tunnels and canyons. Without incident, the trip is two days, but if we run into trouble it will be the last trip we ever take."

"Sounds interesting." Rayn added, with little enthusiasm.

"Lorik, answer me something," Braden spoke, "how will we travel through your country undetected? It seems that none of your race remembers dwarves so I suspect that if we just walk into one of your towns it might cause quite a stir."

"I hadn't thought about it before, but you're right," replied Lorik. "I don't think we will be able to take any of the roads or byways. If we are discovered it will bring up questions better left unanswered." He turned his attention to Aaron and continued. "Sir, I know the northern reaches of Celedon as well as anyone. With your permission, I can guide us when we get back to our land. If we keep to the wilderness, we will avoid any contact. It is a bit more dangerous, but if secrecy is our objective I think it's necessary."

"What do you have in mind?" Aaron asked.

"If I'm right, the river that Garam speaks of will exit the mountains in the northern part of Celedon—somewhere above North Village. We can leave the river and travel undetected around the Shattered Hills."

"I've been in those hills!" Braden said. "They are infested with evil; it's too dangerous!"

"We can skirt the hills to the north and then travel along their eastern border. It is a barren region, little more than scrub grass and open fields." Lorik tried to reassure the dwarf. "Nothing much lives there."

"I suggest we devote our attentions to one problem at a time," Aaron interjected. "Let's get out of this valley first, and then we can concentrate on the next leg of our journey." Aaron's words ended the conversation, and the men rode through the silent, drifting fog.

Another hour passed, and they left the orchard. Ahead of them lay a wide expanse of rolling hills. To the east, shimmering pale blue in the waning moonlight, the Shadow Mountains loomed large. The peaks looked down at the travelers as if they dared them to try and cross. Occasionally, a light shone in some distant home, a signal that the valley slowly started waking. The fog dissipated as they continued, and the early morning air felt crisp and fresh. They crested a hill and looked down to a small village nestled against the base of the mountains. The village teemed with lights.

Braden halted the wagon and peered down to the village below. He and Garam sat and whispered to each other, obviously distressed at the sight of the entire village lit up like a swarm of fireflies. Even from their vantage point, they heard cries and shouts from the townspeople.

"So much for secrecy," Rayn said. "Isn't this just our luck? Just when it seemed that we'd escape, we're stopped dead in our tracks. What's your plan now, Garam?"

"Be quiet," Garam whispered harshly, "your voice carries like the blast of a trumpet!"

Aaron slid closer to Garam and placed himself behind the dwarf. "What do you think has happened?" he whispered.

"I don't know, but we've come too far to turn back. I am sure by now we are pursued, but I doubt that anyone has sent word to the village below. I just don't know what else has stirred up the town." Garam's voice trailed off as he looked down into the distant village. He turned and faced Aaron. "We need more information. I suggest that we drive our cart closer to the village, and the three of you hide here in the back. Braden and I will go into the town and find out what's happened. Afterward, we will return and decide what to do."

"Oh, sure," whispered Rayn, "You two leave us to be found and killed!" He turned to Aaron and gestured toward the two dwarves. "Sir, we can't trust these people! They captured us, imprisoned us, and threatened to execute us, and now we're expected to believe that they are really trying to help us!"

"Private!" Aaron ordered, desperate to keep his voice low. "Be quiet! These two dwarves are in the same mess we are in. We will follow their lead out of this valley and you will do as they say!" With that, all arguments ended, and the three men ducked again into the back of the wagon.

Braden drove down the hill until they reached a small copse of trees, two hundred yards from the village. Quickly and quietly, Braden and Garam stepped from the cart and made their way to the town. Darkness still covered the world, though on the eastern horizon a faint glow appeared over the mountains. Braden and Garam moved with care into the shadows of the trees and disappeared into the darkness.

Aaron peered out from the blankets where he had settled down and watched the two dwarves vanish through the trees. He was amazed at how well adapted they were to stealth. "And they're gone," he whispered.

With a sigh, Lorik looked over the edge of the cart as well. "I hope that it won't be long. Dawn is only an hour away and then nothing will hide us from watchful eyes."

"They left us," Rayn muttered under his breath, anger growled in his words.

After twenty minutes, the two dwarves returned, panting with exhaustion. Braden and Garam climbed back into the wagon and took their place at the front.

Garam looked at Aaron with alarm. "There's been an attack on the village," he said. "I don't know how, but troll raiders attacked less than two hours ago. From what I heard, the trolls came over the mountains. The entire village is in an uproar; we have no hope of passing through undetected."

"What if we wait for nightfall?" Lorik inquired. "We can remain in these trees through the day and pass to the river after the situation has calmed down."

"Perhaps," replied Garam, "but we must believe that there are guards now in pursuit. I don't think we will remain hidden for long. There are just two exits from Hidden Valley, the main passage through the mountains and the river. Once the guards realize that we haven't left by the main road, they will look for us here." Garam paused for a moment. "No," he continued, "I believe that our best hope of escape still remains before us. We must make for the river now or never."

"Then we better get going while it is still dark. It'll be dawn soon," Aaron said as he looked up through the canopy of branches, "less than an hour."

"Well then," Braden said, "if you three will duck down again we'll be off." The three men sunk into the bed of the cart with the blankets over their heads as they hoped to go undetected through the tumultuous village.

Darkness gave way to the bright illumination of the village lights. Through small cracks in the sidewall of the wagon, Aaron watched the chaos that filled the small town. They entered through the main gate of the community, but it was shattered and burned, just a smoldering pile of lumber. Several homes were charred, and two on their right still burned.

Dwarves, both men and women, ran helter-skelter through the road; some carried large buckets of water to try and extinguish the flames, others aided the injured, taking them into a large, two-story stone building on the left of the main road. Amid the tumult, cries and wails of those who lost loved ones filled the air. One young dwarf mother sat on the edge of the road with a small cloak clutched in her arms, screaming for someone to find her children. Her lament ripped at Aaron's heart.

They passed through the pandemonium. Most of the townspeople paid little heed to the cart as it rolled down the main thoroughfare. One or two of the villagers gave them a glance; however, they were able to travel the length of the village without any interference. The wagon rattled through the burned remains of the back gate. Aaron looked through the slats and saw something unexpected. Along the path, just beyond the village wall, a contingent of six dwarves stood guard, three on each side.

Braden kept driving the wagon, moving toward the guards when one of them stood in the road and blocked their passage to the river. Braden looked at Garam. "I hope you have an idea to get us through this," he said.

The dwarf who had stood in the road was stocky, shorter than the rest but broad and firm. His beard was deep black, matted with blood and a large gash stretched from his temple to his jaw. His raiment was torn, and his mail-ringed leather shirt was gashed with claw marks. He looked distraught and worn from battle. The guard raised his hand. "Halt!" he commanded.

"What can I do for you soldier?" Braden asked.

"Tell me," the dwarf spoke, his voice hoarse and weary, "where are you going at this hour?"

Garam quickly answered, "We are going fishing and wanted to get an early start on the day. We are from the city and hoped to try our luck on the river."

The guard leaned on the handle of his battleaxe and shook his head in disbelief. "Goin' to try your luck at the river?" he said, almost chuckling. "Don't you see what's gone on? We've been attacked by trolls, and you wanna go fishin'!" The other soldiers on the side of the road started to walk toward the wagon and held their weapons as if they intended to use them. "I think we need to check out what you've got in this wagon. Get yourselves down from there and let us have a look."

Without warning Garam grabbed the reigns and whipped the horses into a run. They bolted and were soon in a mad dash up the road into the mountains. Quickly falling behind, the six dwarf soldiers ran after them.

"Halt! Stop that wagon!"

Garam paid no heed to the guards and continued to press the horses to run faster.

Aaron sat up from his hiding place and watched the scenery rush past. Alarmed by the change in circumstances, he shouted to be heard. "Garam, what do you think you're doing?"

"They were going to discover you! We need to get to the river before they catch up."

As they climbed higher up the path to the glacial reservoir, Garam pointed back the way they'd come. The first light of dawn had broken over the eastern mountains, and they looked upon the valley below and behind them. Far down the road and still outside the village, a large contingent of dwarves emerged from the orchard groves and ran swiftly towards the town. Much closer, the six dwarf guards pursued them up the path into the mountains.

Through a narrow valley, little more than a crack in the mountainside, Garam drove their cart. Their horses began to pant and sweat under the stress. Dawn's light chased away the shadows, and they saw that they were in a narrow crevice that twisted to the left. Time seemed to slow in the hurried pace, as the horses pressed to climb the mountain pass.

Lorik looked over the sideboard and asked, "How much farther?"

"We're almost there...we will see a lake just around the next bend," Garam said and kept his gaze fixed on their path. Just after he spoke, the wagon began to shudder violently. Aaron looked over the sideboard to see the left wheel begin to separate from the axle. The horses, under the duress of the broken wheel, stumbled in stride and fell to the ground. Everyone in the carriage flew like debris and brutally tumbled along the path.

Aaron gathered himself, scraped and bruised for the experience, and ran back to the wagon. He found Rayn pinned to the ground by the broken transport. Lorik came to his aide and together they freed their companion. The two dwarves hurried and gathered up their scattered belongings. They handed the swords to each of the three men, strapped their axes to their backs and hoisted the bags up on their shoulders.

"Quickly Captain, we must run to the river!" Garam was almost panicked to frenzy as his gaze darted back down the path to watch for those in pursuit.

Aaron, however, was not given to alarm. He strapped his sword around his waist, and began to assess the situation. Rayn was injured. Lorik was dazed but functional. The two dwarves were flustered.

He knew they had a good lead on the six guards. The soldiers were farther behind and posed no immediate threat. So his first concern was Rayn. He went to the private and began to examine his leg that had been pinned under the wagon.

"Can you move, Rayn? How's the leg?" Aaron knelt down to examine the wounds. Blood oozed from an open gash on Rayn's thigh. His arm was bruised and battered but there was no sign of any broken bones.

"I can make it, sir," Rayn said. He grimaced as he tried to stand. "It's just a simple cut." However, when Rayn tried to walk he screamed and collapsed under his own weight. Aaron wrestled Rayn to his feet again, and had the private lean against him to walk.

"Captain!" shouted Garam and Braden together, exasperated.

Garam continued, "We must leave now or we never will! We have no idea what waits for us at the reservoir, and we need time to find a boat and get downstream!"

"Calm down!" Aaron ordered. His authority echoed in his voice. "We won't help ourselves by losing control. Have we gathered all our gear?" Braden nodded an affirmative. "Lorik, can you help Rayn?" Lorik gave a nod of assurance. "OK, let's move out." His hand on his sword, Aaron gave a quick grin of approval, glad to be in command of his circumstances again.

He and his four companions began an ordered march to the river. Garam led. Close behind him, Braden followed with much of the gear upon his back. On his heels were Lorik and Rayn, holding onto each other and desperate to keep pace with the two dwarves. Aaron followed and continued to watch for their pursuers.

As they rounded a corner, a pristine mountain lake nestled in a massive gorge came into view. Glaciers reached to the mountain peaks and supplied the lake with countless rivulets, streams, and waterfalls. The crystal water glistened and sparkled and reflected the spires as pure as any mirror might have done. Trees lined the terrain. Large pine and spruce, fir and a host of others kept vigil around the water. Two rivers flowed out of the lake, one made a noisy exit to the north, as it poured water over a large, tumultuous fall. The other river departed to the south, slow and steady into the heart of the mountains. Garam turned toward the southern river. He followed a well-worn path to the water's edge.

Braden stopped with a shout. "Trolls!" he cried.

At Braden's shout, Aaron ran ahead, his sword drawn for battle. Two trolls, large grey beasts at the edge of the lake splashed in the water. Aaron noticed two other figures there as well; two dwarf children who desperately tried to escape the troll's torment.

The forlorn cry of a desperate mother echoed in Aaron's head as he ran toward the water, outpacing his companions to the shore of the lake. The trolls failed to notice him until he had run his sword through the back of one. With a massive splash, the troll fell face first into the lake and never moved again. The other troll watched his companion fall and threw aside its victim in order to attack Aaron.

Aaron ducked and slashed as he fought in the cold shallows of the lake. Icy water swirled and splashed around his knees. He parried and hacked at his opponent, but could gain no advantage.

When the rest of the company arrived, Garam and Braden rushed into the water, axes ready. Waist deep in the lake, Braden ducked a certain death blow from the troll and chopped at the troll's leg like the trunk of a tree. Sharp as a razor, his axe tore through flesh and bone and completely dismembered the creature. The troll collapsed in a heap into the water, and Aaron plunged his sword through the troll's chest, the final blow.

On the shore, two dwarf children clutched each other, paralyzed with fear. Garam returned to them, his battleaxe in his hand. "Be calm, children, there are no more trolls." As Garam spoke, the dwarf children fell into his arms, sobbing and trembling. He reassured the two and clasped them both on the shoulders to calm them.

"Young ones," he said finally, "we have need of a boat. Have you any that can be spared?" One of the two children stood, still trembling and took them to a fishing boat. It seemed small to Aaron, but it was capable of holding six dwarves. It had been hidden in a large patch of thorny brush, and Braden and Garam struggled to free it.

"Lorik, Aaron!" shouted Braden. "We need your help!" It was a heavy, sturdy vessel, made with thick planks and fitted with broad oars. Together the four of them mounted the boat on their shoulders and with one heave brought the craft to the lake. Rayn watched, as he gathered up the gear.

"All aboard!" barked Garam. "We must depart now!" Rayn sat at the bow, Aaron sat with Lorik on the center plank and the two dwarves sat at the stern. The company cast off and began rowing toward the southern outlet. In a moment, the lake was behind them. As they floated down the river they watched the two young dwarves still huddled on the shore, diminishing in the distance. The group of six dwarves arrived at the lake, but just stood and watched as the boat sped downstream, out of Hidden Valley.

****

Lorik and Aaron rowed hard, swiftly moving through the massive canyon and down the river. Immense grey cliffs loomed over them on either side; huge, sheer stone walls reached to the sky and guarded the river from any intrusion. The sun did not reach into the depths of the canyon and made their journey seem like a sojourn through perpetual twilight. Large pillars of stone stood like sentinels in the water, while a cold breeze blew through the gorge. The mammoth walls of the canyon reached down into the depths of the river with no landing area to moor the boat. No trees, no brush, no foliage of any kind grew along the watercourse, just sheer grey and brown walls of solid rock kept the travelers company along their journey.

Aaron and Braden shivered in their wet, cold clothing. Both were soaked head to toe from their encounter with the troll. Rayn took two fresh cloaks from the bundled baggage and gave one each to his two wet companions. Garam was dripping as well, but had only suffered the water up to his waist as Aaron and Braden took the brunt of the troll's attack. Aaron declined the dry cloak as he and Lorik rowed with such zeal that the canyon seemed almost a blur as it rushed past.

"Captain," spoke Garam, "you and Lorik can quit rowing so hard. We've passed beyond the reach of the guards, and I doubt that anyone will come for us along this river."

Exhausted from the effort, Aaron let his oars rest as ripples of water casually drifted off the boat to the edge of the slow-moving waterway. Now, Aaron took the garment offered by Rayn, gratefully donning the fresh attire.

Their small craft rode very low in the water, and the river occasionally spilled over the gunwale.

"With this water coming in our boat, I don't suppose that we might end up swimming the rest of the way?" Lorik asked Braden.

Braden chuckled at the thought. "Don't worry! This small boat is fit for six dwarves, and there are only five of us. I think that we'll find ourselves safe upon the river for some time."

Aaron looked at Braden as a growing respect filled his thoughts. "Braden," he said, "I was told that you were imprisoned for acts of cowardice. Let me say that you showed your courage today. I am grateful to you."

"Captain," Braden spoke with broken voice, "thank you. I fear that we will all have to find greater courage before our journey is complete."

Aaron nodded in agreement and then turned his attention to Garam who sat silent in the stern and watched the river drift past them. "You said that this river was a perilous journey," Aaron commented. "It seems to me that this is nothing more than a gentle drift along a deep channel of water. What makes you so sure that we won't be pursued along this river?"

"Captain," returned Garam, "we are just a mile along. Right now we are high in the mountains, and the river follows a gentle channel. It will change dramatically, and we will be forced to navigate along paths without light when this river runs through the heart of the mountains and exits out on the other side."

Aaron noticed a distinct look of concern in Garam's dark brown eyes. "Is there something more?" asked Aaron.

"Well, Captain," Garam's voice was hesitant, "I don't know if there is any port along the journey. We may be in this small craft for two days without relief." Garam looked up at the monstrous cliffs that loomed menacingly over them as he spoke.

"I'll tell you this, dwarf," — Rayn's voice was filled with scorn — "it's a site better than being locked up in your prison!" He sat in the bow and rubbed his injured leg.

"Private," injected Lorik, as he spun around to fix his gaze upon the young soldier, "you owe these two dwarves your freedom, if not your very life! I expect better from you!"

"Yes, Sergeant," Rayn said with disdain. He motioned for Lorik to lean closer, "But I'll tell you this," he spoke quiet enough for only Lorik and Aaron to hear, "I won't trust either of them. They are enemies of our land. I don't believe for a moment that they intend to help us or intend to allow us to keep the item that we seek. And I caution you to keep your eyes on them."

Lorik leaned over to speak to Rayn, "Young man," his voice was low and stern, "You will change your attitude, or I'll change it for you. You are under orders and will obey. It is not your place to challenge the captain's authority, and I won't have it! Do we understand each other?"

Rayn nodded, though a glaring look of resentment and anger filled his eyes.

Lorik turned away from Rayn and fixed his attention on rowing the small craft. Aaron gave a quick glance at the sergeant and offered a slight nod of approval. He tried to relax in the confined space of the boat and pondered what to do with his belligerent young soldier.

The companions journeyed silently for several hours. The river moved along, picking up speed as it coursed deeper into the mountain canyon and away from the dwarf realm. Miles vanished behind them without a harbor or inlet to give the travelers relief. Just cliffs; high, rugged cliffs provided the only scenery for them.

"We haven't eaten since we left the city. Braden, will you open the packs and see what we have for food?" Lorik asked.

Braden rummaged through the satchel, and pulled out several cloth-wrapped items and distributed them to the company. Wrapped inside the cloth were dry, cooked bricks of layered bread-wafers. Between each wafer, a layer of some form of fruit provided ample flavor for the meal. Water was plentiful as it swirled all around them, and Lorik took their flasks and filled each one. They ate in quiet rumination, allowing the river to take their craft ever southward.

The day passed without event as the sun drifted across the azure sky and showered a brief display of light into the dim chasm. The canyon narrowed and the waters of the tributary leapt and danced in foamy whitecaps. The river sparkled with the assorted ripples and broke against the cliff walls. The brief glimpse of sunshine was a refreshing break from the grey, half-light. However, the joy was short lived.

"Look! The river is coming to an end!" Rayn

exclaimed.

Aaron glanced up to see what Rayn was pointing at.

A high wall rose in front of them and blocked their way. The strange sight made it look as if the river suddenly came to a violent end. Water buckled against the sheer cliff, angrily pounding against the rock and exploding up in massive towers of waves. To their left a small spit of land carved out of the rock face provided a diminutive landing, barely able to hold the five companions. However, Garam directed them to steer toward the shore. Aaron and Lorik heaved against the current and fought their small craft until it turned toward the refuge and, with some effort, made landfall.

Rayn was the first to disembark the vessel with Aaron and Lorik close on his heels. They heaved their boat higher onto the shore. Afterward, Garam and Braden stepped out of the boat and carried the packs to dry ground. Rayn stumbled, and struggled to walk. He hobbled over to a small log which had washed up on the river's edge, bleached pale by its exposure to the elements, and sat down. Lorik joined him on the large piece of driftwood.

"Is the leg bad?" Lorik asked.

"Just stiff," Rayn replied. "Being cramped in that boat only helped to tighten the muscles. I'll be fine in a moment." Rayn stretched and rubbed his injured leg.

Meanwhile, Aaron and the two dwarves discussed the next phase of the journey. He stood near the river and looked southward to the maelstrom that appeared to be the end of the waterway. He stroked his beard as he pondered the fate that brought him and his men to such a place. "How do you expect us to navigate such a violent current?" Aaron looked over toward Garam as he puzzled over their situation. His voice was anxious and stern and cut through the air like a sword.

"I told you at the outset that this journey was dangerous," Garam replied. The dwarf walked to the shore and stood next to Aaron.

Garam pointed toward the great upheaval of spray. "What you see is the entrance to a dark passage under the mountains. This river has cut a channel through the heart of the Shadow Mountains," he said. "The tumult you see before you is not the end of the river. This is where it plummets into the rock, but I am told that it is possible to navigate the course. Very few have managed it, but it is our only passage. The river is too strong at this point to try and row back, and the cliffs are a much greater danger. We can either stay here or go on, there is no other choice."

That, of course, is obvious, Aaron thought. "The men are tired, and we need a rest. Let us make a camp here in this hollow and continue in the morning."

"That is not a good idea." Garam's voice echoed with a sense of caution. "This is the only location on the river that is safe to stand so it is the one place for any of the wild beasts of the mountains to venture down for a drink. We will not be safe here for the horros have the ability to climb the sheer cliffs. I don't need to tell you the dangers of those beasts. We can remain here for a short while, but not long. It may sound strange, but our safest road will be to attempt the river."

Aaron assessed the river as it rushed into oblivion. He had faced, and perhaps cheated, death before. He looked down at his stalwart companion and a stern determination filled his eyes. "We'll give Rayn a chance to rest and then we leave."

Garam nodded his approval and began to re-pack the gear, storing it under the three bench seats. Before he packed it all, however, he opened a flask of thick, dark liquid and passed the container to each of the party members. "Drink this," he commanded, "it will help us all keep our strength." Braden took it with gladness, as well as Aaron and Rayn who had imbibed the drink on their journey to Brekken-Dahl. Lorik, however, was wary of the concoction and cautiously sipped at the liquid.

Time passed as swift as the river, and, grudgingly, the five companions moved to regain their places in the boat. Rayn, after his rest and the healing drink walked with greater strength; just a slight limp hindered his progress.

"Captain," Braden said, "perhaps it's better if Garam and I took the oars. Both of us are more adept in the darkness and might have a better chance to navigate the river under the mountains." Aaron nodded in agreement and the two dwarves took the center seat. Lorik and Rayn sat hunkered down in the stern and Aaron took the bow.

Garam spoke to Aaron. "You will find a small stone in the pack under your seat. It may be helpful after we enter the cavern." Aaron fumbled around in the satchel until he produced a small, oblong crystal, blue like sapphire, with a slight glow that flickered in the center. It fit well in the palm of his hand, and he tucked it into the inner pocket of his shirt. Patting it, he made sure that the gem was secure against accidental loss and placed his hands on the bow of the boat and prepared to shove the craft into the river.

Aaron fixed his gaze at Garam with a puzzled

look. "How long is it that we will be underground?"

"I am uncertain." Garam said with all sincerity. "We have traveled many miles already for the river is running swift, but it may be more than a day before we see the light of the sun again."

"All right," Aaron said. He braced his legs in the dirt and shoved the boat into the water, hopping in at the last.

****

The power of the river captured their little craft and tossed it through the channel. The heavy rapids burst and beat against the hull as the travelers flowed with the swift current, barely able to maintain control. Before them, a churning turmoil of white water bellowed with an angry roar. Garam and Lorik gripped the oars like weapons against the rushing current. With strength Aaron had never seen, the two dwarves fought against the might of the river and kept the boat from tumbling into a chaotic frenzy of motion.

The spray off the breakers drifted and floated around them and doused them with a continual shower. Aaron looked at his men as worry and desperation filled their eyes, wide with the terror of the plunge that awaited them. The roar of the powerful water crashed into the hollow of the mountain, growing louder as they neared. Aaron turned around to look.

The view terrified him. Before him, the river split into two channels, swirling against a large outcropping of rock that protruded from the middle of the river. Massive breaks crashed against the towering monolith. In a wash of mist and foam, the river disappeared into a black abyss. Aaron sat stoic, knowing it was too late to turn back. The river gripped their small craft with the full force of its power. The five companions held on as they entered the jaws of the mountain, a descent, perhaps, into death.

From behind him, Garam shouted against the roar of the water— "Aaron!" He turned his attention to the dwarf who fought with all his might against the current. "Which channel?" Garam's plea was desperate as he and Braden held the boat against the might of the river.

Aaron looked again at the river's course. "Take the right!" he shouted back.

With a concerted effort, Braden and Garam forced the craft toward the right passage of the river then allowed the current to take them over the falls. "Hang on!" Aaron shouted as the boat plummeted over the edge of the abyss.

The boat descended into the depths of the cavern as darkness engulfed the craft and water rushed against them. The oars were useless so Braden and Garam held the gunwale as the craft pitched and rocked down the powerful torrent. Behind them, Lorik and Rayn held on with firm determination. In the bow of the boat, Aaron gripped the rail with all his strength to keep from pitching over into the maelstrom as he peered into the misty blackness before him.

Then, with a sudden crash, the boat found the bottom of the falls and hit with such force it felt as if it skipped like a stone against the surface of the water. All five held their places as their small craft drifted in darkness. Exhausted and worn, Aaron slumped in his seat, too tired to move. Hundreds of feet above them a small window of light glowed like a hole in pitch-black sky. The sound of crashing water echoed all around the travelers. The river's power was tempered, and slowed so much that the boat casually drifted in the gentle currents.

Time vanished in the absolute blackness of the cavern. Aaron remembered the small stone that was carefully contained in his inner pocket. He pulled it out; a faint, iridescent glow streamed from its core and shone a brilliant blue light all around the craft. The two dwarves looked almost lifeless as they leaned against each other. He watched Lorik and Rayn in the stern of the craft, both of them with their head in their hands. Aaron then looked around and marveled at the sight.

They drifted across a large, deep pool of water, an underground lake that swirled in the constant flow of the river. Outside the sphere of light, the darkness remained. As far as Aaron knew, the water was endless. Their boat drifted in lazy motion. By his dim light, Aaron noticed a large rock wall with a black hole cut into it like some gaping maw.

Aaron gained Garam's attention. "What can you see in this darkness?"

Garam took a deep breath, regained his composure and looked around the cave. "Captain, we are in a large cavern. Water reaches to the walls on every side with just one exit. It is several hundred feet in width, and the ceiling is more than a hundred feet over our heads." There was a collective gasp from all the members of the party when they heard how far they had fallen.

"Is there any place to take rest and regroup?" Aaron hoped, but he had already guessed the answer.

"No, there is no place at all. The water fills this cavern like a basin." Aaron heard the heaviness in

Garam's voice.

"Take us to the cliff wall; at least we can stop for a moment before we venture into the watercourse." Aaron directed them toward the edge of the water and put his hand out to allow their craft to nestle gently against the rock face.

They began to check their gear, and were relieved when they found their packs had survived. Some water had filled the bottom of the boat, but that was of little concern to Aaron, knowing where they had just come from.

"Well," Aaron said, "there's nothing else but to continue on our journey. We've survived thus far, and I will trust to our luck for the remainder of this cruise." The two men in the stern nodded in agreement while Braden and Garam took control of the oars and rowed their vessel back into the river's current.

Once again they found themselves in the main course of the waterway. With steady rhythm, the two dwarves guided the boat with impeccable skill. Aaron used the faint blue light to illuminate their way and found the outlet where the river departed the underground lake. The narrow passage made it difficult for Braden and Garam to use the oars. On more than one occasion they needed to retract them to save them from bashing into the cavern walls. Aaron grew concerned their ship might find itself locked in the waterway, pinched by the narrow channel.

"You said that others have safely navigated this course?" Aaron asked Garam.

"It has been said that others have navigated it," he replied, "but I've not known anyone personally who returned from this underground passage."

"Now you tell us," Rayn said.

For several hours they drifted in the silent darkness. Only the lapping of the water against the boat gave voice to their passage. Then the cavern widened enough for Braden and Garam to put the oars in the water. Aaron held out the stone and watched the moist cavern walls flicker in the reflected light off the water.

Only the constant flow of water indicated the passage of time. To Aaron the journey became a monotony of motion so he took the opportunity to hunker down in his cloak and listen to the rhythm of the water. Braden and Lorik were on the oars and Garam sat in the stern, wrapped in a cloak and sound asleep. Rayn, weary and nursing his injury, slipped into a fitful drowse as well.

Aaron listened as Braden and Lorik quietly talked about their experiences. "It was a difficult time," Braden began as he remembered his life in the Kanton Mountains. "We labored for years to try and excavate the ancient tunnels. It was said that one of the sons of Lord Brekken ventured to retake the Kanton Mountains and was lost in battle." Braden's eyes drifted into the vague darkness. "But tell me about you. What was your life like before all of this?"

"There's not much to tell," Lorik commented. "My family lived in the north. We farmed and kept cattle, a modest life that I wanted no part of. So I joined the ranks of the Royal Guard just after my seventeenth birthday and never looked back."

The two kept up a quiet conversation for some time as they reminisced and tried to outdo each other's stories. After several hours, Braden excused himself from the oar and tapped Aaron on the leg. "Captain," he said, "do you mind if we change places. My eyes will close by themselves if I don't take a break soon."

"Certainly," Aaron replied and handed Braden the stone. With great care the two exchanged places, anxious to keep from falling in the water or tipping the boat.

"Well, Captain," Lorik observed, "I guess it's up to us to keep moving the right direction." Lorik's lighthearted disposition lifted Aaron's spirits. He sat down next to the sergeant and took the oar in hand. Together with Lorik, Aaron gently stroked the water and kept their small craft in the center of the channel.

Aaron glanced at Rayn who appeared to sleep in the stern. Garam and Braden also slept as they drifted along the river.

"Lorik?" Aaron whispered in the dark to his friend.

"Yes, Captain?"

"We've served together a long time."

"More than fifteen years, sir."

Aaron hesitated and gripped the oar even tighter.

"Captain," Lorik's voice was soft and patient. "Aaron," he said, "You don't need to guard your words with me."

Aaron smiled at the friendship he had with the sergeant. He took a deep breath. "I want to let you know that I intend on finding the Book of Aleth, but I won't be taking it back to the emperor."

Lorik grinned. "That doesn't surprise me, sir."

"I've seen too much, Lorik," Aaron said. "I have to know what the truth is and this Book of Aleth might be the key. If I find the book and return it to the emperor, I doubt I will ever get another chance to learn what it has to say."

"You do know that it goes against your orders."

"I know, but I can't think of another way to find out the truth. I can't keep an allegiance to those who have lied to me my entire life."

Lorik chuckled.

"What's so funny?" Aaron asked.

"It's nothing," Lorik said. "It's just that I never doubted that once we left the dwarf city, that you would want to understand this book for yourself. As long as I've known you, your need for the truth has been the driving force in your life." Lorik took a deep breath. "But I want you to know, Captain; I'm with you to the end of this."

Aaron clapped his friend on the shoulder and smiled. "I hoped I could count on you," he said then turned his attention to the business of steering the boat.

****

Trying to keep the boat steady was fitful duty for Aaron. Minimal light and the swift current made guiding their craft difficult and required intense concentration. He envied the dwarves' ability to see in the dark cavern. However, even with the limited view, Aaron and Lorik navigated the vessel well enough to maintain control and keep themselves in the center of the river. The water cut through the mountain, twisting like a serpent. He had no idea how far they had come, but Aaron felt certain that escape was near.

Then the river flowed into another large chamber. The boat slowed to a crawl so that Aaron and Lorik were forced to step up their efforts in order to continue. It was a vast cavity deep in the roots of the mountains. The low ceiling required them to keep their heads down while stalactites reached their massive fingers into the water. Aaron found it difficult to keep the boat on course as the current increased, so he woke both Braden and Garam to take control of the vessel.

The four switched places, with Aaron, again, at the bow. The two dwarves gripped the oars and steered through the menagerie of rock formations. As they weaved through the maze of stone obstacles, Aaron held out the light. Scintillating gems imbedded in the rocky fingers reflected like a subterranean star field. He wondered if he didn't look upon some ancient treasure trove, hidden for ages in the depths of the earth.

Aaron had lost all track of time. He turned to Garam. "How long have we been on this boat?"

Garam looked perplexed as he waived off Aaron's question. "Two days," he said. "Now just listen for a moment." All the men were quiet as they strained to hear what Garam listened to. Echoing through the darkness, the whisper of rushing water filtered through the cavern.

"What's that?" Rayn asked as he woke.

"I believe," said Garam, "that is the sound of our exit."

Aaron looked around and hoped to see the light of the sun, but all was darkness before him. "Garam, Braden, can either of you see the exit?"

The two dwarves looked around. "Captain," replied Braden, "what I see is a large bowl, and we are floating in it. Ahead of us there is a cave and the current runs rather swift in that direction. The water disappears as if over a breach. I can only guess that it rushes out of this cavern through another tunnel."

"Do you think that's our exit?" Lorik asked.

Garam looked at the sergeant. "Yes, I believe it is. But I fear that it might be as bad an experience as when we entered." The wizened dwarf turned to Aaron and inquired, "Ready?"

"I think that we're as ready as we'll ever be. Let's go." Aaron held the blue crystal in his hand as he sat in the bow. Lorik and Rayn sat in the stern and held on tight. The two dwarves gripped the oars and turned their craft toward the tunnel. They maneuvered through the rock formations with such skill that not one stalactite threatened them. Then, in a rush, they plunged into the violent flow of the raging waters.

Aaron watched as the blue-grey walls of stone blurred with the speed of their descent. Swiftly and steadily, their speed increased. He held onto the frame of the boat, desperate not to be cast into the torrent. The dwarves soon gave up on the oars, unable to control their pace. The boat began to shudder in the rapids. Banging from wall to wall, the two oars fractured and ripped violently from their posts. They were now at the mercy of the river.

Faster and faster the river flowed, pounding against the boat. Their small craft was tossed about like a cork, and the five companions struggled just to remain aboard. Waves exploded beneath them and tossed them in the air. Aaron nearly struck his head on the ceiling. Then, down they went. In a violent shake, Aaron lost the blue stone into the river.

Darkness engulfed them. Tumbling through the blackness, the men clung to whatever their hands found.

Aaron watched as a light began to grow. Over the roar of the rapids he heard the thunderous sound of a waterfall. Panic gripped his heart as they rushed toward the light. The exit grew brighter as they neared their final escape. Water splashed around them and filled their boat. Their craft now ran dangerously low in the river. Then sunlight exploded around them.

In a violent expulsion, the men were cast out of the mountain and sent hurtling through the air. Their screams were drowned by the roar of the river as they crashed into violent rapids below. The boat shattered on impact, and each man clambered for the shore. Waves crashed and pounded over Aaron's head as he frantically swam toward the eastern bank of the river.

Lorik was first to reach the land, grabbing the grass and brush against the edge of the water. Garam and Braden washed up on the bank twenty yards down river with Aaron close on their heels. Lorik stumbled to help the dwarves, all of them distressed and worn, yet thankful to be alive.

Aaron noticed that Rayn desperately struggled against the current. Aaron rushed to the edge of the water and grabbed the young soldier by the shirt, hauling him to the shore. Panting with exhaustion, Aaron leaned over and rested his hands on his knees. At that moment, Rayn stood to his feet, drew his sword and slashed at his Captain, eyes wide with anger.

Aaron jumped back just in time as the tip of Rayn's blade sliced the edge of his tunic. "What are you doing?" Aaron demanded as he drew his own weapon from its sheath.

"You dare to ask me what I'm doing." Rayn kept his sword pointed at Aaron's chest. He swung again, and the two weapons rang out as they clanged together. Rayn thrust swiftly at him. "You plan on betraying our emperor and handing this nation over to those vile creatures," he said and glanced toward Braden and Garam. Again he swung his sword through the air, aimed at the captain's head.

Aaron parried and dodged Rayn's attack. He never took advantage but merely defended himself. "Put your weapon away, you don't know what you're talking about," he said. With his own sword, he spun Rayn's blade, and it flew from the private's grasp.

Steam wafted from Rayn with each breath as if his anger boiled within like a fire. He retrieved his sword from the trampled, compacted snow. "I heard you! In the boat, in those dreadful caverns. I heard you say that you will find that book for yourself. You want to find it and depose Emperor Therion. Maybe you plan on setting yourself up as ruler in Celedon."

"Rayn, you're completely wrong. Look around, see for yourself. All our lives we've been taught lies. The things I've been shown have hammered against my heart, and now I must know the truth for myself. If this Book of Aleth contains the truth, I want to know it." Aaron lowered his sword so that the tip of the blade touched the snowy ground.

Lorik walked up to stand at Aaron's side, his sword drawn. "What are you doing, Rayn? Put your sword away."

Garam and Braden followed after, their axes gripped tightly in their hands.

"Think about it, Rayn," Aaron said. "We were taught that the ancient peoples of the past were only myth and legend. But even you must see that was a lie." He pointed toward Garam and Braden who stood behind Lorik. "The proof stands right here!"

"What I see," Rayn said, "is that you are nothing more than a traitor and now you and Lorik stand with these dwarves and against the emperor." He lowered his sword a fraction as his shoulders slumped. "I should have left you when I had the chance. I should have gone to the emperor and reported your failure." A new resolve set into the young man's eyes as his gaze narrowed upon Aaron. "You won't stop me now. I will go to the capital and tell him of your rebellion."

"Don't be a fool," Aaron pleaded. "You won't even make it as far as North Village. You need to trust me."

A sly, cruel smile crossed Rayn's lips. "Trust you? That will never happen again. But I promise you this: once more our swords will cross and in the name of the emperor, I will strike you down." Rayn sheathed his blade and turned south, away from the four companions. He entered the woods and disappeared into the foliage.

Aaron returned his sword to its scabbard, shook his head, and moved to follow the young man when a hand gripped his arm.

"No, Captain," Lorik said. "He won't come back with you."

"But he'll die out here," Aaron said as he looked at Lorik.

Lorik clasped Aaron on the shoulder. "He has made his choice and so have we."

Both men turned around to see Garam and Braden. The two dwarves looked at Aaron with questioning glances under their heavy brows.

"What are your plans now, Captain?" Braden asked.

Aaron walked past them without looking back, a resolution in his stride. "Let's go find the book."

COMING 2012

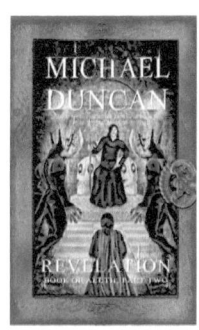

REVELATION: BOOK OF ALETH
PART TWO

Evil Reigns in Celedon...

No longer a captain in the Royal Guard, Aaron now commands a ragtag band on a mission foretold by ancient prophecy, a mission that must not fail.

But Emperor Therion knows of Aaron's desertion, and each step of their quest is fraught with danger and betrayal. From the dark and deadly tunnels of the Shattered Hills to the lofty heights of Kanton's ancient towers, the four band together to restore hope and a future. And as their mission hangs in the balance...a new Protector rises.

Thank you for purchasing this Harbourlight title. For other inspirational stories, please visit our on-line bookstore at www.pelicanbookgroup.com.

For questions or more information, contact us at titleadmin@harbourlightbooks.com.

Harbourlight Books
The Beacon in Christian Fiction™
www.HarbourlightBooks.com
www.pelicanbookgroup.com

May God's glory shine through
this inspirational work of fiction.

AMDG